He ate slowly, his thoughts wandering back over the years he'd been a lawman, then shifting to the present. His life had taken many twists and turns. The best one was the day he'd met Tessa.

Later, with the fire little more than a glow and coyotes yodeling in the distance, he filled his cup with the last of the strong brew and lay back against his saddle to look toward the south, where a few stars were visible. He singled out the brightest sparkler. Wrapping his hands around the cup, he said, "Lead me to them, Tessa. Help me find the men who hurt you."

A gust of wind kicked up and hovered over the fire, causing the flames to flicker and dance. He sat up abruptly. For the slightest moment Jim was certain Tessa's face loomed only inches from his. The easy innocence in her eyes sent a shudder through him. He was suddenly brought back to the present when a pair of coyotes approached the camp. The spell broken, Jim laughed out loud. "I'll be damned."

Loretta C. Rogers's Previous Books

LADY ADEL'S CAPTAIN
THE WITCHING MOON
FORBIDDEN SON
BANNON'S BRIDES
MCKENNA'S WOMAN
ISABELLE AND THE OUTLAW
All are available from The Wild Rose Press, Inc.

Cloud Woman's Spirit

by

Loretta C. Rogers

Cloud Woman's Spirit

Cover Art by *Rae Monet, Inc. Design*

The Wild Rose Press, Inc.
PO Box 708
Adams Basin, NY 14410-0708
Visit us at www.thewildrosepress.com

Publishing History
First Faery Rose Edition, 2014
Print ISBN 978-1-62830-591-3
Digital ISBN 978-1-62830-592-0

Published in the United States of America

Dedication

For my daughter
Jamie:
You are loved!

Prologue

There is never a good day to die. Not tomorrow or next week, and especially not tonight. Jim was coming home. She needed to let him know what these men had done to her father. She needed to tell Jim how hard she'd tried to live, and how sorry she was to leave him.

Tessa Cloud Woman Sawyer drifted in and out of awareness. She no longer felt pain, though she gagged on the foul stench of the men gathered around her. She etched the four leering faces into her memory.

With each slice of the knife, she refused to cry out. It was not the Comanche way, and she was proud to be half Comanche.

The men's voices became a distant drone. She tried to stay focused. She wanted to live. She wanted to live for the sake of the child growing inside her, and for Jim, too.

She lifted her head, turning slightly to stare at the man whose voice reminded her of a buzzing mosquito. He played the skinning knife back and forth from one hand to the other. "C'mon, Fourney, give me another go. Just 'cause you're the youngest don't mean you get special privileges. Stop hogging."

Another voice said, "Put the dang knife away, Blinkey. Why're you always wantin' to slice up pretty ladies?"

Blinkey ran the blade down Tessa's arms. "Don't

know...jest do…that's all."

The one named Ollie shoved his kid brother aside. "You been ridin' long 'nuff. My turn."

Scuffling.

The tip of a dirty boot kicked the boy named Fourney aside. Not the one whose eyes never stopped blinking. Tessa shut her own eyes for a moment's rest.

Mosquito Voice whined, "Hurry up, Bufford. We better skeedaddle before somebody comes."

Bufford yelled, "Stop your whining and go round up them horses in the corral. I'll be there in a minute. And Ollie, tell Blinkey to torch the house."

"What about the ole man?"

"Hell, he's dead. Leave him where he is."

Tessa looked up at the hole in the barn roof. A moonbeam shone through, and she saw the spirit soldiers astride their ghostly steeds. It was her time. They had come for her.

She lifted her voice and prayed aloud. "Great Father Spirit, I beg you to know the faces of these evil men." And then she stared into Bufford Dobbs' eyes. "My soul will not rest until the Great Spirit calls your name and the names of those you call brother. I curse…all of you."

The rotund man with a bulbous nose balled his fist and smashed it against her chest. "Shut your Injin gibberish."

The bones sounded like brittle twigs snapping during a wind storm. Her lungs filled with blood. Gurgling echoed in her ears.

She lay there and felt the wounds open, then lost the feeling in her arms, her legs, as the blood that was left inside her leaked out, the straw beneath her growing moist and warm.

Tessa knew the life was draining out of her. She forced her eyes to remain open as she continued to stare at her killer's face.

Several minutes passed.

A dark cloud shut out the moon's light.

Bufford Dobbs fumbled with the buttons on the fly to his pants as he yelled, "Let's get the hell out of here."

Chapter One

Deputy United States Marshal Jim Sawyer was brought back to reality by a sharp gust of wind that flung stinging sand against his face. He could think of no other place he would rather be headed. Home...and he was damned anxious to get there.

He knelt in the center of the dirt road and grabbed the gelding's front hoof, cursing the delay that would prevent him from reaching the ranch by nightfall. He dug the tip of the knife under a quarter-sized pebble, the cause of the buckskin's limp, and pried the stone free.

Standing, he tugged his hat brim down against the glare of the sun's golden streamers snaking through the firs and cottonwoods as the last vestiges of day fought a losing battle against the night. Dark shadows slowly worked their way along the grassy forest bed of Texhoma, Oklahoma. With aggravated resignation, he slid the knife into the leather sheath attached to his gun belt and prepared for the five-mile walk ahead.

He patted the gelding's withers. "Not much of a bruise, son. I'll give you a break until these boots start pinching my toes. Then you're carrying me the rest of the way home."

The horse flicked its ears forward as if listening. He brushed his head against the man's shoulder. Jim Sawyer laughed. "Yeah, it's been a long two months. I'm as ready as you for a little comfort."

Jim continued to talk. It was what a man did while hunting down renegades, bank robbers, and other nefarious criminals. Nights under the stars got lonesome, and sometimes a lawman might go weeks, even months, with the only human voice belonging to himself. Under his breath he hummed a nameless tune. "I sure am looking forward to cuddling up with Tessa."

The horse grunted and gave a little squeal. Jim harrumphed. "If I didn't know better, I'd swear you understand every word I'm saying."

Tall, lean and rawhide tough, Jim Sawyer was thirty-three now, and sometimes felt fifty. After two months of chasing down Curly Joe Smith and Shug Grier, his bones ached. He looked forward to a hot bath, a home-cooked meal, a smoke on the porch with Joe Hennessey, his father-in-law. Most of all he longed to hold his young bride in his arms. He grinned and hoped she'd like the blue gingham dress and matching shawl packed in his saddlebag. Yep, blue would compliment her complexion.

Feelings swirled through his heart at the vision in his head of the first time he'd seen her. Part Comanche, with hair the color of a raven's wing, she wasn't beautiful in the way a man would describe a white woman but more like in the classical sense. He congratulated himself for having found such a woman out here on the frontier, a woman who was easy on the eyes, respectable, loveable, maternal, and a credit to her race. Perfect! What more could a man want in a wife?

An owl belled across the dusky evening. Another answered in the far distance as quiet settled over the countryside like a comfortable blanket. Only the shuffling of the buckskin's hooves broke the silence.

In the dim light Jim noticed a blurred movement on the southern horizon. Out of instinct he stopped to watch until the shadowy shapes began to be identifiable; horses and riders moving in and out of the meandering line of trees that marked the course of Rock Creek. As best he could estimate from the distance, there were four of them—not Indians. Trappers, maybe, though there would be little reason for trappers to be in the area. The riders were about a mile away. Their presence made him a little edgy.

Jim squinted his eyes trying to bring the riders into focus. One was leading an appaloosa with unusual markings, easy to spot—and it sure looked like his wife's mare.

The question left him with a slight tingling sensation at the base of his skull, like a doubtful dog whose hackles were stirred by an uncertain sense of danger.

Torn between laming his horse and the urgent desire to get home, Jim swung into the saddle. "Rest time is over, son." He gigged the buckskin into a gallop and headed north.

Dusk changed to a pale glow emanating upward from behind a dark and distant rise of land. He spurred the buckskin into a run. When he topped the rise, Jim saw the roaring flames.

No matter how much he pushed for more speed, he felt the buckskin begin to falter. By the time he'd entered the ranch yard and hauled up on the reins, it was obvious the horse favored the right leg, barely able to place pressure on it. Damn, when it came time to put a bullet through an outlaw's black heart, Jim didn't blink an eye, but it hurt him to the core knowing he'd deliberately injured the horse that had carried him faithfully for many a year.

In the cool September evening, heat drew Jim's attention toward the house. Flames swirled furnace-like from the windows and front door, roaring skyward in great eddies of sparks and smoke. An explosive combustion sent pieces of shard through the air. One struck Jim's cheek, nearly cutting the flesh to the bone, while another tore through the leather vest to pierce his shoulder. The gelding squealed with pain as fragments of glass pinpricked its body.

Putting the horse in a spinning turn to avoid the splintering projectiles, Jim spotted the silhouette against the red blaze of the moon—the body swinging by a rope from the beam above the double barn doors. He rode within a few inches to recognize his father-in-law, the wrinkled and weathered face twisted grotesquely above the hangman's noose, hands tied behind his back, eyes bulging, mouth agape.

Oblivious of the pain from his face and shoulder, Jim unsheathed the knife at his waist and, standing in the stirrups, reached up to slice through the thick rope. The blade dropped from his hand as he wrapped his arms around the body and gently let it slide to the ground. Knowing the old man was dead, Jim leapt from the saddle and raced toward the house.

Running full speed, he collided with the heat from the burning structure as though the high temperature were a soft wall. He was engulfed in it for a moment and then sent reeling backward, his arms raised to protect his eyes. As soon as he recovered his breath and his balance, he once again dashed forward, only to be sent reeling backward again.

In anguish, he dropped lump-like to the ground and stared at the house while it burned and collapsed into a huge pile of sparks and glowing embers.

He rocked on his knees, his wounded arm dangling by his side, as he screamed her name, "Tessa...Te-e-essa!"

****

Jim flinched away from the hand that touched his shoulder. The voice sounded far away. His cheek throbbed. He reached up to touch it. Pain. His left arm refused to move. He tried to lever himself upward, but his numb legs remained twisted beneath him.

He was confused. It seemed like hours had passed. Why was he sleeping in the yard? Why did his shoulder feel as if a hot poker had stabbed him?

The voice came again. Closer this time. "Jim...it's me, Lettie...Lettie Edwards."

He squinted through the darkness, using the moon's light to focus on the woman's solemn face. "Lettie?"

"You're hurt bad, Jim. There's a hunk of glass stuck deep in your left shoulder. I'm afraid it's close to your heart. And your cheek is laid open like a gutted fish. Gonna leave a powerful scar."

His voice was thick and husky. "Don't fret yourself over me. I've had worse."

She harrumphed, then placed her arms beneath his. "I doubt it. Can you stand?"

He clenched his teeth against the painful effort. The awakening circulation in his legs was comparable to the sharp, stinging prickles of a thousand needles as he used the woman's strength to help him stand. He teetered unsteadily, as yet unable to stand alone, and allowed the woman to slip an arm about his chest to half support him.

Numb with shock, he pulled from her embrace. "Who did this? I was always careful not to lead anyone here. That's why the ranch was in Joe's name instead of mine."

"Lots of meanness in this world, Jim. Hank and I came as soon as we saw the flames."

"Bastards hung Joe."

"I know. Hank took care of him. Said for me to stay with you while he tried to pick up a trail. We both know it's too dark to see anything. C'mon now, we gotta get you to the doc's."

Still unsteady on his feet, Jim stared at the smoldering ruins. Nothing of the house remained. His emotions were raw, and his voice sounded hollow; even to himself. "I couldn't get to Tessa. The fire was too hot." A sob tore from his throat. "Oh, God, I should've tried harder."

A breeze caused a cloud to shift away from the moon, and a shiver rippled through him. The light was enough to reveal Lettie Edward's sorrowful face. Jim's lawman nature didn't miss her subtle glance toward the barn.

A sense of hope overtook him. With a growl he pulled away to escape her grip. White-hot pain seared through his left shoulder. He cradled the injured arm against his chest and held it with his good hand as he staggered with stiff-legged steps toward the barn.

Lettie grabbed at his shirttail. "No, Jim. You don't want—"

With a defiant snarl, he cut her off. "Dammit, she's my wife."

Lettie's last words followed him. "—to see her like that."

Lantern light lit the barn's interior with a soft glow. His eyes marked the length of rope that still dangled from the beam above the gaping doorway. A pair of workworn boots stuck out from a front stall. Without looking, he knew who lay beneath the horse blanket.

Snatching the lantern from its hook and holding it high, he called, "Tessa…answer me."

The top of his head itched, the way it always did when the odds were stacked against him. Yet there was every reason for him to believe his wife was still alive. His gaze swept the empty stalls as he half walked, half staggered down the center aisle. He called again, "Tessa?"

And then the icy fingers of dread chilled his entire being. His breath hitched in his chest, and it was difficult for him to breathe. He hung the lantern on a nail at the stall's wide entrance and then lifted his good hand to sweep away the blood that trickled down his cheek to drip from his chin and to stain the front of his shirt.

He stiffened as the footsteps neared. Lettie's touch irritated him; setting off a quickening temper.

She whispered, "Don't look at her, Jim. Tessa wouldn't want you to remember her this way."

His gaze swept the older woman squarely and then back down to the one moccasin-clad foot sticking from beneath a canvas tarp. The other foot was bare.

His voice soft, seeking a different approach through the thick mire of her chastening, he said, "I know you mean well, Lettie. You have to understand… she's my wife. I need to know how badly the bastards hurt her."

Lettie Edwards' eyelids dipped briefly. She gave a nod to convey her acceptance of his request.

Drawing in a fortifying breath, he hesitated before entering the stall, then moaned as he eased to his knees. He blinked several times to chase away the little black spots that danced in front of his eyes. The buzzing in his ears grew louder. Somehow it seemed appropriate for him to lie down and die next to his beautiful Tessa.

Steeling himself, he clasped the corner of the canvas tarp and pulled it back. His throat convulsed as he swallowed the bile threatening to spew forth.

The moon emerged from a blanket of clouds. Its light shone through a hole in the barn's roof, casting a pattern across the dead woman's face. He had always meant to repair the crack. He cocked his head as if listening to Tessa's voice scolding him for not helping her aged father replace the missing shingle—and then she would smile, wrap her arms around him, and chatter like a happy magpie, filling him in on all that had happened while he was away chasing outlaws.

Two months ago, she'd stood in the yard, holding his hand while he leaned down from the saddle to plant a kiss on lips that reminded him of ripe berries. She'd smiled up at him and patted her stomach. *"Don't you go getting yourself killed, Jim Sawyer, 'cause this baby needs more than a grandpa to help raise him."*

Hearing that he was to become a father had been the happiest day of his life. He would remember her just that way. And on lonely nights he would have the memory of their loving to keep him warm.

Now, his heart squeezed in his chest, hurting to the point he expected it to burst. As much as he wanted to die, he would survive. Yeah, he would live—live to hunt down the animals who'd destroyed his family.

Time froze as he leaned over her battered body. His fingers trembled and his brow creased in a pained frown as he tenderly touched the discolored swelling on her forehead.

Long lashes lay like dim shadows on her cheeks. Her hair formed a dark, tumbled halo over her bare shoulders. Her dress had been ripped and lay like a useless rag, exposing her nakedness, the swelling curves of her bosom bare to his scrutiny. She reminded him of a sleeping child, harmless and innocent. He allowed his gaze to linger on her face and then skimmed it down to the flat of her belly, where the little mound from the child she'd carried was no longer visible.

Clenching his teeth, he steeled himself and called on his strength as a lawman to harden his emotions, and then leaned slightly closer to study her more carefully. Blood glistened like wet paint down her abdomen and down her legs. Bruising had turned to purple welts. Her arms and ribcage were crisscrossed where she'd been slashed with a knife. He prayed she had died before suffering such heinous brutalization.

And then he spotted the small mass between her legs. He wanted to touch it, to hold it in his hands; to tell the unborn fetus how sorry he was that he hadn't been home to protect his family. He solemnly vowed he'd search to the ends of the earth to find the crazed misfits who had done this. And he vowed to make them suffer just as his loved ones had suffered.

With the agony of the sharp length of glass embedded inside his shoulder, he could not lift his wife to hold her in his arms to say goodbye.

Dizzy with pain, the last he remembered was the keening wail of a wounded animal, not recognizing the sound as his own cry.

Another moment and he was lost in darkness.

Chapter Two

A rooster crowed and Jim became aware it was not for the first time. He'd no doubt slept through the sound earlier.

A cool breeze swept in through the open second-story window, carrying with it the sharp alkaline scent of the river. Jim opened his eyes to an unfamiliar sight. Squinting at the strange, soft glow, he realized it was morning, and he couldn't remember the last time he had seen the light of day.

Rolling on to his side, he winced at the throbbing. He tried to sit up, groaning at the strain it placed on his aching muscles and the crushing pain in his shoulder.

He shifted to lie on his back, a shockingly painful ordeal. What the devil had he done? And where on earth was he? And why couldn't he move his left arm?

He looked around at the small square room with its small square fireplace. The walls were adorned with blue floral wallpaper, its planked floor with a latch-hooked oval rug next to the bed. There was one door, and on the opposite wall, a window covered with frilly curtains. Between sat the bed he lay on, a bedside table, and a cane-backed chair.

His head throbbed viciously as he tried to recall what had happened to him. He remembered the heat, the flames, and the mournful wail of an animal. His memory remained blank other than that.

He was tired and in too much pain to give a damn. He didn't even have the strength to worry about the footsteps he heard outside his room. When he opened his eyes, a tall spare woman with brown hair streaked with gray stood beside the bed.

"Lettie?"

Lettie Edwards, a woman past her prime, set the tray she carried on the bedside table. "It's about time you rejoined the living."

"Where am I?"

"At the boarding house. I wanted to make sure you were taken care of proper." She reached behind Jim to plump the pillow. "Doc Hubbard removed a piece of glass from your shoulder long enough to've killed an ox. Said it missed your heart by a thread—a plumb miracle, if you ask me."

Her tart words didn't quite cover the concern etched on her features. She leaned forward and gently pulled aside the binding to study the wound. Jim glanced down at the angry redness around the stitches. "Don't see any sign of infection. For now, all we can do is keep the wound clean and pray until Doc gets back."

Jim wanted to close his eyes, to drift into nothingness, to shut out the pain. "Where is Doc?"

The touch of her hand cooled his forehead. He opened his eyes. She clicked her tongue, a faint frown marring her brow. "A bit feverish, if you ask me. Doc had to ride over to Five Corners. It's Missus Anderson's time. Number eight, and the youngest not even a year old." She tsked again. "Somebody ought to tie Slybie Anderson's wing-wanger in a knot."

Jim grimaced at the woman's comment. Part of him wanted to reach down to protect his own manhood.

Instead he touched the bulky bandage on his cheek. "What happened?"

"Don't you remember?"

He gave Lettie a bleary stare. "If I did, I wouldn't be asking."

"Time enough for the telling. Right now you need to think about the healing."

"Did someone tell Tessa and Joe I'm here? Tessa's expecting me home. I don't like to give her any more worry than the job of a deputy marshal already brings with it."

Lettie's voice was bland when she answered. "Hank took care of everything."

She mixed two spoonfuls of milky liquid with a glass of water and reached behind Jim's good shoulder to help lift him forward. "Doc said to give you this to help with the pain. There's time enough later to talk about what happened."

Jim gagged as he swallowed the chalky substance. "Tastes like sheep-dip. What is it?"

"Laudanum."

Lifting the tray from the table, she set it across his lap, then unfurled the blue checkered napkin to tuck under his chin. "It's been a spell since you had any nourishment. I've made my special chicken soup. It's good for what ails you. Let's get a few spoonfuls into you before the laudanum takes over."

He grunted as he pushed higher on the mattress to settle more comfortably on the pillows. He closed his eyes, then opened them again when the spoon touched his lips. The rich broth helped revive the tired weakness invading his body. "I'm not helpless, Lettie. I can still feed myself. Don't you have cookies to bake or coffee beans to grind? Anything's better than your hovering like a vulture waiting for me to curl my toes under."

Lettie gave a snort and dipped the spoon back into the broth. "You're a leftie. Which means you're 'bout as awkward as a dancer with two right feet. I don't want you dribblin' all over my good coverlet. So quit your fussin' and open wide."

Acquiescing, Jim obeyed. Between bites, he tried to ask questions. "Why am I here, Lettie? How come somebody didn't take me to the ranch?"

Lettie lifted the napkin and wiped a dribble from the corner of his mouth. "Time enough for answers when you're up to it. Now, c'mon and finish up this broth before it gets cold."

Nourished by the soup, and exhausted from the effort of sitting up, Jim closed his eyes and succumbed to a drug-induced unconsciousness. He thought he whispered, "Tessa."

Through a whirling haze, he heard himself calling her name; he watched from the fringes of the netherworld as he strode down the barn's walkway, and suddenly the terrible scene of his father-in-law dangling from a rope and a vision of his wife's battered body rushed through him like floodwaters breaching their banks, drowning his senses and making it difficult to breath. He tried to open his eyes. He didn't want to see, but the images rose before him, erupting into his mind so vividly that he could neither stop them nor deny them.

"Jim…Jim…it's Lettie." She shushed him in a soft voice. The cool, damp cloth on his forehead soothed him.

He struggled to bring her face into focus. "I was

dreaming about Tessa."

"Are you in pain? Do you need more laudanum?" Lettie Edwards was already mixing the cloudy concoction. As before, she placed her arm behind the pillow to help lift him forward as he swallowed. He grimaced as he lay back.

"I saw Tessa, and what those bastards did to her." He strained to rise up on his good elbow only to collapse against the pillow. He sucked in a sharp breath against the red tides of pain that seared through his shoulder. He lay there, his chest heaving, the beats of his heart thundering in his ears. He fought against the effects of the laudanum. "Tell me it was a dream, Lettie. Tell me when I get home Joe will be sitting on the porch smoking his pipe. Tell me..." His voice drifted off as he fought the murky haze threatening to drag him into the bowels of darkness.

The force within him was trying to pull him down into oblivion, into nothingness, darkness, death. He refused to die, and struggled against it.

Lettie dipped the cloth into a pan of water and wrung it dry. She wiped the beads of perspiration from his face. Her voice was distant to his ears. "God help those sinners once you're able to use your gun hand again."

****

Alone in the bedroom, Jim solemnly stood in front of the window, his heart heavy and his eyes moist with unshed tears. His left arm still cradled in a sling mirrored his raw emotions. He felt as numb and useless as the fingers on his gun hand. Eighteen days had passed since his beautiful wife's death. He'd been unconscious and unable to attend her funeral. He sorely missed her and his father-in-law.

Beyond his grief, fresh and wrenching was the overwhelming sensation of remembering. He'd once had a family—a loving one. Not anymore. The knowing made him want to crawl back into the laudanum-induced void.

He tormented himself by recalling Tessa's soft ebony hair and how the strands felt between his fingers. He imagined, yet again, how the curves of her figure looked in the doeskin shifts she wore, and how she would feel, naked, beneath him. He smiled at the thought.

A bottle of whiskey and a glass sat next to the bed. He poured a drink and looked at the amber liquid. He lifted the glass to his mouth. Not a drop of alcohol crossed his lips. He tossed the liquor into the fire, admiring the burst of flames that disappeared as soon as it started. Just like their time together, he thought wryly of his beautiful wife. He paused then, still astounded at how much he ached for her.

Walking to the mirror, he barely recognized the pinched face with hollow eyes that stared back at him. He touched the row of black catgut stitches that puckered the flesh on his cheek.

The voice startled him. "You always were a little too pretty for a deputy marshal. The scar will add character to your face."

Doc Hubbards' image reflected in the mirror. Jim closed his eyes against the throbbing in his cheek. His words were a dry, harsh croak, struggling up from his throat. "It's a forever reminder of what was taken from me."

"Terrible thing, Jim. If you let it eat on you, grief

will destroy you. Tough as it may sound, Tessa would want you to get on with your life. So would Joe."

Jim frowned. A piercing pang of longing spread through him. The doctor's words gave him little comfort. "How soon before I can use my arm?"

"Don't go getting rambunctious. Wound that deep takes time to heal properly."

"How long, Doc? Every day I'm laid up is a day longer it'll take me to pick up the trail of those animals who murdered my family."

Jim watched the doctor pour himself a drink, then gulp it in one swallow. The old man shook and grimaced as if the whiskey were liquid fire. "I've seen my share of suffering, Jim. And seen my share of dying, too. Even so, I can only guess how the anger is eating at your insides. If you plan to do what I think you're planning, then give your arm time to heal. Either that or learn to handle a gun with your right hand."

Jim's upper lip twitched into a snarl. "I'll ask again. How long...a week, a month?"

The pudgy doctor heaved a sigh. He poured another drink and held the glass forward in a salute. "I see you're hell bent on self destruction. All right, then. Stitches in your face can come out in a day or two. But that shard of glass came a hair's tip from puncturing your heart. It tore through muscle and ligaments and blood vessels. All that needs time to heal, the way it should. In another two weeks, you can shed the sling, then try simple things like feeding yourself. I can guarantee a fork will feel as heavy as a shovelful of horse manure. Trying to pull a revolver out of its holster will take longer. You'll most certainly need to push through the pain."

Jim reached out with his good hand to clamp down on the doctor's when he reached to pour another drink. Doc Hubbard shrugged his shoulders and released a deep sigh. "I read in one of my journals about a new study where working joints while submerged in water helps the injured limb to relax, but winter's coming on. The creek's already too cold for man or beast."

"What about a tub filled with hot water?"

Doc Hubbard rubbed his chin. A smile flitted across his puffy cheeks. "Anything's worth a try. You can either wait another ten days, give or take, or…take up a profession that doesn't require two hands."

Jim's heart beat heavy against his chest. Time was wasting, the trail of his wife's murderers growing colder by the minute. A searing pain greeted him when he shifted his arm inside the sling.

A knock sounded on the door. Marshal Hank Edwards poked his head in. "Lettie sent me with a lunch tray for you, Jim. Fried chicken, buttermilk biscuits, gravy, and a pot of coffee."

He set the tray on a table, then poured two cups of coffee and handed one to Jim. "Doc, Lettie's got a plate waitin' fer you in the kitchen."

The doctor grabbed his satchel. "Come to my office day after tomorrow, and I'll remove the stitches from your cheek. In the meantime, wiggle your fingers, maybe move your hand up and down, but keep your arm in the sling. And cut the laudanum in half. We need to start weaning you off it so you don't become dependent on it."

Jim sank to the chair. He lifted the cup of coffee. "Yeah, sure, Doc. Thanks." His voice sounded hoarse when he looked at the man sitting across from him.

"Any news?"

Hank Edwards tugged the end of his graying goatee and pursed his lips as he shook his head. "Sorry as I can be, Jim. Except for the hoof prints of a pigeon-toed horse, it's like them fellers turned into a puff of smoke and disappeared."

"Sure as I'm sitting here, it's Tessa's mare I spotted the day of the..." Jim choked on the word *murder*. "Spirit Dancer is pigeon-toed."

"It's been more'n two weeks, Jim. You know how quick a trail goes cold."

Jim merely nodded.

"One thing in your favor, we haven't had any rain. Maybe the wind hasn't blown dust over the hoof prints."

Jim lifted one muscular shoulder in a shrug.

A silence passed between the two men.

Expelling a weary sigh, Jim closed his eyes, the pinch in his heart growing. His mind flashed to his wife's lifeless body. With effort, he unfroze his muscles to look at his long-time friend and mentor. "Maybe Doc is right—maybe I won't regain the use of my gun hand. Do me a favor, Hank?"

"If it's within my power, you've got it."

Jim ran his thumb across the fingertips of his left hand. The numbness was still there. He flexed his fingers. They worked. He rotated his wrist, and flinched when pain streaked up his arm. "Tell Delbert, down at the gun shop, I need a double-barrel shotgun...sawed off, and a swivel holster, so all I have to do is raise, point, and pull the trigger."

The old marshal raised an eyebrow. "You giving up on regaining the use of your left hand?"

"Nope, but until I get the use back, I need all the advantage I can get. A sawed-off greener ought to give me the edge I need."

Hank harrumphed. "Danged right."

Jim walked to the window. He looked off into the distance toward a hill where an oak tree stood with its massive canopy. The ever-present ache between his shoulder blades knotted itself tighter as he focused on two lone grave markers.

The echo of boot heels against the bare wooden floor distracted Jim. He turned. The marshal stood at the opened bedroom door. "Sorry, Hank. Didn't mean to shut you out."

"No offense taken. Time to make my rounds. I'll check on you tonight and let you know what Delbert says 'bout the shotgun and holster."

Jim nodded his thanks. A festering was growing inside him. The need for vengeance was like water behind a dam before the sluice opened. Time was wasting, and the scum who murdered his family were getting farther and farther away.

He turned toward the bed, but the muffled voices outside the bedroom door stilled him. He strained to hear Lettie's words. "How does he seem to you?"

Hank replied, "Calm. Too danged calm."

"You don't think Jim's about to do anything foolish?"

Jim envisioned the old marshal placing a reassuring hand on Lettie's shoulders. "Let's just say it'll be a sorry day in hell when he catches up with those yahoos."

"I worry about his frame of mind, finding Tessa the way he did."

"Man's gotta do what a man's gotta do, Lettie."

"I know, but it doesn't make me feel any better. What if he goes and gets himself killed?"

It seemed to Jim that it took longer than a few seconds before Hank answered. He almost stepped closer to the door, but the old man's voice stilled him. "There ain't too many rewards on this here earth. A man's reward is how well he chooses to die. I 'spect if Jim takes a bullet, he'll die the best way he can—with his boots on, wearin' his badge, and thinking of Tessa."

The fading footfalls on the stairs assured Jim that Lettie and Hank were no longer outside his door. A little voice played around inside his head as he walked to the bed.

The mental wheels grew in a slow clacking racket until exhaustion from planning his revenge overtook him. The bed springs creaked when he sat down. It had been days of unparalleled torture. He found no rest in his lonely bed. He missed Tessa's warmth and her softly curving form snuggled against him; he missed reaching out and touching her in the middle of the night; he missed holding her in love. He missed her with an intensity that left him weak.

Chapter Three

Jim stood in front of the mirror. The weight he'd lost during his convalescence had left him a gaunt man with deep-set lackluster eyes and a look that forbade all familiarity.

An October wind whistled around the boarding house, a lonesome sound that matched his mood. A month since his injuries, and he still struggled to lift the Colt .44 from the holster draped over the cane-back chair.

He tucked the revolver inside his saddle bag. Then, gritting his teeth against the pain, he forced his left arm to swing the modified gun belt around his waist. He fumbled with the buckle, flexed the fingers on his left hand.

"Damn it all to hell." He balled his hand into a fist, then opened it wide. "Work…damn you…work."

Beads of sweat popped out on his forehead as he struggled to make the fingers secure the narrow leather straps and buckles in place, until he had the swivel holster rigged to his right leg. He walked around the room, testing the weight of the sawed-off shotgun. He crouched into a gunfighter's stance to swivel the weapon upward. He was slow with his right hand—awkward.

He lifted the brown bottle from the table, poured a glass of water, and stirred in two spoonfuls of laudanum, then grimaced as he chugged the bitter liquid. The bottle was half full. He corked it and dropped it into his coat pocket.

After slinging the saddlebag over his right shoulder, he settled his hat low over his face, low enough to hide the jagged scar puckering his cheek. His hand rested on the doorknob as he stood in quiet contemplation. He patted the bottle of painkiller in his pocket and vowed to wean off. He'd heed the doctor's words about getting addicted. A lawman depended on his raw instincts, relied on his cunning and quick thinking to stay alive. He had men to hunt down, men to kill. Without a backward glance, he slipped from the room.

****

His shoulder ached where the shard of glass had pierced dangerously close to his heart a month earlier. Jim sat back in the saddle and bunched the collar tighter around his neck against October's chilly morning breeze.

He shifted an appreciative gaze down at Lettie and Hank Edwards. "Thanks for all you've done for me, Lettie. Wish I knew how to repay your kindness."

Lettie's expression was serious, contemplative. After a brief time, she nodded. "May God keep you safe, Jim. My prayers will be with you. And may God have mercy on those wretched souls when you catch up with them." After a second, she added, "I don't think He'll hold it against you if you help them on their way to Hades."

Marshal Hank Edwards harrumphed as he tugged at the tip of his gray goatee. "Sorry as I can be that I can't ride with you, Jim. What with Ernie taking a bullet in the kneecap, and Melvin down with the croup, I'm the only one left to mind the town."

"Sometimes it's better to ride alone, Hank. This is personal—between me and them—when I find 'em." Jim darkened his expression. He flexed the fingers on his left hand. "When I do find them, there'll be hell to pay."

Hank drew a long breath. Jim studied the old man's face. "Spit it out, Hank, before you choke on whatever's stuck in your craw."

The old marshal's mouth firmed into a thin line. "There must come a time when good men commit evil. Ride for justice, Jim, not for revenge. Tessa and Joe wouldn't want it any different. Personally, I don't care how you bring 'em in—slung over a saddle or alive long enough to swing from the end of a rope. All I ask is that you stay within the law. The men you're after are animals, there's no denying it. Jest make dang sure you don't become one yourself."

When the marshal shifted from one foot to the other, Jim didn't miss the carefully guarded grimace. "Your hip giving you trouble?"

"Gittin' old is danged inconvenient." Hank placed a hand on his wife's shoulder as if for support. "Man lives to be my age and still wearin' a badge, he's 'bout outlived his time on this earth. I'd hope to pin my marshal's star on you when I retire. Guess I can wait 'til you get this job done."

Jim took in the older man's features. Sixty, face weathered by the sun, silver-gray hair, eyes once a brilliant blue now faded and cloudy. He sat in silent contemplation for several long seconds. Sixty years old...hell, most lawmen never lived to see thirty-five.

He gathered the reins, his jaw pulling taut. "Don't know how long I'll be gone, or if I'll live to make it back. If a better man comes this way, pin your star on him."

A heavy quiet slowly enveloped the three friends. Jim tipped his hat, and backed the gelding away from the hitching post.

"Where's your star, Jim?"

He pointed to his heavy jacket. "Out of sight. Pinned on the underneath of my vest."

Hank nodded his satisfaction. "One last word of advice, Jim. Always keep the sun to your back."

Jim let a smile lift one corner of his mouth as he glanced from Lettie's teary smile to Hank's concerned frown. He touched the brim of his hat, signaling his goodbye.

****

Low clouds bumped and bruised the sky. Jim smelled the rain coming on the edge of the wind. Weather would soon become his enemy, wetting the land, washing out the most obscure clues left by the men he sought.

The cemetery was small, and with the last fading vestiges of summer it seemed drab and somehow forlorn.

He stood at the two graves nestled beneath an oak tree. In spite of the crisp morning air, a cold sweat broke out across his forehead. He didn't know if it was from the overwhelming grief threatening to consume him or from the exertion after weeks of confinement. Pulling the hat from his head, he knelt between the two mounds of dirt.

"I came to say goodbye, Tessa. It may be a while

before I get back this way again. If it takes the rest of my life, I'll find the men who took you and your father…and our baby…away from me. Maybe I'll take a bullet and join you up there in the blue beyond. It's lonely without you, my sweet girl. Sometimes, at night when the town is asleep and all is quiet, I think I can hear your voice. If only you knew how much I miss holding you in my arms."

An ache of loneliness built in his chest as his fingers slowly traced the curved letters on the headboard. His mind flowed easily into the natural channel of remembering Tessa, and he relaxed his tightly held restraint, allowing his thoughts to wander where they would. He sat back on his knees, recalling an afternoon in a meadow of wildflowers where he and his young wife had lain entwined. The aromatics of the flowers had drifted through his senses while he reveled in their intimacy. The dusky-hued breasts, sleek limbs, and bronzed nakedness whetted his appetite until he was driven to touch, taste, and possess. In their brief time together they had savored the full measure of wedded bliss. Now she had been snatched from him.

He leaned forward and brushed crisp, brown leaves from around the wooden grave marker. The words carved simply read: Tessa Cloud Woman Sawyer. Loving wife. 1853-1873.

His breath hitched in his throat when he read the words and repeated her Comanche name—*Cloud Woman*. A strong breeze rustled the branches of the oak tree. For a moment it felt as if invisible arms had embraced him. He thought he heard Tessa's voice on the wind and caught a faint whiff of lilac scent. He thought he heard her say—*I'll always be with you.*

Though Tessa was part Comanche, she'd never lived among the tribe. Joe had bought Tessa's mother from a couple of trappers who'd taken her captive and were using her for more than cooking their meals. Malnourished and just plain worn out from abuse, the young woman had died a few days after giving birth. Joe Hennessey called the baby Cloud Woman after her mother, named her Tessa after his wife who'd died in childbirth years before, and then gave the newborn his name. He'd loved the little girl as if she were his natural daughter, and raised her in a white man's world.

But there was something mystical about Tessa. Something even she couldn't explain. She had a way with wild creatures. Perhaps she had spoken to him from the netherworld. Perhaps she would lead him to her murderers. A half-chuckle escaped Jim's lips. Perhaps he was suffering from the effects of too much laudanum.

Jim stood. He brushed leaves and dirt from the knees of his pants. Situating the hat on his head, he looked down at his father-in-law's grave. "Sorry as I can be, Joe, that I wasn't there when you needed me the most." A grievous sigh shuddered from Jim. His voice hitched. "You and Tessa take good care of each other."

A coldness congealed in Jim's heart. Gathering the reins, he toed the tip of his boot in the stirrup and swung into the saddle. Gigging the bay gelding into a canter, Jim rode down the hill and away from the graveyard without looking back over his shoulder.

It took an hour to cover the few short miles to the ranch he'd shared with his family. Stopping at the edge of the yard and seeing the burned-out remains of the house filled him with a rush of emotions. He was unprepared for the sudden flood of memories that almost overwhelmed him. Lowering his head so that his chin touched the collar of his heavy jacket, he took a moment to recover.

He rode past the house and dismounted, letting the reins drag the ground. Part of him didn't care if the horse wandered off. His anger rose as he strode toward the barn. He stopped at the door. Visions of Tessa's battered body wouldn't allow him to go inside. Changing direction, he walked around the structure, taking his time, using the toe of his boot to flick away a clump of dirt here or there. From time to time he squatted to smooth his hand over a hoof print or to check a rock to see if the edges had been scraped by a boot. He found nothing out of the ordinary. Inside the corral were many hoof prints—scattered—the dirt maimed by running horses.

Finally, a clue. Joe raised horses. He and Tessa gentle-broke them for the Army, and a few they sold to the livery in town to use as carriage horses. These weren't wild broncos. They were handled every day until completely gentle. Joe didn't sell mares to the Army, only geldings. These were geldings that didn't run and kick up their heels unless they were panicked.

The hairs at the base of his skull prickled. Something didn't feel right, but what? He turned, slowly, deliberately. His deep voice bellowed his frustration. It seemed the birds stopped their twittering to listen.

"Damn it all to hell! It's right in front of me. Why can't I see it? A sign, I need a sign."

A strong breeze toppled the hat from his head. When he bent to retrieve it, a dust-devil whirled the hat just out of his fingers' reach, propelling Jim forward. Not a man given to goose bumps, his arms prickled when the perfume of lilacs wafted around him. Closing his eyes, he inhaled Tessa's familiar scent. Impossible. His gaze drifted toward the charred ruins where the house once stood. Nothing remained, not even his wife's precious lilac bush.

He squinted against the sun as he looked up at the sky. "Tessa, is that you playing jokes on me?" He shook his head, thinking his question ridiculous. Nah, he didn't believe in ghosts.

Snatching the hat, he slapped it against his thigh to rid it of dirt, and settled it on his head.

He paused for a half-second. The clue he needed was staring at him like a huge grin. The large wooden gate to the corral was swung wide. He'd walked through the six-foot opening without giving it a second thought.

Like a bloodhound who'd picked up a scent, he studied the ground and was careful not to scuff his boots against the dirt. He followed the singular line of prints. The top of his head itched. He needed to remember something. Think...think.

Then it dawned on him. The horses had been rope-tied to one another and led out in a single file. This is what he'd glimpsed the evening of the fire. The distance had been too far for him to realize it was riders leading horses. All except for the one rider who separately led a liver-spotted appaloosa.

Horse thieves, who'd committed rape and murder. Horse thieves who would try to sell the stock for whatever price they could get. Horses that he could easily identify. Every horse Joe Hennessey owned had a notched ear. "There's nowhere you bastards can run. Not now."

The question that begged answering was whether these men had scoped out the ranch and planned to steal the horses, or had they happened on the ranch and committed their crimes as an afterthought? Either way made no difference to Jim.

Part of him wanted to fault Hank for not spotting the hoof prints as a clue. The other part rationalized that Joe raised horses. This was a ranch, and at any given time, on any given day, there were horses walking over the property.

Jim had found his clue. He had one thing left to do. He clenched his jaw as quick strides took him to the storage shed. The door hung open. Another clue. Joe was a careful man. He'd never leave the door unlatched. Jim allowed his eyes to adjust to the darkness. It took a mere second for him to spot the empty space where a can of coal oil had sat. Now he knew why the house had burned so rapidly. The bastards had probably ransacked it, taken what money they could find, then splattered it with coal oil before setting a torch to it.

But why hadn't they burned the barn, too? Had they wanted him to find Joe and Tessa? Were these men he knew, who held a grudge against him? Still, how did they know to associate him with the ranch?

Questions...questions. They beat inside his head like angry hornets.

He slowly reached down and gripped the handle of a second can with his left hand. The muscles in his arm protested against the weight. He gritted his teeth as pain almost caused him to drop the metal container. He forced himself not to switch the can to his right hand. Blowing out a fortifying breath, he used both hands to tilt the can so that it trailed a line of flammable fluid as he walked to the barn, stopping at the door. He rubbed a finger along the still puckered edge of the scar that marred his cheek: A forever reminder of his loss, and of the mission that lay ahead of him.

Gathering his emotions, he walked down the barn's wide aisle, sloshing coal oil on both sides of the stalls until he reached the rear door that led outside to the corral. He tossed the empty can back inside the barn. Reaching into a pocket, he withdrew a match. He swiped the sulfur head against the weathered door, tossed it to a pile of hay. The flame didn't catch. He cursed as he struck another match. This time, he stooped and touched the timid flicker to the dry straw. Fire flared. Its thirsty tongue lapped at the puddles of coal oil, and like a glowing blue snake it slithered in and out of each horse stall until the entire structure was ablaze.

Jim stepped back from the heat and watched. Watched as fire shot through the weathered wooden roof. Watched until the sides of the barn collapsed like a deck of cards. And still watched as the heated tongue found its way to the trail of oil that led to the storage shed.

Cans filled with coal oil exploded like cannon balls. The ground vibrated, the air filled with stifling fumes, and flames pirouetted and leaped like exotic dancers.

Mesmerized, he didn't feel the heat, and watched until the last flames died to white hot embers.

It was all gone now. The house, the horses, the

barn, the shed...Tessa and Joe. The land was still his. He didn't think he'd ever return to this place.

Jim gathered up the reins of the gelding, mounted, and rode off toward the stand of trees where he'd first spotted the riders. Riding at a slow but steady pace, five miles seemed to take forever. He remembered how he'd called on the strength of his faithful buckskin, asking the horse to endure the pain of an injured hoof. No longer able to sustain the weight of a rider, Buck had been given to Lettie, and she'd promised to let the animal live out the remainder of his days without a saddle on his back.

Jim needed the stocky bay he now rode instead, with its broad chest and sturdy legs. With all four hooves being black, there was no fear of hoof rot. The animal was built for stamina. Jim wouldn't push for speed until it was necessary. He didn't know how soon he'd catch up with the miscreants. He didn't know how far he'd have to travel. He had time. Time to calculate how to carry out his own brand of justice.

His left arm ached. When he cradled it against his chest, the pressure pushed against the badge pinned to the underside of his vest, a reminder that he was a United States Deputy Marshal. He growled his aggravation and gigged the horse to a faster pace.

Jim reined to a halt under the shade of a tall cottonwood near the edge of the grove and dismounted. He ground-tied his mount, frowning as he contemplated where to look for more clues.

He walked a few feet, searching the ground, and then he knelt on one knee to examine a pile of horse chips. He lifted one of the round globs and squeezed. Months old, it crumbled like dust as it sifted through his gloved fingers. They had been here—the men who murdered his family. This pile of dung was left from one of the horses. It wasn't much of a clue. He'd take what he could get.

Grabbing the bay's reins, Jim walked a steady and straight path, searching, ever searching with the eyes of a lawman for what ordinary men didn't see. A broken twig that had dried and now dangled limp and lifeless. Coarse, black hair snagged on tree bark where strands of a horse's mane had tangled and caught.

An owl hooted from nearby. Jim paused, frowning at the knot that tightened his stomach. He looked through the maze of trees in the cottonwood grove. Light filtering between the canopy of leaves, dark and eerie, set him on edge. He shook aside the uneasy feeling as he moved along.

He tried to ward off the guilt that plagued him. After a mile, he came upon another pile of dried horse droppings. It appeared the men he was after had headed toward Rock Creek with their string of stolen horses. He reckoned the men figured they'd gotten away with murder since no one was trailing them. And they had, but that was their mistake. He was trailing them. These men would head for a lawless town, to a saloon, a lot of whiskey, and maybe a little horse trading.

Jim turned the bay gelding toward the creek.

He followed the trail until nightfall, when it disappeared into the darkness. After tethering his horse, he removed a sack of oats from his saddlebag and proceeded to feed the hungry horse a well-deserved meal. He checked the gelding's hooves for small pebbles or thorns. "You're a bit green, but you'll learn." He gave the horse a firm pat on the rump before seeing to his own needs.

Jim ate some of Lettie's provisions as he rested against a tree, sorely aware of his cold bed. He reached into his pocket and withdrew the bottle of laudanum. Though the night air chilled him to the bone, perspiration peppered his forehead and pooled beneath his armpits from the ceaseless throbbing in his shoulder. His arm felt too heavy to lift, the tips of his fingers numb to the touch.

The temptation to swig the medication rode heavy. He held the bottle forward and saluted the night. "Here's to pain, and sorrow, and the devil himself."

His body fatigued, his mind in turmoil, he lifted the bottle to his lips. A wind kicked up. Why did the liquid inside the bottle suddenly smell like lilacs? The rustling leaves reminded Jim of chittering cicadas. Never a man who easily spooked, his heart tumbled against his chest when the wind dipped a tree limb down to knock the hat off his head.

Maybe he was going a little crazy. First imagining he heard Tessa's voice when he knelt over her grave. Then at the ranch, the wind blowing the hat from his head and skittering it as if pointing him to clues, and now knocking the hat from his head to distract him from swilling the strong opiate. Jim corked the bottle and dropped it into his pocket.

He remained quiet for a time. He would try to sleep now. "Okay, Tessa, I guess the pain's not so bad that I can't live with it."

At dawn, he was off again, cursing the green-broke gelding under him and wishing for his trail-hardened horse.

Although years of tracking outlaws had perfected

his patience, Jim found this time the miles dragged by at a frustrating pace. Revenge for Tessa kept him on edge in an odd way, as if he were fighting a losing war with useless weapons. He was so anxious to find the men he had to curb himself from riding the horse to its death.

When the poor beast started puffing and blowing, Jim stopped by a creek for a short rest. He cupped his hands and drank his fill, then rose to prowl restlessly along the stream's edge. After a bit, he pulled some jerky from his saddlebag and chewed absently. It tasted like boot leather. By all that was righteous, would nothing ease this unfamiliar ache? He sank down on the bank, feeling as though his chest were a bellows from which all the air had been sucked.

He missed her.

Her quiet strength, her sometimes foolish but clever wit, her gentle pride—all these made up the Comanche woman known as Tessa Cloud Woman. And Jim missed them.

When she smiled, revealing impish dimples, and turned those huge dark eyes upon him, it seemed as if, somehow, everything in the world was right. The knowledge that she was gone forever opened a new ache in his heart. With a low growl of sorrow, Jim finished the rest of the jerky.

He told himself it was only natural to shoulder the blame for the deaths of Tessa and Joe. After all, there were many he'd put behind bars, and plenty of vengeful relatives of those he'd brought in across the saddle. He should have known it was only a matter of time before someone figured out he had a family.

Deciding he'd allowed enough time for the horse to

rest, Jim tightened the girth on the saddle and swung up. By the time he reached the outskirts of Twin Forks, night had fallen again, and the ache in his arm filtered through his entire body, even into his soul. Numerous times in his life Jim had been bone-weary on the trail, sick of sleeping in the open, chilled and hungry. This evening there was something more to it. Anxiety had crept into his blood, tainting his every thought and action.

Chapter Four

A gust of cold wind swirled around Jim. He turned the collar of his heavy coat up to cover his ears and took in the town with a glance. Main Street was hardly more than a wide path churned and rutted by horses' hooves and wagon wheels. Prairie grass grew under the protective edges of storefront sidewalks, and the planks in the sidewalks were cracked from the summer sun and the winter rainstorms.

After sweeping the streets in every direction and detecting no signs of danger, he eased out of the saddle to tie the bay to the hitch rail and then pushed open the tall, swinging doors of the Twin Forks saloon. He took two steps into the smoke-filled, crowded room before letting the panels rattle shut behind him. Rather than give the impression he was seeking information, he paused inside the door to survey his surroundings. The ceiling was low, the room long and narrow, with the space broken by two stout posts that supported the upper floor. A solid bar, pockmarked from a multitude of brawls, angled across one corner from the hall, while the open area was crammed with small tables and crude chairs. A good many of these were filled with patrons, and a pair of shabby characters leaned against the bar. A more sensitive nose might have turned away from the stench of sweaty bodies, soured ale, tobacco, and the rancid contents of two large spittoons, but Jim was no pampered gentleman. He had seen both sides of the world around him.

He strolled across the room and selected a dimly lighted table, where he pulled out a chair facing the door. Almost before he settled into it a squat Tonkawa squaw ambled to his table. "You want to eat?"

"What you got?"

"Rattlesnake stew. Plenty good." She smiled a toothless smile and rubbed her rotund belly.

He nodded. "What's the best drink you got in this place?"

"Ale. It's the only thing can't be watered down much."

"Cold, and in a clean mug."

The woman's broad brow puckered into a deep furrow. "This ain't no fancy hotel, mister. You get whatcha get."

She offered another grin as she held out her hand. "Pay first. Two bits."

Jim reached into his pants pocket and flipped a quarter on the table.

She moved away. Beneath the ragged hem of her stained brown dress, her loose moccasins made a slight flip-flop sound on the floor. Her appearance seemed very much a part of this desolate life. Sizing up each man in the room, Jim idled until the Indian woman returned with his plate and a frothy mug.

Jim sampled the ale and wrinkled his nose at the acrid taste of the brew. If this was the best drink in the house, he mused with repugnance, he would be hard-pressed to order a second glass.

With unhurried ease he settled back in the chair, the low-crowned hat still upon his head. "I'm lookin' to buy a couple of horses. Don't need to be saddle broke, but I'd pay more if they were."

"Cherokee Charlie. Him always got horses. Easy to find if he's drunk. Today, he's drunk." She pointed to a man face down at a table, an eagle feather sticking out from a battered slouch hat.

"Where does he keep his stock?"

The Tonkawa woman shrugged. "Here and there."

Jim shoved a spoonful of the stew into his mouth. He'd had worse food on the trail, so he used the warm beer to help the greasy goop slide down a bit easier. The woman's reply, *here and there*, most likely meant the horses were stolen.

Not knowing how long before his next hearty meal, he forced himself to finish the plate of congealed swill and swallow the beer before he ambled out of the saloon. He stood in front of the hitch rail, where he stretched and scratched as if he had all the time in the world. The five o'clock shadow on his face itched. He yearned for a shave but knew a beard along with the horrible scar on his face were both good disguises. Twin Forks was a hole in the wall and, like all small settlements, a place where strangers became the center of attention. To his advantage, he'd never trailed outlaws to this flea-bitten burg.

He hawked a wad and spat. Might as well impress the person across the street peering through the window of the local whorehouse. He mentally counted the buildings. Six. No bank, no sheriff's office, no livery stable. A town destined to die or to be ruled by outlaws.

Settling the hat tighter on his head, Jim gathered the reins and lazily stepped into the saddle. He backed the bay away from the saloon, and then made a show of drawing the tail of his coat back to expose the sawed-off greener strapped to his right leg. Might as well let the peeping toms know he wasn't someone to mess with. A lasting impression might work to his advantage if the citizens considered him a man on the run.

A squat, piggy-eyed man wearing wire-rimmed glasses and a bowler on his head stepped from the weather-tired brothel. "You passing through, mister, or got business?"

"Who'd be asking?"

The man, looking decidedly uncomfortable, made a dry cracking sound in his throat that might have been the beginning of a cough. "I'm Peabody J. Hiers, mayor of Twin Forks. I make it my business to know what strangers are up to."

Jim moved his right hand to rest on the shotgun's twin hammers. "Looking to buy some horses. Feller told me I'd find Cherokee Charlie in this wasteland you call a town. Said the Indian had good stock. Don't reckon I can do much business with a drunk."

The mayor's hand trembled as he adjusted his glasses. "You don't look like a horse dealer, more like a bounty hunter."

"Man can't help the way he looks."

"We had some trouble a while back. Four men rode in...shot up the place. Carved up a couple of the girls, and didn't pay for all the beer they swilled down. We're a bit skittish of strangers. You understand."

"These men...you know any of 'em?"

"If you ain't a bounty hunter, then what's your interest?"

Jim shrugged. "None, really, just passin' the time of day."

"I'm thinking maybe you're a lawman."

"Done told you. I'm just a man looking to buy some good horse stock. 'Pears I ain't gonna find it here." How far should he push his luck with questions? "Why didn't your sheriff throw those men in the calaboose?"

He detected Peabody J. Hiers' slight flinch. "Four against one ain't great odds."

Jim drew his top lip into a sneer. "Meaning a town full of cowards hid behind locked doors while one lone man got himself killed. Well, Mayor Hiers, you and the good citizens of Twin Forks ought to be mighty proud of yourselves."

He turned the gelding.

Hiers called out, "If you don't want to wait for Charlie to sober up, his shack is about ten miles east."

Disgust souring the rattlesnake stew on his stomach, Jim looked directly at Hiers, then hawked and spat a wad that landed on the pudgy mayor's dusty brogan. He shrugged, not overly concerned about insulting the man.

Eyes narrowed in aggravation, Jim touched a spur to the gelding's flank. At the edge of town, he pulled the horse to a halt. The rancid fat from the meal burned its way up his throat. His stomach rumbled, then cramped, giving him only seconds to lean over the saddle to soil the ground. It felt as if the bottom had fallen out of his belly. Gulping breaths and blowing them out, he uncorked the canteen and swished water around the inside his mouth, then spat.

The air was heavy and dense and cold, yet hot sweat pooled beneath his armpits. He reached inside his coat pocket. Damn, his shoulder ached, and damn, he needed a dose of laudanum. His hand trembled as he pulled the bottle from his pocket. The young gelding pawed the ground, showing his impatience at having to stand still.

The jarring caused Jim to cradle his arm close to his chest and shut his eyes against the pain. He sat there, feeling weak and shaky, his stomach still rebelling. Maybe he should have listened to Lettie. She'd warned him it was too soon to get back in the saddle. Doc had warned him about the debilitating effects of cutting off the laudanum cold turkey. He felt like hell and wanted to drag himself to the nearest bed. His words came between gasps. "Just one swig, Tessa. I promise."

He used his teeth to pull the cork from the bottle. Lifting it to his lips, he forced back the gag as the bitter liquid seemed to cling to the back of his throat. Replacing the cork and then dropping the bottle back into his pocket, Jim shut his eyes, inhaled the crisp air, and blew out slowly.

The gelding tugged at the bit and squealed as it danced in a circle. Jim allowed the horse to move into a canter. He wished things were different for him, wished he wasn't a man always trailing outlaws, with danger and trouble blocking his path at nearly every turn. He raked through his memory, trying to figure out who could possibly know he was married and owned a ranch. The same answer kept coming back—except for his closest friends, no one.

His anger mounted.

For several moments he stared off into the distance. He veered off the trail and halted in a small hollow between several low hills. There were no trees, but various shrubs ringed the area. He dismounted and, shivering from pain, cold, and exhaustion, moved off toward the brush to gather wood for a fire.

Crouching over the pile of limbs and twigs, Jim selected a few of the smaller pieces, bunched a handful of leaves and moss in the center, and placed the nest-like arrangement to one side, then thumbnailed a match into life. After laying it on the tinder, he blew gentle puffs until the small flame grew stronger life, and shortly he had a fire going. While a cup of hot coffee would have done much to make the dragging hours more endurable, he passed on the idea. Curling into a ball, he allowed the soothing effect of the laudanum to work its magic.

When Jim opened his eyes, morning had come and gone. He sat up with an abruptness that caused a swimmy feeling in his head, his body stiff from sleeping on the ground and heavy from the aftereffects of the drug. Glancing around, relief settled over him when he spotted the gelding cropping snatches of grass. By some miracle, the horse hadn't wandered off.

Walking to the crest of one of the hills that encircled the hollow, Jim spotted a dilapidated shack and a pole corral that wouldn't hold a herd of sheep, much less wild mustangs. He studied the surroundings, then squinted as he glanced up. The sun was straight up in the sky. Close as he figured, it was two o'clock. He decided to bed down and nap until the Indian showed.

Gathering the canvas coat closer to his chest, he crossed his legs and lay listening to a meadowlark whistling vigorously as if trying its best to brighten up the patches of dirty gray clouds hanging around the horizon.

He slid the hat down over his eyes, released a deep, sad sigh, and settled in for a long wait.

The bay gelding huffed a squeal. Jim thumbed the hat back and cocked an eye toward the horse. Flicking ears and flared nostrils was enough to give reason to rout Jim from his resting place. In two long strides, he settled a calming hand over the horse's muzzle to keep it from whinnying. He soothed the animal with soft words. In somber contemplation, he watched the distant rider swaying back and forth in the saddle. An eagle feather sticking up from a slouch hat alerted Jim that his wait was over.

Stroking the horse's neck, Jim crooned, "Quiet, Red. It's not time to show our hand yet."

He scooped handfuls of dirt to put out the fire, then used the toe of his boot to scatter the ashes. Confident the fire was out, he stepped into the saddle and swung the horse in the direction of Cherokee Charlie.

Holding the antsy gelding to a walk, Jim snorted when the Indian slumped forward, arms draped on either side of the brown-and-white pinto. He followed the slow-plodding horse, half-expecting the old man to slide to the ground.

When the pinto stopped in front of the shack, it became obvious this was a well rehearsed routine for horse and rider. Jim gathered the frail body from the saddle. "C'mon, ole timer. Let's get you out of the weather and some coffee into both of us."

A bloodshot eye peered at Jim. "Who're you?"

"If you're Cherokee Charlie, I'm looking to buy some horses."

The old man leaned against Jim for support. "No have horses. You got whiskey?"

Jim chuckled when his answer was greeted with a snore. The old man had fallen into a drunken stupor. He half helped, half dragged Charlie into the cabin.

Inside, the adobe chinking between the gnarled logs had fallen out, allowing the icy wind to moan through the cracks, and the roof sagged. In the corner of the one-room structure sat a bunk with a corn shuck mattress that had long since been chewed to rags by field mice.

Charlie collapsed on the bunk. Jim folded a moth-eaten blanket over the man. When he'd started a fire in the old iron stove, he went outside to unsaddle the horses and turn them loose inside the pole corral. From one side of his saddlebag he scooped a handful of oats for each horse. Then, spotting a well, he drew a bucket of water.

Within an hour he had a lantern burning inside the cabin and a pot of stew simmering on the stove. The stew had come from one of several cans Lettie had packed in a gunnysack, along with potatoes, onions, a canister of coffee, flour, a sack of sugar, a slab of bacon, and a couple loaves of home-baked bread she had sliced and wrapped in oil cloth.

Her words brought a smile to his face. *What with winter coming, you might freeze to death, but at least you won't starve.*

When the stew and coffee were ready, Jim found a couple of chipped enamel plates and tin can coffee cups from the jumble on a shelf behind the stove. After wiping the plates clean on his sleeve, he dished up stew for both of them.

The old man's stench filled Jim's nose when he doused him with a bucket of cold water. He sat up, spitting and sputtering and spouting words Jim didn't understand.

Charlie made a feeble attempt to unsheathe the knife at his belt. The effort was too much, and he sank back to the cot. "What you want? Charlie have nothing left for white man to steal."

"First, my name is Jim Sawyer. Second, I'm not a thief. I'm looking for men who could've passed through here with a string of half-broke horses. I heard you were a mustanger and might have done some business with them."

Charlie lifted bloodshot eyes at Jim. "Food smell good. Eat first. Talk later."

From the loud rumblings coming from the old man's stomach, Jim surmised it'd been a while since Charlie had eaten. He laid a thick slice of bread on a plate and handed it to Charlie.

Ravenously hungry, the old man scooped up a spoonful of stew before it was cool enough to eat. He grunted between mouthfuls, and then reached for the tin can filled with coffee, wrapping his hands around it for warmth. As if desperate to get some of the hot liquid into his bone-chilled body, he alternately blew on it and slurped it, saying between blows and slurps, "Men come. Bad men. They have horses with notched ears." He used his finger to cut an invisible V through the air.

Jim's spoon stopped midway to his mouth. His heart thudded against his chest. He'd never known anyone other than his father-in-law to mark horses this way. Joe was of the mind that rustlers knew how to alter brands, but never a cut V. "Notched ears?"

Charlie swigged more coffee. He dragged the sleeve of his shirt across his mouth. "Yeah. I seen

49

plenty brands afore, but no notched ears."

"What makes you say these were bad men?"

Charlie lifted the calico shirt and pointed to the yellow and green bruises rimming his ribcage. Old bruises that took a long time healing. "Men ride through here. They have whiskey. They toss Charlie back and forth like a ball. They pistol-whip. Stomp him with heels of boots. Hurt Charlie bad. Steal horses, too." His voice carried a forlornness to it.

"How long ago?"

"Charlie old. All this talk make head hurt."

"It's important."

The old man rubbed the sides of his head as if easing an unseen pain. "Don't know. Little more 'n a month. Maybe less."

When they were both finished with their stew, Jim collected the plates. He refilled the cups with the last of the coffee. He rolled himself a cigarette and passed the makings to the Indian. A month, horses with notched ears. This was no coincidence. All he needed now were names.

Charlie's voice cut through Jim's thoughts. "Why you want to know about these men?"

"They stole something of value from me."

"Horses?"

They'd stolen something more valuable than horses. These men had murdered the two people who had meant everything to him. He circumvented the question.

"Did they have a liver-spotted appaloosa mare in their bunch?"

Charlie's eyes widened. "Me want to trade for spirit horse. She not much good—have pigeon toes. She no like the fat man or the skinny man. She try to bite. She kick the skinny man plenty hard. Sent him rollin' in the dirt." His laughter turned into a raspy spasm of coughing, and then silence.

The quiet echoed inside Jim's ears. Tessa's mare. "These men have names, Charlie?"

"Dobbs. All of 'em."

"How many?"

Charlie looked at his hand, then one by one held up four fingers. "This many."

"Which way did they go?"

"Cain't say. Charlie passed out long time from beating."

"Did you try to track them when you were well enough?"

The old man lay back on the cot and crooked an arm over his eyes. "Charlie old man. He tired now. Want to sleep."

Immediate snores filled the small space. Jim figured it was safe to catch a few winks himself. He dragged the chair to the corner and reared it against the wall. Settled with his arms crossed over his chest, he'd drifted to that place between wakefulness and sleep when Charlie yelled out, "For-neigh."

He leaned over Jim and with fetid breath wheezed, "I heard the fat man call one of them For-neigh."

Jim allowed the front chair legs to fall to the floor. He rolled the names around in his head. He'd run across a lot of outlaws in his time and had looked through hundreds of wanted posters. The name Fourney Dobbs didn't sound familiar.

"That's good, Charlie. What about the others?"

"Somethin' wrong with the skinny man's eyes. He

51

do this?" Charlie pointed to his eyes as he repeatedly blinked them. "Him called Blinkey. Fat man—him Bufort."

Fourney, Blinkey and Bufford Dobbs. "You said there were four?"

Charlie settled back down on the cot. "No hear name. Him have eyes like coyote." He heaved a sigh and pulled the threadbare blanket up to his chin. "No more talk. Charlie sleep now."

Jim resumed his position in the chair. He smiled, as if he'd been given a great gift. The one blemish to the gift was not knowing which direction Dobbs and his brothers headed. He gave the matter considerable thought. Colorado, Kansas, or Texas—that was the question. He lowered the chair legs to the dirt floor. Instinct told him the Indian knew. He reached into his saddlebag and withdrew the pint bottle of rye. Bending over the supine figure, Jim dribbled whiskey over the old man's lips.

Both eyes opened. A thirsty tongue searched for more of the fiery liquid. "This what you're looking for?"

Charlie sat up. He reached for the bottle. Jim held it out of reach. "Nope, not until you tell me which direction Dobbs rode."

"I tell you...I don't know."

"And I tell you that I see the lie in those black eyes of yours. You're a mustanger, Charlie. You said yourself you wanted the spirit horse. A mare like that doesn't come along but once in a lifetime. Why haven't you gotten on that pinto of yours and trailed after her?"

"I think a little whiskey might jog my memory."

"Nope. Talk first. Which direction did Bufford

Dobbs and his brothers head?"

Watery black eyes seemed to plead for the nectar inside the bottle Jim held. "True, me want spirit horse. I'm a no-good drunken Indian. That's why I not go after the mare. Can't get far down the road without needin' the firewater to calm the demons that make my body cry out for more." His voice rose to a begging whine. "Gimme that bottle. Me need whiskey...bad."

"Not until you tell me what I want to know."

"Ho-kay. I trail 'em about five miles or so. They go northwest. Unless they double back to the east. You give me bottle now?"

Jim poured a quarter of a cupful and handed it to Charlie. "Colorado? I figured they'd head for Texas."

"Not Texas. Brothers argue 'bout going to New Mexico. Bu-fort say too many wanted posters for them to pass through Texas. They go to Colorado, or Kansas, maybe, and lay low for a while."

"Did they say anything about killing a woman, Charlie? Think on this. Think real hard before you answer."

The Indian stiffened. The lines around his mouth hardened, and a look of resignation came into his hazel eyes. It was the first time Jim noticed. He took a closer look and wondered which one of Charlie's parents was white. Another shrewd glance revealed the features of a man who wasn't as old as he first appeared. By Jim's best estimation, the Indian's weather-leathered face and years of slugging down whiskey betrayed his real age.

Charlie stared off toward the trees and swore deeply. "They cut up one of the town whores pretty bad. Wasn't satisfied with just the one. Found a decent woman. Left her in a bad way. I reckon you could say they killed her. She hanged herself. From shame, is what I heard."

Somewhere off in the trees a rain frog uttered its harsh, forlorn call. Another answered. Jim and the Indian listened silently, and then after a few moments Jim stirred. He handed Charlie the bottle. "I reckon you earned it, old man."

Charlie pulled long and hard until he'd half-emptied the pint. He drew a tattered sleeve across his mouth, then stumbled back to the cot. He belched. "Wa-wasn't always a no-good, drunken Indian."

Snores broke the silence. Jim resumed his position in the chair. He pulled his hat down over his eyes. Every man has his demons. He wondered which ones haunted Charlie.

Before the sun touched the sky, Jim left several slices of bread, a can of beans, an onion, and enough coffee for several cups where the old Indian would find them.

Chapter Five

Jim considered it almost providential that the old Cherokee had provided names and without knowing had verified these were the men he sought. Leaving a few days of food was worth the information.

The bay's gait was smooth and fluid, all his movements harmonious, and his hooves moved with a swiftness that made up for the time spent in Twin Forks and at Charlie's. Jim figured the Dobbs bunch would ride toward Texas, despite Charlie's report. With fewer towns and more open areas, the high country made sense. A string of stolen horses would bring a hefty price from outlaws and Indians alike, with no questions asked.

Charlie had said Colorado, but the tracks seemed to double back northeast toward Kansas. Jim knew both territories well. He removed a coin from his coat pocket. "Well, Red, heads—we ride to Colorado. Tails—Kansas. You call it, son."

The horse squealed and pawed the ground. Jim chuckled as he flipped the coin into the air, then caught it. He opened his hand. Tails.

With renewed energy, he turned the big horse toward Kansas.

The sky, clear when he had ridden from Charlie's, had quietly clouded until it was now thickly overcast. The first sprinkles dripped from the brim of Jim's hat.

Rain and cold mixed with dodging hostiles didn't make for good company on the long ride to the border. The trees and shrubs all around him began to resound with the hard patters of raindrops.

The drizzle soon increased to a storm, and Jim cast around for a shelter. He pulled up in a shallow coulee. Dismounting, he untied the slicker from behind his saddle. It took a moment to shake out the folds. By the time he slipped it on he was soaked to the skin. Despite the wetness of his clothes, the garment collected steam from his body, offering a temporary warmth.

He reached into his saddlebag and withdrew a handful of oats, extended his hand, and allowed the gelding to nibble through the meager meal. "Take care of your horse first, and you'll always have a loyal friend who will carry you far." These were his father's words, and Jim had always abided by them.

Leaning back against the face of the bluff, he drew out the makings for a cigarette. Holding a hand close to the match to shelter the flame from the rain, he lit the end, drew in a deep drag, and held it a second before releasing the puff. He thought about his father, a Pennsylvania farmer who had loved the soil as much as he'd loved his family. It was a good farm, not large, but able to sustain a reasonable living. Then the war had come, leaving his parents and sisters dead, and the land ravaged. Barely fifteen, Jim had sold the land for less than its worth and headed west.

After years of drifting, a drunken brawl landed him in Hank Edwards' jail, an angry lad of seventeen trying to be a man. Lettie had taken him under her wing. He'd paid his fine by toting food to the prisoners, sweeping, mopping the jail floors, washing dishes at Lettie's boarding house, until Hank had declared the debt was paid and handed him a badge.

None of that counted for anything. It was the crosses on a naked hill that left his emotions raw.

Jim stirred to glance at the sky. The storm had ended, leaving everything around him sodden, under rainclouds still waiting to empty their contents without notice. Deciding against making a wet camp, he brushed water from the saddle and swung up. The slicker gave some protection from the wet seat, but he was already soaked to the skin, and the change was hardly noticeable.

He clucked the big horse into motion. The gelding had about five or six hours of going in him. Hell, they both did. He was certain the Kansas border was about a hundred and fifty miles away. If he recalled correctly, he was two or three days from the Goff River.

If the rain persisted, the creeks would continue to rise, the trails would turn to mud, and his travel time would increase. He broke out of the trees into a string of low, rolling hills. A movement to the left drew his attention and brought him up sharply.

Riders.

He swore under his breath when he counted six of them coming fast. He swung off the trail, inbred caution forcing him to be circumspect, and halted in a small, shoulder-high cluster of scrub oak and junipers where he had the flat side of a butte to his back. He snapped the sawed-off shotgun from its breakaway holster. He liked its heft, and the damage it would do, albeit at close range. The cold gunbutt warmed quickly to his big hand. The horses came into view.

Hunching lower to the saddle, he figured the riders

would pass a half dozen strides or so in front of him. Fortunately the growth in the area was thick, and unless the horse beneath him set up a ruckus he should go unnoticed. He was in an ideal position to spring an ambush if he so desired, and the thought did enter his mind, but he brushed it away. Ambush wasn't his style. Besides, a scattergun with only two loads wasn't much protection against six.

The moments ticked by with aggravating slowness. He whispered to the bay gelding to keep quiet. Jim clamped his left hand over the twin hammers of the shotgun to muffle the click and cocked the weapon. If it came down to a shootout, he'd be forced to open up on the nearest man, and then, during the resulting confusion, gig the gelding into action to make a run for it. The trees and thick shrubs limited his vision. With luck and the element of surprise on his side, he should be able to get away.

The head of a horse bobbing wearily up and down came into view. Jim tensed, tightened his grip on the butt of the greener. The neck of the animal appeared, and then the rider. The gelding shifted beneath Jim. He swore softly, then whispered to calm the animal. A brave rode past. He sat hunched forward, his leather shirt a dull brown in the weak sunlight. A rifle lay across his legs, and he looked to be dozing.

Jim flattened against the saddle and the gelding's neck. The riders passed within a half dozen strides in front of him. He soothed a hand against the gelding and felt the nervous quivers. He didn't much cotton to the idea of killing if it could be avoided. Killing came with the duty of wearing a badge.

A second Indian appeared, and then a third, all

asleep. He guessed from their demeanor it was a hunting party returning to their village. A fourth brave rode into view, this one with a deer slung over the withers of his horse. Two more riders passed, each with a carcass hefted across their horses. One pinto jerked its head upward, eyed Jim's position. His breath stilled in his throat as he reached forward and laid a hand on the bay's neck. The pinto lowered its head as if too tired to whinny. Judging from the men's clothing and hair, Jim knew he was in Kiowa territory.

He yearned for the soothing effects of a cigarette. The longing evoked a memory of Cherokee Charlie pleading for a shot of whiskey. He blinked away the image. Knowing the scent of tobacco would alert the hunting party, Jim stilled his urge.

He was glad the men he'd encountered were weary braves returning home from a hunt. He didn't relish a shootout, or losing his scalp.

He waited a good hour before moving from the safety of his position. As he traveled he fell to thinking about the Dobbs brothers. With the information supplied by Cherokee Charlie regarding the notch-eared horses and the violation of the women, Jim had no doubts these were the men who had murdered his wife and father-in-law. He'd fight the Dobbses to the death if necessary. A man had the right to avenge his family— to bring peace to himself.

Jim realized he needed to move faster and keep a sharp watch on both sides as well as the rear. He rode steadily, putting in long days that often continued into the night. He saw no more of the six braves or any others, and there was only a splatter of rain now and then. He had no precise idea of where he was, but he'd know for sure once he reached a small stream called Dead Man's Creek.

It was a landmark for him. Once there, with his bearings established, he'd be faced with the decision that had occurred to him earlier—should he head for Colorado or turn to the opposite direction, enter Kansas, and hope to run across a plow-pusher or a town hostler who might have bought a horse or two from Dobbs.

Colorado offered towering, thickly forested mountains, along with deep canyons in which the brothers could hide. But that was many miles away, and with few opportunities for profitable horse dealings.

Kansas was only a week's ride. Jim decided to trust the coin toss. Once he reached the creek he would cross the border, and another river with which he was familiar. From there he'd head for small towns. Towns who accepted riffraff without question.

Clouds began to build early in the day, and the smell of rain once more filled the air. He was crossing wide and open country now. Cover was scarce. The hills were low and rolling. Only occasionally did he come across a deep arroyo that lent him safety from hunting parties.

It occurred to him as the bay plodded wearily along that he could cut sharp right and head into the panhandle of Indian Territory. A haven for outlaws, it lay like a barrier between Oklahoma and Kansas. Under usual circumstances, a man fleeing from the law could find safety there. Jim had no legal jurisdiction in the territories, and his life wouldn't be worth a plugged nickel if he was caught wearing a badge. His scalp prickled at the thought.

Rain fell shortly after noon and continued

sporadically for the rest of that day, ceasing only when the soggy clouds masked the sun's descent behind a craggy range of hills.

Damp, chilled to the bone, and bone-weary from hours in the saddle, with no indication of where to search for the Dobbs gang, Jim drew the bay to a halt beneath a small cottonwood tree. The big horse was as played out as he. After picketing the gelding, Jim poured a measure of grain from his diminishing supply onto a patch of dried grass in front of the bay, then turned to his own needs.

First laying out his tarp and blanket for the night's sleep, he then rustled up an armload of twigs and small branches, built a low fire, boiled up some coffee, warmed a couple of slices of bread, and topped off the meal with fried fatback. He was getting low on food and would soon need to visit a settlement to replenish his supply.

He ate slowly, his thoughts wandering back over the years he'd been a lawman, then shifting to the present. His life had taken many twists and turns. The best one was the day he'd met Tessa.

Later, with the fire little more than a glow and coyotes yodeling in the distance, he filled his cup with the last of the strong brew and lay back against his saddle to look toward the south, where a few stars were visible. He singled out the brightest sparkler. Wrapping his hands around the cup, he said, "Lead me to them, Tessa. Help me find the men who hurt you."

A gust of wind kicked up and hovered over the fire, causing the flames to flicker and dance. He sat up abruptly. For the slightest moment Jim was certain Tessa's face loomed only inches from his. The easy innocence in her eyes sent a shudder through him. He was suddenly brought back to the present when a pair of coyotes approached the camp. The spell broken, Jim laughed out loud. "I'll be damned."

The coyotes tucked tail and slunk away like dark shadows blending with the night. Knowing their natural fear of men, Jim figured the scent of fried meat had attracted them to investigate his camp.

For some reason he felt better. Finishing off the coffee, he rolled a cigarette, smoked it down to a mere stub, and shortly thereafter crawled into his blanket. He checked the loads in the shotgun, keeping it tucked close. It wasn't four-legged coyotes that concerned him.

He went over each detail of the night he'd returned home to find his house burned to the ground, family massacred, until he stopped trying to work out the improbable and gave in to the seductive tug of sleep.

Despite his exhaustion, Jim tossed and turned for several hours, trying to make sense of his jumbled thoughts. Tessa's death cut too close to the bone, opened avenues that ran to his gut, and left him planning different ways to torture the Dobbs brothers. He wanted them to suffer, wanted to hear them beg for their lives, the way he was certain Joe and Tessa had pleaded.

He nestled tighter into the blanket to ward off the deepening chill, waiting as the night dragged on. Even while he was sleeping, something in his senses kept track of the ordinary night sounds around him—the chorus of tree frogs, the chirruping of crickets in the high grass.

The gelding huffed a squeal, snorting and blowing several times. The sound sent an alarm through Jim's sleeping body. He came awake enough to pull the blanket away from the shotgun. Thumbing back both hammers, he wrapped a finger around one trigger. He strained to see through the darkness. The shadow was no coyote.

"Show yourself...easy-like...or I'll cut you in two with buckshot."

"Must be losin' my touch. Indian 'sposed to sneak up on white man."

"Charlie?"

"Yep."

"What the hell you doing following me?"

Cherokee Charlie moved into view. He squatted and stretched his hands toward the fire's dying embers. "Got nothin' else to do. Thought to help you track men who stole your horses."

Jim eased the shotgun's twin hammers back into place. "I never said they were my horses, or that they were stolen."

Charlie cut a grin toward Jim. "Didn't have to. Spotted the notched V on your gelding's ear."

"Where's your pinto?"

"Tied next to that big bay of yours. Got any whiskey?"

"There'll be no whiskey if you ride with me, Charlie. I won't risk getting killed because of a drunken Indian. You savvy?"

Charlie harrumphed. "Reckon so. Don't mean I have to like it."

Jim settled inside the blanket. He pulled the hat down over his eyes. "Get some shuteye. We've got a long day of riding ahead of us."

Chapter Six

Two days later, Jim and Charlie camped at Dead Man's Creek. Jim tossed a small branch on the fire. Embers deepened into the glow of blood as the flames licked skyward. Early evening yawned into night while the fire burned down to gray cinders.

Jim poked the ashes with a long twig. "Supplies are 'bout gone. We'll ride into town tomorrow to restock, do some nosing around, ask a few questions. No saloons, Charlie."

"Not even one drink to scare off the shivers? My hands are tremblin' somethin' fierce. Don't know if I could hold my gun steady if I had to use it."

"Make your choice, Charlie. Either stay out of the saloons or ride on back to where you came from."

Charlie sat cross-legged. He gathered the edges of the blanket around his shoulders. "Your eyes are like ashes of a dead fire...cold but still deadly. Who killed your soul, Jim Sawyer?"

Jim paused for a moment, the cup halfway to his lips, giving time to consider the answer. He desperately sought within himself to tamp down the fury, and chafed at this unexpected question. It took a decidedly strong effort on his part to keep from telling the old man to go straight to hell.

The countryside grew hushed as if waiting for his answer. The air hung in breathless suspense.

Jim lit a cigarette and drew deep, holding the smoke in his throat before blowing it out. His eyes shifted toward the direction of his ranch. He missed Tessa's dimpled smile, her graceful movements, her silly patter, and the air of innocence that clung to her despite her hot passions.

His jaws ached with tension as he recounted the events that led up to this day…related how the shard of glass had impaled his shoulder, and the month it took to heal enough for him to strike a cold trail. He swung between anger and irritation.

"I miss her, Charlie. I miss the way she argued with me, and the way she fussed over me." He paused to savor the memory.

She was gone—forever.

Something inside him broke. He clamped his jaws tight. Lawmen didn't cry.

A cold breeze stirred the night, drawing Jim back to the present. He turned his face into the fitful wind to feel the tingle of misty droplets on his cheeks. It would snow soon.

He stared at the man seated close to the fire, hugging its stingy warmth. "You have a family, Charlie?"

The Cherokee leaned forward to stir the coals. His breath eased out in a ragged sigh. "Once."

"It's none of my business. No need to torment yourself."

"Sometimes talkin' is good medicine. Been long time since a white man cared to know 'bout ole Cherokee Charlie."

Ole Cherokee Charlie. The morose in the man's voice struck a deep chord and prompted Jim to ask,

"Which part of you is white, Charlie?"

The question caught the Indian off guard. There was no denying the look of surprise. "My mother. How did you know?"

Jim pointed his coffee cup forward. "Your eyes. Sometimes they're greenish yellow, other times blue. My wife's mother was full Comanche. The only way to know Tessa had white blood was her eyes. They were as blue as a summer sky."

Minutes crawled past. Jim figured the silence was Charlie's way of saying his past was nobody's business, but then he spoke, his voice a monotone as if recalling was difficult. And his speech was different, too, almost as though he were a different person, the person he was in his memory. "I was born in North Carolina. I lived in a two-story house with large white columns. My mother gave piano lessons. Her name was Penelope Ann. She was called by her full name. My father was a saddle maker. My white grandfather owned a dry goods store. My Cherokee grandfather owned a farm. By white man's standards, we were wealthy. We were a happy family. When gold was found in Georgia, land speculators came to take away what was rightfully ours. Instead of protecting what belonged to the Cherokee, the government betrayed the people.

"I was nine years old when we were put into wagons and hauled away. Many were placed in chains and forced to walk. My father begged my mother to stay behind where she would be safe. I was too young to understand how he knew the hardships we would face. She agreed only if she could keep her son. It did not matter to the soldiers that I was part white. They said I was Cherokee, and all Cherokee must leave North

Carolina.

"I will never forget the tears that stained my grandmother's cheeks as she clung to me, begging the soldiers to let me stay.

"For three years we walked. When we left North Carolina, many of the people prayed for life. By the end of the first year, many prayed for death. My grandfather, my father, and my mother died on the trail.

"When I was old enough, I took a wife. She was Choctaw. A good woman. We were happy. But life was not so good. There was no work on the rez. No work, no money to buy pretty things for a pretty woman. I was good at breaking horses. A man came to hire Indians. He gave me a job on his ranch, but he say no women allowed.

"I was gone a long time. When the job was over, I returned to the reservation. My woman, they told me, had taken up with a white man and gone away. I didn't blame her for wanting a better life.

"I took more ranch jobs breaking horses. Even worked for the cavalry, once. Took a liking to the white man's firewater. The strong drink worked its magic and helped me forget I was just another dirty half-breed. Most times couldn't stay sober. Can't break horses when you're drunk. I know. Got the shit stomped out of me, more 'n once. Got fired more 'n once, too. Nobody wanted to hire a drunk, Indian or not. After that, I drifted, caught a few mustangs to break and sell. Just enough for drinkin' money. You know the rest."

Cocooned in the blanket, Charlie lay back, curled in a ball, on the ground.

Jim placed another branch on the fire. He reckoned Charlie's age about fifty. A man with a lot of years left in him.

He closed his eyes and filled his lungs with the scent of wood smoke and damp earth. Every man had his own bag of sorrows to tote around. "Did you ever come across your wife, or learn of her whereabouts?"

Charlie laughed sharply. "Yeah. Found her whorin' in a saloon. She wasn't pretty no more. All used up. Didn't even remember me."

The night ebbed to tranquility, each man lost in his own thoughts. In the ensuing silence, Jim peered at the lump on the other side of the campfire.

"Charlie, do you believe in spirits?"

The man propped on an elbow. "We Indians put great store in spirits. Why you ask?"

Jim shivered inside as he spoke. "Sometimes I think I hear Tessa's voice, when it's really the wind. A few nights ago, I thought I saw her face in the fire. A couple of coyotes wandered into the camp then, and in an instant the spell was broken, and she was gone."

"I'm no shaman, Jim, but I don't believe what you heard was the wind. I think her spirit is angry at the way she was forced to leave this earth. Her spirit won't rest easy 'til you find those men. You plan to kill 'em?"

Jim's answer was cold and deliberate. "Killing would be too easy. I want them to suffer before they die. I want them to remember what they did to my wife."

Charlie answered with a slow nod of agreement before he shifted positions, rolling so that his back was to Jim.

"You talked different—just now."

"What you mean? Charlie always talk same."

"Nope. When telling about your family, you spoke

near perfect English."

Like the night shadows lengthened, so did the silence. Jim figured this was the old man's way of telling him to mind his own business.

"To the day she died, my mother continued to teach me. She said education would take me far. She was wrong. I am what is expected—a dirty, drunken, no-good half-breed."

The bitterness in his voice was evident.

"You have a name other than Cherokee Charlie?"

"Does it matter?"

"Nope. Just wondering."

"Haven't spoken it in a long time. Charles Ashwin. Charles for my white grandfather. Ashwin is Cherokee for Strong Horse."

"Good to know you, Charles Ashwin."

Jim rolled onto his back to gaze up at the stars. A slow grin spread across his face as his eyes settled on the star that glittered the brightest.

Chapter Seven

The town of Canton proved little more than ambitious lines laid out in the dust. Jim and Charlie stood beside the old trading post, surveying the collection of shacks, tents, and half-completed buildings that foreshadowed a town that had died before it lived.

Jim kicked at a clump of mud. "Town's not much. Just the sort of place that would attract a band of thieves with a string of stolen horses." He gave a look around. "Let's go in and see if we can scare up some breakfast."

"Yeah. My ribs are plumb stuck to my backbone."

"Afterwards, you mosey on over to the livery. See if the hostler has any notch-eared horses, or if any riders passed this way with about twenty or so geldings. With the exception of an appaloosa mare."

"Where'll you be?"

Jim faced Charlie squarely. "At the saloon."

Charlie's shoulders stirred. "Yeah, no liquor. You done told me."

Jim clapped the Cherokee on the shoulder. "Sober's not so bad once you get used to it."

Charlie followed behind Jim as they entered the building. The aroma of perked coffee greeted them.

A balding man wearing a soiled white apron looked up from his paperwork. "Howdy, gents. What can I get you?"

Jim said, "You got any food to go with two cups of coffee?"

"To be sure. We've got fried sowbelly, biscuits, and might scare up a couple of eggs."

"My friend and I'll each have a plate. Make the eggs fried, good 'n' done."

"You betcha. Sit anywhere you like." The storekeep hollered, "Belvadeen, got a couple of hungry drifters. Hustle up two plates, and kill the eggs." He walked to the potbellied stove. To keep from burning his hand, he used his apron as a hotpad as he lifted the kettle and poured two mugs of steaming coffee.

"How long you fellers planning to stay?"

Jim wrapped his hands around the mug. The heat warmed his cold hands. "Oh, long enough to buy a few supplies. Maybe stop at the saloon and wet my whistle."

Charlie cut Jim a mean eye.

"If you give me a list, I can fill your order while you're eating."

"All right. Two pounds of flour, slab of bacon, two pounds of dried beans. A dozen potatoes. You got any canned peaches?"

"Sure do."

"Four cans of peaches, two pounds of ground coffee, box of matches, tin of tobacco, and a package of cigarette wrappings. Two small sacks of oats."

The woman named Belvadeen set the plates of food in front of Jim and Charlie. "I got some honey if you'd like it for your biscuits."

Jim tipped his hat. "That'd be right nice, ma'am."

The storekeep said, "I don't keep grain. You'll

have to get it from the livery. Old man Vanderbeeker'll do you right."

"This Vanderbeeker, he do any horse trading?"

"Some, I s'pose. You fellers eat up while I fill your order."

Once the man was out of earshot, Charlie leaned forward. He kept his voice low. "Nervous kinda feller, aint he?"

Jim stuffed his mouth with biscuit, giving it a thoughtful chew. "Living in a town like this is cause enough to get nervous when strangers pass through."

The storekeep appeared, his arms laden with sacks of goods. "Ah, say, I-I need to tell you gents, I don't deal in credit. C-cash on the barrelhead."

Jim swallowed the last of his coffee. "I can pay."

"Yes, of course. I-I didn't mean to imply—"

"Stand easy, mister. Get the bill ready, and I'll settle up."

"Your friend... He don't talk much, does he?"

Jim grinned at the nervous man. "Only when he has something to say."

Once outside, Jim and Charlie divided the goods and loaded their saddlebags. They surveyed their surroundings. A few bedraggled Kickapoo Indians squatted against a building, blankets draped around their shoulders. Two men on mud-spattered horses rode toward the saloon and dismounted.

"I'll meet you at the livery in 'bout an hour. That ought to give me enough time to ask questions without arousing too much suspicion." Jim reached into his pocket and flipped a five-dollar gold piece. "Keep whatever's left after you pay for the grain."

Charlie's hand closed over the coin. There was an

edge to his voice. "I ain't no charity case."

Jim turned toward the saloon. "Never said you was." He glanced over his shoulder. "Another thing. If there's rewards on those ole boys, I'll split it with you."

Charlie offered a ghost of a smile, then headed toward the large barn with a sign hung over the door—Vanderbeeker's.

The November wind kicked up, and Jim lifted his collar. Muttering an oath, he flexed the fingers on his left hand. The fiery tingles seemed to crawl up his arm and settle deep inside his shoulder. He rubbed the throbbing ache.

He stood just outside the Two Bits saloon, opening the door an inch to look around before entering. Satisfied there was no one who would recognize him, he entered and sidled up at the end of the bar, where his back was to the wall and he had a clear view of the entire room, including its front and back doors.

The barkeep removed three dirty mugs. "What'll it be, friend?"

"Little early for beer. Got any coffee?"

"Friend, I got coffee, beer, panther piss, cactus rum, and firewater. If it's coffee you're wantin', then it's coffee I'm servin'.

Jim turned his attention toward the two strangers who had ridden in earlier. On second glance he noticed one of them dressed as a man and carried a gun like a man, but the hip on which the holster rested had an unmistakable roundness to it. A cold fist squeezed his gut. He pulled his hat down lower on his forehead and peered beneath the brim. A closer look verified his suspicion. *He* was definitely a *she*, and not just any woman, but Katie Em.

She was fifteen when he'd arrested her for stabbing a man to death. Later, when he found out that Katie Em was exacting retribution against the man who stole her virginity, he let her go. As far as Jim knew, she had gotten her life in order, married, and had a passel of young'uns. But here she was ten years later, packing a long-gun on her side, with a man who might have passed for a sodbuster in his bib overalls and slouch hat.

He did a mental search of the last Wanted posters he'd looked through. Either the man was a stranger to Oklahoma, or there were no warrants against him. Jim pretended not to know Katie Em. The last thing he needed was a loud reunion announcing him as a do-gooder lawman.

As luck would have it, she glanced his way, and Jim was sure there was a flicker of recognition and surprise in her eyes when she saw him, though she acted otherwise.

The barkeep set a mug in front of Jim. "So here's your coffee. Steaming hot, and strong enough to eat the rust off nails."

Jim flipped a nickel onto the bar. The man scooped up the coin and, laughing at his own joke, moved to wait on another customer.

It appeared Katie Em and the sodbuster were engaged in serious conversation, their voices hushed, heads close together. Then she clapped the man on the back, turned, and headed for the door. She gave Jim a follow-me look. He took his time sipping the bitter brew. The barkeep pegged it right when he said the coffee was strong.

After a suitable length of time, Jim made his exit.

He looked up and down the dirt road, wondering where she would head.

"Psst…psst."

He turned at the sound.

"Outhouse. It's a double-holer."

She disappeared down the alley. He took his time following. When she entered the door of the first privy, he went into the second. The wall dividing the two holes was thin enough to hear without straining. He could hear her peeing.

"That you, Jim Sawyer?"

"Katie Em. How are you?"

"Not good, Jim. You see that polecat I'm hooked up with?"

"Looks like a bad one."

"That ain't the half of it. He's into some deep shit."

"How come you're riding with the likes of him, Katie? After I let you go, I figured you'd find yourself a decent man, settle down, and raise a family."

"Things don't always work out the way you hope, Jim. But, listen, I ain't sittin' in this stinking crapper 'cause I want to catch up on old times. You did me a good turn all them years ago. I figure I owe you one."

"Seems I remember the promise you made." Jim peered through the half-moon opening in the door, keeping an eye on the saloon and the street. "As young as you were, you said you always paid your debts."

"I do if I can, but you've got to give me your word on something. Promise you won't let 'em know it was me what told you."

"Once given, I never go back on a promise, Katie."

A long silence followed on the other side of the partition, and then Katie said, "You ever hear of a group named Dobbs? There's four of 'em. Brothers."

For a moment Jim was certain the stench inside the outhouse had sucked all the air out of his lungs. "Why do you want to know?"

"Cut the crap, Jim. You know there ain't no such things as secrets. Me and the Jensens was passing through Texhoma. I was in the saloon. Everybody was talking about the fire, what happened to a certain Comanche woman, and that she was the wife of a certain deputy marshal by the name of Jim Sawyer."

"Why are you telling me this, Katie?"

"What those men done to your wife brought back a bunch of my own hurtful memories. If'n all they done to her is what I heard, it weren't right."

"How do you know about the Dobbs brothers?"

"I'm plumb ashamed to admit that we threw in with them and helped steal a few horses. Spent a couple of weeks with 'em. Fellers always got liquored up after a raid. Tongues got to wagging. The more they drank, the more bragging them Dobbses done 'bout that night at your ranch. I tell you, Blinkey Dobbs, he's wicked with a knife."

"What were you and the Jensens doing in Texhoma?"

"Pfft! Why're you askin' when you already know we were gonna rob the bank? When I found out it was your town, and what had happened to your wife, there weren't no way I was gonna steal from you. Enough had already been taken."

"Where are the Dobbses from, Katie? There's no posters on them."

"Said they was hill folks from Kentucky. Got into some trouble, somethin' about a feud, and was told to skedaddle and never come back. They drifted down to the Brazos and stayed in Texas for a while before moseying on into Oklahoma. From what I recollect, they never leave any live witnesses, and they always strike small farms. Places where there ain't guns to fight against them. They steal what they need—clothes, food, money. Bufford, he's the oldest, and the only one his mama didn't drop on his head. He don't let the brothers go into town. He goes when need be."

"Where is Bufford Dobbs and his brothers now?"

"May have already crossed into Kansas. Maybe not. There was some talk about ridin' all the way to Canada. Thing is, Bufford knows the law can't touch 'em in the territories. Just depends on how horny they get, if they go looking for a woman. Anyway, I'm telling you so's you don't have to go traipsin' all over creation and maybe never find 'em."

"This sodbuster you're riding with—the two of you up to no good?"

"Aw, shit, Jim. We're on our way to rob the bank in Ada."

"You've done me a favor, and now I'm not supposed to send a telegram to warn the sheriff?"

"If you do, and if Lonnie or any of his bunch finds out, my life won't be worth a fart in a rainstorm."

"How in the hell did you get mixed up with Lonnie Beecham?"

"Well," she said, "times're hard, and I sort of teamed up with Ruben Thompson. You heard of him?"

Jim sifted around in his memory and came up with the name and face of a kid on a Wanted poster, but the reward was so low that only a few telegraph offices had put them up.

"Ruben is…well…he's my kid brother. We have different pa's. Don't make no difference—kin is kin. Ain't that so?"

Jim knew it was a question that didn't need answering. He heard the ripping and wadding of paper. He figured Katie was about finished with her business when she said, "Ruben wants to get in good with Lonnie, maybe get to be a member of the gang. Personally, I think Lonnie and his boys are a bunch of no-good egg-sucking sumbitches, but the kid… Well, I sort of tagged along to look out for him, as best I can."

"What moniker does your brother use?"

"Aw, he fancies he can outgun and outride any man. He's just a snot-nosed kid of nineteen, but he don't like to be called Ruben. Guess you can figure why. Calls himself Tex, which is a hoot, 'cause we're Okies through and through, and he ain't never been to Texas.

"By the way, Ruben dresses in all black, and wears double holsters, but he couldn't knock the ears off a donkey if it was to come up and kiss him on the lips."

The sounds she was making indicated she was ready to leave. "Tell you the truth, Jim, it wouldn't hurt my feelin's if Beecham and his bastards got what's comin' to them. But leave me and Ruben out of it, y'hear? I want your word."

"Don't worry, Katie," Jim said as he heard her lift the latch. "I'm grateful to you. I won't forget this."

"I owed you. Now we're even. Wait a spell before you leave. Cain't afford to be gone too long. It might make my guard dog suspicious. Good luck, Jim. Give them Dobbs bastards the killin' they deserve."

Jim watched through the quarter moon in the door

as Katie Em strolled down the alley and turned in the direction of the saloon. She had grown into a fine-looking woman, but time and hardships would soon take its toll on a wild outlaw girl.

Chapter Eight

By the time Jim reached the end of the alley, two riders were riding past, one on a long-legged gray, the other wearing bib overalls and astride a roman-nosed chestnut. Katie Em went without saying goodbye, and with not so much as a nod in his direction, and Jim stood and watched her go. The look on her face was a mingle of disgust and shame.

There was one thing he remembered about Katie. She could talk the bark off a tree. The memory brought a smile. In the confabbing department, she hadn't changed.

He shifted his weight to one leg, looked up and down the deeply rutted dirt road like a man trying to decide which direction to choose.

The morning sun cast a shadow moving in his direction. Without turning, he said, "What'd you find out at the livery?"

Charlie came to stand next to Jim. "Wha-ho, thought sure I had you this time. Don't think my white blood knows the Indian part of me is s'posed to sneak up on people without them knowing."

More concerned with what he had learned from Katie and what Charlie might have learned from the hostler, Jim shrugged away the comment and walked toward his horse. Charlie followed, matching him stride for stride.

"Vanderbeeker had a horse with a notched ear. Said he paid fifty dollars for it. Bought it from a feller named Bufford. He didn't know if that was the man's first or last name."

Jim stiffened at the news. "Did he get a bill of sale? Did he know where Bufford was headed?"

"Whoa, slow down, pardner. One question at a time." Charlie shrugged. "Didn't think to ask 'bout a bill of sale. Vanderbeeker wanted to buy more horses, but Bufford said he couldn't spare any 'cause he'd promised the string to a buyer, and the only reason he was selling that one is he was runnin' short on cash. As far as to where he was going, the old man said Bufford spent a couple of hours in the saloon. Then he headed north toward the territories."

"When was that?"

"'Bout a month ago. You figure this Bufford is the same as Dobbs?"

The sun was high now, and the wind had died down. The fist twisting Jim's gut was as cold as the brisk air. "Reckon so. My guess is, he and his brothers aren't in a great hurry, otherwise they would have crossed into Kansas by now. You ever hear of Rattlesnake Junction, Charlie?"

The Cherokee grimaced as if a shiver shook him. "Bad med'cine, that place."

"Yeah. Let's go track down some killers and exact a little...justice."

The subject died there. Jim turned his eyes in the direction of hoof beats coming fast. A tightness filled his throat. Four of them. Something in the way they rode told him these were no ordinary cowpokes heading for the saloon to wash down trail dust.

Within seconds, before either Jim or Charlie could react, one man rode up the steps and inside the trading post, guns drawn and blasting away. The other three riders galloped past, firing as they rode. A bullet nicked Charlie's cheek before he fired two hurried shots from his .38, one of which hit a rider in the shoulder, knocking him backwards out of the saddle.

Jim, finding himself a momentary target, found his feet and, moving like a dancer, sprinted up the steps. A shotgun blast echoed in his ears, and a panicked horse nearly bowled him over as Jim entered the trading post.

A kid dressed in black lay thrashing and screaming on the floor, clutching the bloody hole in his chest. The nervous storekeeper held a smoking shotgun. "I-I had to do it. Why, he ain't nothing but a kid. You saw it, didn't you? I-it was either him or me."

Alerted by the sound of running footsteps, Jim swung his sawed-off greener around to bear on Katie Em as she appeared in the doorway. Cherokee Charlie was three steps behind her.

Jim looked around for a moment to get his bearings. "There a sheriff in this town?"

"Last one we had was run off two years ago. Ain't no law within fifty miles of Canton. If I had the money, me and my missus would have pulled out a long time ago. Decent folks know the town's reputation and cut a wide berth. This here is the last straw."

Katie cried out, but her cry was lost amid the screams from the boy on the floor. She shoved past Jim to kneel next to her brother and pull his head onto her lap. The explosion had knocked his hat off. She was weeping.

Jim said, "Better take care of that wound, Charlie."

The Cherokee pulled a bandanna from his pocket and wiped the trail of blood from his cheek. "Storekeep, you got any sulfur to put on this?"

"Yeah, sure." The man laid the shotgun on the counter and reached up on a shelf for a container. With trembling hands he offered it to Charlie. Then, shaking his head, he said, "I ain't never killed nobody before."

Jim knelt next to Katie. "I'm sorry."

She said, "Me and Pruitt was barely out of town when I seen 'em. Knew they was up to no good. I yelled, but Ruben just put the spurs to his horse. I didn't want him marked for this."

She brushed a lock of hair off the dying boy's forehead. "But what chance did he have? A ma who was too worn out and beat down to care what happened to her only son and a pa that was meaner'n a rabid wolf. I tried to tell Ruben there was more to life than being an outlaw. He just couldn't see it."

The boy coughed. Little bubbles of bloody foam collected on his chin, and then it was over. Jim pressed his hand to the woman's shoulder. "What can I do for you, Katie?"

"Help me get him across the saddle. I want to take him home to bury next to ma. She'd like that, I think."

Jim looked around. "Charlie, go bring up the gray and the black."

He turned back to the woman. "What about you, Katie Em? You're not marked for the outlaw life either."

She gave him a long wavering look. "I got no place to go. Ruben was the only kin I had. Cain't hardly read or even write my name. Whorin' ain't my style, so what else am I good for 'cept robbin' banks?"

Jim said, "Hey, storekeep, grab the boy's legs and help me tote him outside."

Once down the steps, Jim tied the kid's body, face down, on the black gelding. Katie mounted the grey. The storekeeper handed her the boy's hat. "Sorry as I can be, miss."

She offered a wan smile. "Don't fret yerself, mister. If not for you, then sooner or later it'd be some sheriff or a posse."

Once again, Jim turned his eyes toward the young woman. He leaned close so that his words were for her only. "Once you've taken care of the burying, head on to Texhoma. Go to the boarding house and tell Lettie Edwards I sent you. She's a good woman, Katie. She doesn't hold judgment against anyone until they prove her wrong. If you're a mind to live a decent life, Lettie is the one to help you."

"Don't reckon I want any help from a Bible-thumping do-gooder."

"Lettie would laugh at that because she's neither of those things. She wouldn't want it told far and wide, Katie, but life wasn't always kind to her, either. In her younger days, she was a saloon gal. That is, until she married Hank."

Katie smiled faintly at Jim's reassuring tone. "You mean she married a marshal? *That* Hank Edwards?"

"Life doesn't always offer second chances, Katie. Hank's a good man. If there's no Wanted poster on you, he'll hold no judgment either. If you are wanted, then he'll do the best he can to help you."

She glanced around at her brother's body draped over the saddle of the black horse. "Lots to think on, Jim. Seems I owe you, again."

Offering a wooden nod, Katie gigged the gray horse and rode away, leading the black.

Charlie came to stand next to Jim. "Handsome lady. 'Pears you two know each other."

Jim looked toward the woman cantering away. She had a tall lean body with small high hips, and two blonde pigtails that draped from beneath her hat and flapped against the back of her coat. Any observer could tell from the way she sat her horse that she was a woman of quiet pride, strong and independent.

"Our paths crossed...a long time ago."

"That a polite way of sayin' you don't want to talk about her?"

Jim's shrug was one of resignation, not indifference. "There's nothing to talk about."

Charlie pressed the kerchief to his cheek. "In that case, how're you at sewing? This crease needs some stitchin'."

"I'm a fair hand. Let's get it done. Then afterwards, I reckon you've earned yourself a beer."

"Wha-ho! Maybe I ought to get shot more often."

"One beer, Charlie."

The two men gathered the reins of their horses and walked toward the livery. Charlie said, "Beer don't ease the pain like whiskey."

"All right, a beer with a whiskey chaser. Then we've got a job to do."

Once inside the long narrow barn, Jim asked the hostler if he had a needle. Vanderbeeker produced one used for stitching leather and asked, "This do?"

"Looks 'bout right. Got any whiskey to purify it with?"

While the hostler went in search of a bottle, Jim

plucked a long strand of hair from the tail of Charlie's horse. "You know this is going to hurt like hell?"

Charlie snatched the bottle from Vanderbeeker's hand. "In that case, I need a little something to help deaden the pain."

Later, Jim sat with his back against the wall of the Two Bits saloon. Charlie nursed the beer in front of him.

The buzz around the tables was all about the shootout and how the storekeeper had taken down an outlaw with a double-barreled shotgun.

Charlie flinched when he touched the wound on his cheek. "Why you 'spose a kid would do a fool thing like ridin' his horse into a store and shootin' up the place?"

"Trying to make a name for himself. By the way, the man you killed was Gus Moses...Augustus Moses. Robber of banks and stagecoaches."

Charlie lifted the mug and drank until he'd drained the last drop of its contents. He sleeved away the foam on his lips. Then he tilted his head to one side. "I've got me a sneaking suspicion 'bout you, Jim Sawyer."

Jim lifted his own mug and, looking over the rim, said, "Yeah, what's that?"

"There's more to you than a man huntin' down a string of stolen horses and wantin' to exact revenge on a bunch of yeller egg-suckin' dogs. I s'pect..." He leaned forward and cocked his eyebrows upward.

Jim sat quiet for a long moment. The tone of his voice offered a harsh warning. "What is it you suspect, Charlie?"

The Cherokee laughed. "Nothing. Nothing at all. Guess it's the liquor gettin' to me."

The legs of the chair scraped against the wooden floor as Jim pushed it back and stood. "There's a good bit of daylight left. Let's saddle up."

Chapter Nine

After following a narrow trace, the road swung around to the northeast, a pale purple horizon ahead. A warming sun now beat on Jim's broad back, baking away the pain in his shoulder. To his right, the shrub-dotted land dropped off to a deep gully. To his left the terrain rose to a ridge that climbed to a peak a few miles beyond.

Jim drew great breaths of the clean, bracing air. He and Charlie had ridden several miles in silence. Reading the ridge, Jim drew in the bay gelding's reins, then held up his hand as a signal to stop.

Charlie said, "I hear it."

Gunshots disturbed the quiet, continually thundering on the afternoon air. Jim looked down into a shallow valley-like area. The slope fell away from the hill where he and Charlie had halted, ran on to meld into a narrow swale, and then became flat. There were oaks, black walnut, and pine trees and ragged brush.

Charlie stood in the stirrups. "Look. Wagons. Two. Be lucky if they don't overturn at the rate they're pushin' those horses."

In the center of the swale and skidding sideways on the muddy ground, the wagons raced toward the trees. Riding alongside in an obvious attempt to prevent the settlers from getting to the protection of the woods were seven men, triggering their weapons at the onrushing wagons.

Retaliating gunfire came from the lead wagon. Abruptly the man on the seat sagged forward. The rifle he held slid from his grasp and fell to the ground. Almost at the same time a shotgun in the hands of a woman crouched in the front of the seat of the second wagon added its booming blast to the fight.

There was an urgency to Jim's voice. "Looks like a man and a woman attempting to hold off some outlaws."

"Yep, but looks like the man's done for." Charlie swore as he pointed toward the second wagon. "Wha-ho, another woman."

"C'mon, Charlie. Let's even the odds a little."

Bracing himself in the saddle, Jim thumbed back the hammers of his sawed-off shotgun and started down the muddy slope. He'd have to leave it to the sturdy bay horse to make it safely to the bottom. He'd be plenty busy reloading the twin barrels of his weapon. Problem was the greener wasn't much good for long distance. As he came into range he snapped off a shot at the nearest outlaw. The rider he fired at, a lean, dark, bearded man wearing a tattered duster and a large-brimmed hat, looked startled when Jim's load of buckshot caught him in the chest. He toppled from his saddle and hit the ground with a bounce.

Another rider cut sharp and yelled something to his partner. Both then wheeled left in a direct line for Jim and Charlie. Instinctively, Jim grabbed the .44 from his holster. Steadying himself, he leveled his weapon at the nearest rider—a ferret-faced man clad in a faded Union uniform. Ignoring the bullets fired at him, Jim targeted the outlaw and pressed off a shot. The man clawed frantically at the saddle horn to keep from falling as he slumped sideways. The remaining rider pulled away, while the man in the uniform followed, and together they doubled back along the mud-rutted road.

Jim yelled, "Charlie, circle around. Get to the women. I'll take down those two."

Charlie popped off two quick shots at the remaining outlaws. He crouched low against his pinto's neck and raced across the intervening bit of rain-soaked ground toward the wagons, now halted side by side. He circled to the rear of the vehicles and pulled the pinto to a sliding halt.

In three long strides, Charlie made it to the front of the nearest wagon and climbed up onto the seat. An elderly woman held a man in her arms. Anxiety marked her face and her breathing was labored. She gave Charlie a tight look. "Go ahead, you've done killed my man. Might's well get it over and take me, too."

"I'm here to help, ma'am. Name's Charlie."

She sniffled. "He's dead. They killed him."

Charlie hunkered down behind the dashboard and reloaded his gun. "Sorry as I can be, ma'am."

He looked across to the other wagon. The woman with the shotgun peered over the dashboard. She offered a quick nod as she reloaded the double-barreled weapon in her hands. Two more heads popped up, both with pale strained features. The one with the shotgun yelled, "Get down." The two heads disappeared in the bed of the wagon.

An outlaw rode past, hanging on the offside of his horse so as to offer no target at all, firing his gun from under the animal's neck. Long, black hair flowed from beneath a cavalry cap. Charlie muttered under his breath, "Kiowa dog."

Another, a younger man, crouched low in the saddle, triggering rapidly. Charlie swung his attention back to the outlaw riding by at top speed. It was the Indian again, hiding behind the body of his horse. Charlie picked a spot, an exposed portion of the man's leg, and fired. It was a difficult shot. He knew he had missed an instant after he'd fired.

The younger man wheeled and came in fast. Charlie raised his pistol, squeezed the trigger. Nothing happened. He checked the loads. Four bullets remained in the cylinder. Misfire.

"Ma'am, quick, gimme your shotgun."

The woman groaned as she handed Charlie the weapon. "Oh, no, looks like another one riding into the mix."

With a quick glance in the direction she pointed, Charlie said, "No ma'am, that's my pardner, Jim Sawyer."

A scream came from the second wagon. Charlie twisted about. The woman with the shotgun rocked back. A spot of red spread out to stain the front of her plaid dress. Like a rag doll, she crumpled behind the seat.

The elderly woman next to Charlie screamed, "Oh, my lord! Those murdering scoundrels! Look what they've done to my daughter."

In an effort to keep her from scrambling out of the wagon, Charlie grabbed her around the waist. "You wanna get yourself shot?"

"My other two daughters are over there. They need me."

"They need you alive. Leave this wagon, and

you're just another dead body."

While Charlie popped the cylinder from his .38, he heard the Kiowa yell, "Death to the white-eyes!"

Without warning, an explosion filled Charlie's ears. The sound seemed to overpower his brain. White-hot pain sliced through his head. He turned to see what had hit him, but the world around him faded to darkness.

****

Jim steadied himself, peered through the hazy blue gunsmoke and, leveling his .44 at the oncoming rider, squeezed the trigger. In that same instant the pinto the Kiowa was riding lurched, and the bullet meant for the rider drove into its straining body. The horse seemed to wilt and abruptly collapsed.

Swearing under his breath, Jim shifted his attention toward the young rider heading straight toward him. His left arm trembled from the strain of holding the heavy gun. The strength had abandoned his fingers until he feared he might lose his grip. He dropped the reins over the saddle horn to use his right arm as a support. He braced his left arm and thumbed back the hammer on the .44, took aim on the rider, held the gun steady, and rapid-fired two shots that exploded in his ears like a single cannon blast.

Yelps followed the explosion as he whipped the gun around, thumbed the hammer, and fired on the Kiowa, who had managed to pull himself free from the fallen horse. Acrid gunsmoke filled Jim's nostrils. The slug distorted the man's features as he gripped his chest and fell backwards.

Darkness was closing in, and with it came a chilled, damp wind. Jim looked at the bodies littering the muddy ground. In the distance, three riders disappeared behind a line of hills. He hoped the men hadn't ridden off to plan a new attack, although he guessed there would be no more fighting tonight.

He trotted his horse to the lead wagon. "Hello, the wagons!"

A female voice called out, "Are you a friend of the Indian?"

"I'm Jim Sawyer. Cherokee Charlie is my partner."

The older woman climbed over the wagon seat. "Are they gone, Mr. Sawyer?"

"For the night. I can't say about tomorrow."

"Your friend, Charlie, he took a bullet to the head. It's pretty bad. He needs a doctor."

A young woman holding a shotgun walked from behind the wagon. She hefted the weapon to her shoulder. "Don't trust him, Mama. It could be a ruse."

"Hush your mouth, Ada Mae." The older woman scolded her daughter. "I'm Mildred Collins. Folks call me Millie. This is my youngest. She tends to be more outspoken than necessary. Her sister Cora Beth is tending your friend." Tears rushed to her eyes, and she lifted the hem of her apron to cover her face. "And…and Bernice was the oldest."

Ada Mae put an arm around her mother and drew her close. She looked up at Jim. "Understand that I'm not apologizing for what I just said, 'cause I still don't know if I trust you. Anyhow, will you help me bury my sister and pa?"

Jim looked more closely at the girl standing in the failing light. Her face was pinched with tension, and dark circles of fatigue shadowed her eyes. He figured her for not more than sixteen. What possessed a man to bring four women west, and without the protection of a wagon train?

"If you have a shovel, ma'am, I'll take care of the burying. I'd be much obliged if you and your daughter could scare up a meal and some coffee."

Millie Collins patted her daughter on the shoulder. "I'm not usually given to fits of weeping, Mr. Sawyer. We'll gladly share what we have with you."

She told the girl to round up a shovel for Jim, then help put supper together. Before he went to digging, Jim leaned the spade against the wagon and went to stand at the rear of the second conveyance. He spoke before entering. "Miss Collins, I'm Jim Sawyer and have come to check on my friend. I'd like your permission to come inside?"

Cora Beth pulled back the canvas. In the lantern light, her delicate features were serious. Off in the trees an owl belled, and another answered, their music a contrast to the blasting of gunfire only moments ago.

"I'm Cora Beth, and I'm afraid I don't know much about doctoring. The wound is deep where the bullet plowed through the top of his head."

Charlie lay with his eyes closed. The girl had torn strips of petticoat and used them to bandage the wound. His breathing was shallow.

"Are you a gunfighter, Mr. Sawyer?"

Jim squatted next to Charlie. He placed a hand over the Indian's heart and felt the erratic beat. "No, ma'am. I'm... What I mean is, Charlie and I are horse buyers. We were on our way to see a man about a string of mustangs when we spotted those outlaws attacking your wagons." He figured a half truth was better than an out-and-out lie. He still needed to guard his identity.

After a brief silence, Jim said, "Where are you folks heading?"

Cora Beth heaved a heavy, dejected sigh. "Well, as Mama told you, we are the Collins family, and we're from Alabama. My uncle bought a ranch in Colorado. Pa promised to buy in partners with his brother. That's where we were headed. Now, with Pa and my sister Birdie gone, I don't know what Mama plans to do. What would you do, Mr. Sawyer?"

His first inclination was to tell them to turn around and go back to Alabama. On the practical side, three women alone wouldn't make it. He was surprised the family had made it this far with their scalps intact.

"I can't advise you, Miss Collins. That's a decision you and your sister need to make with your mother. Right now my concern is to make sure we're ready if those outlaws decide to make another go at you."

Cora Beth placed her hands to her mouth. Her blue eyes widened, her fear evident. "Do you think those awful men will really return?"

"Can't say for certain." He excused himself. "'Preciate you taking care of Charlie. If you'll pardon me, I've got some burying to do."

Jim stepped down from the wagon. He grabbed the shovel and strode to where the two women had built a fire and were frying bacon and potatoes. "Ma'am, I'll call when I've laid your man and daughter to rest, if you'd like to say a few words."

Millie Collins wiped her hands down the sides of her dress. "Seems like Hiram and me have been together our whole lives. If pains me to leave him out here in the wilderness. And Birdie…Bernice—" Another stream of tears sprang forth like from a broken

95

dam.

His own loss still fresh, he felt the woman's sorrow. "Yes, ma'am." He walked off into the fading light.

An hour later, after a brief ceremony, Jim returned and looked over the wagon stock. Good sturdy horses built for pulling and going long distances. Fine animals, all of them.

"I don't know what we'll do without Pa," said Ada Mae. "Besides doing all the heavy work, he handled Butch and Buster. They have real hard mouths. It takes strong arms to drive them."

Jim settled down with a plate of food and a steaming cup of coffee. "You have any problems before this with outlaws?"

Millie Collins said, "No, this is the first."

Jim used his fork to point through the darkness. "I noticed your wagons made deep ruts. You're carrying heavy. Maybe the outlaws thought you had gold stashed beneath the belly-boards."

Millie Collins' voice carried a defensive edge. "I don't give a tinker's damn what they think. We don't have no gold, just a few precious pieces of furniture, trunks for our belongings, food for us, and grain for the horses.

"Mr. Sawyer, my daughters and me, we can't turn around and go back to Alabama. Not alone. Do you... I mean, could we hire you to escort us to Colorado? We'd pay, of course."

An uneasiness filled Jim. It appeared to be growing darker, and he guessed clouds were gathering for more rain, and he was convinced Bufford Dobbs and his murdering brothers were getting farther away. An already cold trail was growing colder. Soon there'd be no clues, and he'd have to depend on sheer luck and lawman's instinct to track down these criminals.

"Mrs. Collins, it's November. The way the weather's acting, it might snow any day. I've been to Colorado. This time of the year, there's already frozen snow on the ground. You've got good, sturdy stock, but pulling wagons up and over steep passes is dangerous enough in the summer, but more so when the trails are wet and slippery. My best advice is to head north into Kansas. You're only a week away from Medicine Lodge. It's a fair-sized town, with a doctor."

Thunder rumbled off in the distance. Millie Collins waited until it had finished. "You'll guide us to this town?" He supposed he should tell the women he couldn't escort them to Medicine Lodge, and explain why. They had experienced a recent loss. Surely they would understand why he needed to be on his way.

"Our lives are in your hands, Mr. Sawyer." He glanced toward Cora Beth when she spoke. She had slipped quietly from the wagon to sit next to her mother. Like the other Collins women, she had blue eyes and hair the color of wheat.

Ada Mae stiffened. Her face hardened. "Don't beg, Cora Beth. We Collinses don't ever beg. That's what Pa always said. We've come this far without any help!"

"But we had Pa and Birdie then," Cora Beth said. "Don't forget that."

Jim pulled his hat lower over his eyes. For his own sake, leaving these women on their own was the smart thing to do. Yet he couldn't find it in his heart or conscience to abandon them.

He glanced up at Millie Collins.

"By jingle if I'll leave a bunch of women and a wounded Indian on their own. Be ready to move out before the sun rises." Taking up the reins, he led the bay to the edge of the camp. He unsaddled the animal, pulled the feedbag over its head. He then pulled the makings from his pocket and rolled a cigarette. He inhaled deeply before releasing the smoke.

Ada Mae followed him. She offered an icy stare. "Are you going to be giving the orders from now on?"

Jim quirked a smile. "Count on it."

The young woman nodded. "I'm still convinced you're an outlaw. I'll have my shotgun handy every minute. If you make one false move, I'll blow your head off."

"Ada Mae!" Millie Collins scolded. "I'm sorry, Mr. Sawyer. I don't know what's come over that girl." She pointed her finger toward the wagon. "Get yourself to bed, daughter...now! I don't want to hear another peep out of you."

He heard Millie Collins' deep sigh. After the long, frightful day, the women were no doubt close to exhaustion. He tipped his hat. "I'll stand the first watch. I'd appreciate it if you'd spell me in about three hours."

Jim used the heel of his boot to crush the cigarette stub into the mud. He walked a distance from the wagons and settled against a tree, rolling his shoulder to ease the pain. *If I had any sense at all, I'd mount up and leave these women to fend for themselves. Nothing but trouble.*

A chilling wind whispered through the trees. A pine cone fell on the brim of his hat, knocking it forward. Jim chuckled. *Okay, Tessa. I'll stick it out until I get them and Charlie to Medicine Lodge.*

Chapter Ten

Jim sat in the dark shadows of the trees. The rifle rested in the crook of his arm. He thought about Tessa. His life had gone through many alterations in their abbreviated time together. He had never really noticed flowers or their sweet scent until she had pointed them out to him. Through his years as a lawman, he had watched many sunsets but had never appreciated the changing hues until sitting with Tessa in the porch swing. It seemed she saw beauty everywhere she looked. He closed his eyes and listened to the whisper of the wind through the trees and the music the dry, crisp leaves made as they rubbed against each other. He longed to hear Tessa's laughter. He missed the way her soft voice had filled his heart with bliss.

His eyes and throat stung as if he still smelled the smoke from his burning house. He had wanted nothing more than to lie on the ground next to the body of his sweet young wife, close his eyes, and never wake up. Until he apprehended the men who had taken her life, every reason dictated that it was his duty to live.

"Mr. Sawyer?" Cora Beth's voice brought Jim's mind back to the present.

Swallowing his bitterness, he stood. She appeared a ghostly apparition in the moonlight. He stepped from the dark cover of the trees. "Has Charlie regained consciousness?"

"No, I'm sorry." She held a cup forth. "This is the last of tonight's coffee. It seemed a shame to let it go to waste."

He accepted the mug. "Mighty thoughtful of you, ma'am."

A faint smile tugged at her lips, the first of the day. "You must be a kind man, Mr. Sawyer."

"What makes you think so?"

"You could have ridden away without a second look. Instead, you not only helped lay my pa and sister to rest, you also buried those outlaws. You could've left them for the buzzards."

When he didn't offer a response, Cora Beth said, "Well, I just wanted you to know we thank you."

He responded with an abortive laugh. "I'm not much good at receiving compliments, ma'am. I guess it comes from years of riding alone."

Jim watched the way she fidgeted with her hands. Her voice seemed extra quiet. "May I be so forward as to say that there is something about your friend, Charlie, that touches my heart. A person's true soul bares itself while they are unconscious. Is Charlie a good man? Does he have a family?"

Jim lifted his shoulders in a noncommittal shrug. He hadn't known the Cherokee long, but did judge him to have a loyal nature. "If you're asking what I think you're asking, all I'll say is Charlie is well into his prime. Anything else about him is his business to tell."

Cora Beth's lips trembled like a child's. Her voice held an icy tone. "I have passed my twenty-fifth year. In that time I have buried a husband and two babies, and now a sister and father. A hard life has stolen my youth, Mr. Sawyer. I don't need you or anyone else patronizing me. All I did was ask a simple question."

She turned on a heel and her irate strides slapped against the mud beneath her boots. Jim called out, "His name is Charles Ashwin. In Cherokee, Ashwin means *strong horse.*"

Cora Beth paused long enough to let Jim know she had heard.

****

At daybreak and fully spelled from his watch, Jim tightened the cinch on a sorrel that had belonged to one of the outlaws. The animal had wandered into the camp and seemed content to stay with the wagon animals and the two saddle horses.

"Ada Mae, this animal seems gentle enough for you to ride. I'll handle the team of hard-mouthed geldings. Your mother will drive the second wagon, while Cora Beth tends to Charlie."

"I want to ride the Indian pony."

"Nope. Not without Charlie's permission. Besides, Indian ponies are a bit temperamental. Tend to have a mind of their own. Like a certain young lady I've recently met."

The girl gave him a wan, unenthused smile. "People are always bossing me around. Ada Mae do this…Ada Mae do that. I can't wait until I can strike out on my own. And when I do, believe me, I ain't looking back over my shoulder."

She lifted her foot to the stirrup and with Jim's help managed to climb into the saddle.

He glanced around. The women had broken camp and hitched up the teams as he had directed. Through the gloom and misting rain, he cast a quick look at the other vehicle. Climbing up into the wagon, he gathered

101

wet lines in his gloved hands. Before settling on the hard seat, he called out, "Ready, Mrs. Collins?"

Millie Collins raised her hand, signifying she was all set. Jim touched the brim of his hat in a brief salute. He released the brake and, slapping the team smartly on their rumps with the reins, sent the wagon lurching forward in the dark, damp morning.

They drove steadily for a distance of two miles, the wagons slipping and sliding over the muddy ground. Jim swore under his breath at the slow pace they were being forced to maintain, but under the current conditions it was the best he could expect.

Ada Mae rode up beside him. She leaned close to hand him a woolen blanket. "Here, Mama said to give you this. Maybe it'll help keep you a little bit dry. At least until the rain lets up."

He accepted the cover and placed it about his shoulders, drawing it close to his body. "'Preciate it," he said as he strained to look ahead, trying to avoid gully ruts and low slopes that without notice could cause a wagon to overturn. Visibility was limited to only a hundred yards beyond the bobbing heads of the team. As the lines seesawed back and forth, he wondered about the outlaws, and Bufford Dobbs, and if he'd ever catch up to the brothers. He wondered, too, about Charlie. Would the Cherokee live or die?

The sorrel trotted along beside the wagon. He called out to make his voice heard. "Ada Mae, why weren't you traveling with a wagon train?"

The girl said, "We were, until the sickness happened. Pa said us being healthy, he didn't see any reason for us to stick with them and possibly catch the illness ourselves. We cut off from them and continued on alone."

"What kind of illness?"

"Don't know. Some said it was the pox, others said scarlet fever. There was even talk of cholera. All I know is there was a bunch of sick folks. I'm glad we didn't stay. Pa said with all the—" A vivid flash of lightning, followed almost immediately by a crack of thunder, split the dawning day and drowned out Ada Mae's last words.

The storm was moving closer, Jim realized. He brushed at the water lashing his face and covering his eyes. He lifted his voice. "Ada Mae, ride closer to the wagon. You need to get inside."

Her eyes widened, the fear evident. "You mean jump from the horse to the wagon? No, I can't."

He challenged. "What happened to that sassy girl who was going to leave the first chance she got and not look backwards over her shoulder?"

"Don't go mocking me. I might fall and get crushed under the wheels before I have a chance to leave. Besides, what about the horse?"

Jim scooted to the end of the bench seat. "Don't worry about the horse. He'll follow along. Now, take your left foot out of the stirrup and lean as close as you can. I'll grab hold and swing you aboard."

When she hesitated, he scolded, "Dammit, girl, do as I say."

Ada Mae squealed as she reached out and grabbed the two strong arms that lifted her from the saddle and pulled her across Jim's lap. A stabbing pain sifted through his still tender shoulder, causing him to grit his teeth as he scooted over to make room for her on the seat.

"Best you get in the back," he said, as the wagon tipped dangerously to one side. "Find a blanket and wrap yourself in it. And stay put. There's no need for you to get any wetter."

Leaning out from under the canvas arch, the girl appeared with a blanket draped over her head and clutched tight at the neck. "I hate this place. We had a nice farm back in Alabama. With Pa gone, I don't know what's going to happen to us…and where's the damned road?"

Jim glanced back. Through the gray veil of rain he saw the second wagon, rocking and jolting close behind. "Cussing isn't becoming of a young lady. Do it again and I'll stop this wagon and wash your mouth out with muddy water."

"You cussed. How come a man can do stuff and get away with it? Just 'cause I'm a girl don't mean—"

His voice gruff, Jim snapped out, "Get back inside and don't talk."

So far they had all been fortunate. Neither wagon had broken an axle or lost a wheel, and the laboring horses were holding their own in the slippery mire. Jim leaned forward, straining to see the ground ahead. He expelled a sigh of relief. He thought he spotted wagon tracks ahead. It proved to be a fairly well used road, and Jim was grateful for the break. He immediately swung the wagon onto the track. Again he glanced back. Cora Beth held the reins. He guessed she had relieved her mother from the constant strain of sawing the reins back and forth, fighting to keep the team steady.

Traveling became easier. The horses pulled without straining now. Rain continued to come down in almost impenetrable sheets, while lightning and thunder to the north increased. It appeared they were heading into the storm rather than moving away from it. He was aware of the hazards of traveling through hill country during a fierce thunderstorm. Small washes became raging rivers carrying loose brush and uprooted tree trunks to knock aside anything in their path.

The wagon lurched drunkenly sideways as a wheel dropped into a hole created by rushing water. It came with such force that Ada Mae screamed. Jim pressed himself hard against the seat, wet hands clutching the water-slicked leather reins.

He snapped an order. "Ada Mae, shift to the other side of the wagon. Do it now."

He slid to the right, hoping his and the girl's weight would act as a ballast while he struggled to bring the wagon back to an even keel.

Lightning continued to rip through the day, and thunder reverberated without ceasing. The weather seemed intent on bringing their journey to a disastrous end.

"Can't we stop?" Ada Mae yelled, her voice scarcely audible above the noise of the storm and the rattling of the wagon. "I-I'm afraid for Mama and Cora Beth."

"Too dangerous. We've got to find some higher ground." Jim paused, turned, and looked back. Despite rain slashing at his eyes, all but blinding him, he made out the dim shape of the wagon behind. In the eerie light, Cora Beth's face looked strained and frightened as she, too, gripped rain-soaked leather reins and strained to hold her team of horses steady.

Abruptly the front wheel of his wagon hit something solid. The horses seemed to sprint forward as the wagon snapped and then leveled out.

Sliding to one side of the seat and leaning outward, he yelled to make himself heard over the rain's deafening roar. "We've hit flat ground. Ought to be easier going for a while."

They had traveled another quarter of a mile when Ada Mae poked her head through the canvas arch. "Cora Beth says to stop when you think it's safe. I think she's all done in, Mr. Sawyer."

Jim nodded as he strained to see the road ahead. The rain had slackened, but the gray cover persisted. He was having difficulty keeping the team and wagon in the ruts. Now and then it was necessary to swing wide to avoid a washout.

"Just as soon as I can, Ada Mae. We're all about done in. The horses, too."

The girl's voice seemed to plead for Jim to understand her concern. "About those outlaws. Do you think they'll want to seek revenge against us for killing their partners?"

"Not unless they know you folks are carrying a large sum of money or other valuables. If that's the case, then yeah, they'll risk this weather to come after you. Do you?"

She blinked. "Do I what?"

He managed a wry smile. Without knowing it, the girl's expression had revealed the truth. Her family had something of value, and the outlaws knew it. He'd bet his badge that something was money. "Let's hope the rain continues until we cross into Kansas. Medicine Lodge is only a few miles from the border. Maybe we can reach town before the outlaws return."

The downpour continued to hammer at them, aided

now by a chilling wind that buffeted and rocked the wagon. Rain had soaked through the wool blanket. The wrap no longer offered him comfort, for he was soaked to the skin. He fought to keep his teeth from chattering from the cold, and from the pain in his shoulder.

An hour later, the downpour slacked off. Patches of moonlight appeared through the night-darkened clouds. Jim drew the team to a halt. The ground on either side of the road looked too soft and wet to support the wagon. He decided the ruts were solid, and safer than pulling off the road.

Cora Beth and her mother had hiked up the hems of their dresses to slough through the mud toward Jim. Millie Collins said, "Are we safe here for the night?"

"Safe enough, Miz Collins."

"Good." She turned to her daughters. "Cora Beth, Ada Mae, see if you can scare up enough twigs and small branches to build a fire. Supper won't be fancy, Mr. Sawyer."

"Ma'am, right now my stomach feels like it's stuck to my backbone. Whatever you sling together suits me fine. I'll tend to the horses. They've surely earned their keep today." He turned away, then back again. "'Preciate it if you'd call me Jim. After what we've been through, no need to continue formalities."

"All right, Jim. Now, what about the outlaws?" Millie Collins wanted to know.

"I expect they're holed up somewhere trying to stay dry. We're all tired, and the horses are near done in." He searched the horizon. "My guess is we'll see no action tonight."

He hesitated for the slightest moment. His face was close to hers, his mouth grim. "About that, Miz Collins.

You and I need to talk."

Millie averted her eyes. "Yes, I guess we do."

"How much money are you carrying?"

Though she tried to hide it, he didn't miss the slight shift in her eyes. "How did you know?"

"Men like them don't attack for no reason. Of course, you do have two daughters who might bring a fair price from the right buyers."

The woman looked around as if searching for listening ears and prying eyes. Her voice a mere whisper, she told him, "Near five thousand dollars."

Although Ada Mae had earlier let it slip, he asked, "How did those men know you had money?"

Millie Collins ran a trembling hand through her hair, her fatigue obvious. "I'm not sure, and I genuinely hate to admit it, but I think Ada Mae might have done a little bit of bragging. There was a young man on the wagon train. She was sweet on him. He'd often ride off and not return for a couple of days, always with the excuse he was scouting for game or Indians, or some such. Anyhow, we began seeing riders off on the horizon. It wasn't until the sickness struck the train that we left. I begged Mr. Collins to stay, if for nothing else but safety in numbers. He insisted if we stayed we'd catch the sickness, too, and probably die before reaching Colorado. We were only three days out when those awful men attacked."

"Uh-huh. For all our sakes, I hope you've hidden it in a safe place. If they take me down, those men won't stop until they've torn the wagons apart, and done worse to you and your daughters."

"Oh, don't you worry, Jim. It's safe all right." She leaned forward in a conspiratorial manner. "Did you notice how heavy the horse blankets are?"

She winked and gave a tsk-tsk. "Now, if you're satisfied, I need to see if I can get a fire going. My taste buds are hankering for a strong cup of coffee."

"What about Charlie?"

"When he wakes up, he'll have one powerful headache. How much longer to Medicine Lodge?"

"If the rain stops, two, maybe three days. There's a doctor in town."

"Good, 'cause Cora Beth and I have reached the end of our doctoring knowledge. We've cleaned the wound and wrapped it. Doesn't appear the bullet did more than crease his scalp. I can't figure why he hasn't come to yet."

Jim nodded his understanding. "After I take care of the horses, I'll stop by the wagon and check on him."

Two hours later, after a supper of heated canned beans, fried potatoes, and coffee laced with a shot of Alabama elixir, Jim nestled down inside the wagon for some shuteye. He'd stripped down and hung his wet clothes inside the wagon to dry out. With a set of clean clothes from his saddlebag, he donned a damp pair of long underwear. Cocooning himself inside a quilt, he figured as he dropped off to sleep he wouldn't miss much. If there was any action, gunshots would be his alarm clock.

Chapter Eleven

It seemed to Jim he had slept for only seconds when the wagon was suddenly flooded with light and someone was calling his name.

"Jim...Jim, wake up." Cora Beth held a lantern high as she called his name. "You said to let you know if there was any change in Charlie."

"Yeah, sure." Jim said, prepared for the announcement that the Cherokee was dead. "How bad is it?"

"He's coming to, looks like."

"Give me a couple of minutes to get dressed." Jim bounded off the cot, scrambled into his clothes, and left the wagon without stopping to brush the sleep from his eyes. He jumped to the ground and with long strides reached the second vehicle, where he found Cherokee Charlie semiconscious but at least alive. A sense of relief flooded Jim. And why not? The Indian had been at death's door and now had come back. He was puzzled by the bond he felt with the man.

His head swathed in bandages, Charlie's first coherent sentence to those looking down at him was, "What the hell is everybody looking at? You'd think I'd died or something."

Jim asked in a matter-of-fact voice, "Is there anything I can do for you, Charlie?"

A long silence followed. Then Charlie closed his

eyes. Thinking he had gone to sleep, Jim rose to leave.

The Indian squinted through one eye. "Yes."

Jim resumed his squat. "What?"

"Whiskey. Lots of whiskey. It feels like a herd of ponies stomped all over my head. Hurts like hell." He shifted his gaze toward the three women. "Beggin' your pardon, ladies. Didn't mean to cuss."

Jim patted the man's shoulder. "I reckon you've earned yourself a drink or two." He turned to Millie Collins. "Ma'am, how about a shot of your Alabama elixir?"

The woman nodded and got to her feet. The wagon squeaked as she stepped down from its bed. "It's in the water barrel. Best to keep it cool. Stuff's so powerful it's prone to explode when it gets hot."

The woman's comment caused both men to quirk grins at each other.

Charlie reached up and touched the bandages on his head. His effort to sit up seemed to take a toll on his energy, and he lay back on the cot. "I…want to say—"

Whatever Charlie intended to speak was interrupted when Millie Collins reentered the wagon. "Help prop him up, Jim. I'll hold the cup for you, Charlie. Even though I've laced it with a bit of honey, it's powerful potent. Got a kick like a mule. I daresay, it'll ease the pain and help you sleep."

"I don't want to sleep, ma'am. If I lay here too long, I might die. Need to get on my horse."

Jim placed a strong arm around Charlie's back to hold him upright while he sipped the half-cup of liquor. "You've got a serious head wound, friend. Your time to die hasn't come, not yet, so take it easy until we get you to a doctor."

Charlie gasped and grimaced as he swallowed. "Wha-ho! This is damn good firewater." He glanced around. "Sorry 'bout my language, ladies." He nodded toward Jim. "Could I speak to you...in private?"

Millie Collins grabbed the lantern and beckoned her daughters. "Come on, girls. We can take care of our personal needs and leave these two alone for a bit."

In the dim moonlit space it took a moment for Jim's eyes to adjust. Charlie lay like a dark shadow. His voice was hushed. "I visited the spirit world, Jim, and while I was there I saw Cloud Woman." He reached out and gripped the front of Jim's shirt. "The spirit world is a powerful place...a place the white-eyes do not understand. What about you, Jim? Do you believe in the place beyond the sky?"

Had it not been for his short time with Tessa and witnessing otherwise unreal events through her eyes, Jim would have denied any belief in spirits and netherworlds. "Tell me about Tessa."

He leaned forward to hear Charlie's words. Words for his ears only. "She is with you. You will hear her in the wind, see her in the clouds. She may even appear in the form of an animal. You are not to worry, for her spirit will lead you to those who did her evil. It is good we go to Medicine Lodge. One you seek is there."

"How did you know we are going to Medicine Lodge?"

"Cloud Woman told me. Her spirit is uneasy. She cannot rest because those men murdered her child. She seeks revenge."

Charlie's words faltered. He closed his eyes. The silence that followed became awkward by the time Millie Collins rapped on the side of the wagon. Jim got to his feet. He answered in grim satisfaction. "Charlie's resting. It's time we all get a few hours' sleep."

Jim stalked off into the shadowy outline of trees. From steely outrage to downright consternation, he wrestled with a plethora of emotions. He had only given the Cherokee a brief sketch of what had happened that night at the ranch. The one thing he had not mentioned was the little mound lying in the straw that would have grown into a son or a daughter had Tessa lived.

He looked toward the moon and one bright star. A frigid puff of air chilled him. The freshness of it brought back the memory of the first time he'd seen Tessa. He'd happened upon her bathing naked in a stream.

She had smiled at him and said, *Aho, I knew you would come.*

How did you know it was me and not another man?
I saw you in my dreams. There was no other.

The loss of her haunted him. Now there was new hope. Come the morning, life would begin anew. Quietly, he returned to the covered wagon and, not bothering to remove his clothes or boots, settled once again on the cot. He pulled the quilt tight around his body with one last thought. *The Dobbs brothers better watch out. 'Cause their asses belong to me.*

****

The road was slick and gullied in many places. Anything faster than a slow walk was out of the question, and cognizant of the predicament the Collins women would be in if they lost one of their wagons, Jim drove the weary team of geldings with care.

The rain had passed on, relieving them of that worry. His biggest concern was that the outlaws could return with reinforcements to rob the women of their money. He also knew these criminals wouldn't leave anyone alive.

Ada Mae's voice disturbed his thoughts. "Why do you supposed those men haven't showed up yet?"

He looked at the girl astride the sorrel trotting alongside the wagon. "It's anybody's guess, Ada Mae. They're around here somewhere. Could be the flooding has made travel difficult for them. Thing is to keep a watchful eye, and sing out if you spot any unusual movement."

The right front wheel dropped off into a deep rut in the road that Jim had failed to see, and the wagon lurched forward, silencing the conversation for several minutes. He slapped the reins hard on the horses' rumps to keep them moving until the wagon leveled off.

"Your ma said you were sweet on a young fellow who rode with the wagon train. One of those outlaws appeared to be only a few years older than yourself. Could he be the same fellow you had set to give your affections to?"

Ada Mae snapped out her answer. "Who I give my affections to is none of your business, Mr. Sawyer."

"So, he was one of the men. It's written all over your face, girl. Don't go forgetting he's one of the men who killed your pa and sister."

"You don't know nothing about it. If you love somebody strong enough, you can change them."

Jim hi-yupped the team. His voice was thoughtful. "I once knew a man who found an orphaned bear. He treated the cub like a pet. Took real good care of it. That little guy followed the man everywhere, just like a puppy dog."

Ada Mae offered a quizzical look. She shrugged. "And what does that have to do with Johnny Joe?"

Jim hid his smile by looking off to the east. She had not only let his name slip, but verified Johnny Joe Moody was one of the outlaws. Yeah, he thought he'd recognized the kid, and if the wagons made it all the way to Medicine Lodge, Jim planned to alert his old friend the sheriff.

"The point is, Ada Mae, the cub grew into a full grown boar bear. One day the bear turned on the very hand that had shown it kindness. Killed that man and ate him." Jim's voice was blunt. "Just like a bear is a predator, Johnny Joe is an outlaw, and nothing you can say or do will change that."

The girl made a noise of disgust. She spurred the sorrel forward to gallop away from the wagon.

They were moving through tall pines and firs, and despite the clearing sky, dark clouds hung heavy with the promise of more rain. There was considerable thick brush growing alongside the roadway. This set Jim on edge. The tall growth provided an ideal hiding place for outlaws.

In the middle of the afternoon, Jim pulled the team off the track and into a clearing. He set the brake and jumped down to help the women and to check on Charlie. After conversing a few minutes with the Cherokee, he approached Millie and Cora Beth. "I'm concerned about Ada Mae. She didn't much like what I had to say about Johnny Joe Moody. She rode off in a huff. Her not returning concerns me."

Cora Beth said, "What about Johnny?"

The expression on Jim's face caused Millie Collins to groan. "Oh, no. Do you think he's one of the men who attacked us?"

"I know it for a fact. Sorry as I can be, ma'am."

Cora Beth whirled about. "Here she comes now."

Ada Mae climbed out of the saddle and tossed the reins over a wagon wheel.

Millie's face went chalk white. "Where were you?" Angry lines deepened her features.

Jim only half listened. He turned his attention to loosening the harnesses on the horses and slipping the grain bags over their heads.

He heard Millie say, "Thank heaven you're all right. I don't want you riding off like that again. It's not safe."

Cora Beth cut in. "You went looking for Johnny, didn't you? Answer me, Ada Mae. Didn't you?"

The younger girl whirled around. "So what if I did? I didn't find him. I don't know what you're so upset about. I'm here, aren't I?"

Cora Beth grabbed her sister by both arms and shook her as if she were a rag doll. "Because he's an outlaw. Because he's responsible for our father and sister lying back yonder in cold, unmarked graves. That's why I'm upset. How could you be so...so disloyal to Mama and me?"

The girl shouted, "At least I'm not mooning over a dirty, stinkin' Indian."

From the corner of his eye, Jim glimpsed the older woman draw back her hand. The slap's echo caused him to turn around in time to see a sobbing Cora Beth rush to the wagon where Charlie lay recuperating.

A wind kicked up, sending sparks from the fire Millie had banked to brew coffee. Ada Mae squealed and swatted at the flames traveling along the hem of her dress. A thin cloud of smoke no bigger around than a buggy whip spiraled around the girl.

Jim rushed forward. He removed his hat to beat out the feeble flames before the girl's entire skirt ignited.

Millie swore quietly. "I swear, I've never seen such a thing. That bitty wisp of smoke almost looked like the figure of a woman." She rubbed her eyes. "I believe the strain is getting to me." She turned with a trembling sigh. "I don't think I can stand much more, Jim."

Jim laughed without humor. Millie hadn't imagined what she'd seen. The hairs on the back of his neck prickled. Maybe Charlie wasn't hallucinating when he claimed Tessa's spirit remained close by.

"Tomorrow, Miz Collins. Tomorrow, if the weather holds, and if we don't stop for a noon break, we should make Medicine Lodge by dark."

Millie Collins ladled water from the barrel into the coffeepot. She scooped in ground coffee from a sack and set the pot on a flat rock she used for gathering heat. "Ada Mae is old enough to know what she wants. It'll break my heart if she chooses to go after that Moody boy."

Jim touched the woman's shoulder. "It will be a hard life if she does."

Millie heaved a sigh. "Are we moving on today, Jim?"

"No, ma'am. The horses need the rest. We can make up the time by pulling out at first light."

Millie faced him squarely. "I'm sorry if Ada Mae said the wrong thing about Charlie. I believe he's a good man. Just as you are, Jim."

"Forget it," he said. "Young'uns have a habit of pinning a label on a man whether he deserves it or not.

If it's the wrong label, then it's just his run of bad luck."

"Are you referring to Johnny, too?"

Jim scratched his jaw. "I'm sorry to say, I've come across a couple of Wanted posters bearing his name and likeness."

The subject died there.

Later, when he was alone in his blanket, Jim considered the incident with the unusual way the fire had caught the hem of Ada Mae's skirt, and how the smoke had wrapped around her. Laughter rumbled in his chest as he shifted to a more comfortable position. He wondered if Tessa had given him a little rehearsal of what was to come, and if she was now listening. *Tell you the truth, Tessa, I'll be glad to get rid of their company. Don't get me wrong. They're nice ladies, but I've got a job to. And I'm ready to get to it.*

Chapter Twelve

It was well after dark when the wagons rolled down the main street of Medicine Lodge. Jim guided the lead team to the rear of the livery stable. Millie Collins pulled hers next to his.

"Thanks be, I'm all done in, Jim. My arms feel like lead weights. I never thought seeing a town would fill me with such delight."

"I know Ed Lauder. He owns the livery and won't mind if we camp here for the night."

A voice in the dark called out, "You all wait a bit till I can get a light going."

"That you, Ed?"

"Who might you be?"

"Jim Sawyer." Jim hoped the old man wouldn't greet him as "Deputy" or "Marshal." He jumped from the wagon seat to land lightly on his feet.

A match flared in the darkness. It was followed by a yellow glow that spread through the interior of the large livery. Jim hurried toward the light. Keeping his voice low, he leaned in close. "Ed, I'd be obliged if you didn't mention that I'm a lawman."

"Working undercover, are you?"

"Something like that."

"Whoever these folks are, won't hear nothing from me. My word given."

Jim clapped the old man on the back. "I've got

three women and a wounded man. Miz Collins' husband and daughter were killed by outlaws attacking them, and my friend, Cherokee Charlie, took a bullet to the head while helping defend the women."

Millie, Cora Beth, and Ada Mae came to stand next to the men. Ed's voice held a chipper tone. "Jim, the lights are still on over to the boarding house. These ladies look as if they could use a good meal and a soft place to lay their heads."

Millie said, "Oh, it sounds heavenly."

"Well, then, that settles it. Jim, you unharness the teams, and I'll escort these ladies and get them settled. Back directly to help you with your friend."

Less than twenty minutes later, Jim opened the gate and led the horses into the corral. He went inside the livery and scooped sweet oats into two buckets. After filling the feed troughs, he cut the cords on a bale of hay and scattered it for the horses. "You fellows have certainly earned a feast and a mighty good rest."

Ed Lauder yelled out, "Jim, I woke the doc up. He's expecting you. Can your friend walk a couple hundred yards or so?"

Charlie said, "Ain't no need to talk like I'm not here. I can make it. What about the women?"

"Oh, Miss Annie, she owns the boarding house, she'll fix 'em right up. Don't you fret none 'bout that. Said she'd even fry up some extra pieces of chicken and taters to send over for you two."

With a man on each side to support him, Charlie managed to make it down the boardwalk and up the stairs to the doctor's office, where he collapsed on the bed.

Doctor Schuyler adjusted the spectacles on his

nose, then set to cutting away the homemade bandage from Charlie's head.

After examining the wound and giving a few hmms and humms, the doctor said, "You're a lucky man. If the bullet had gouged a bit deeper it would have penetrated your brain, and you'd be a corpse."

"How soon can I be up and about my business? Laying around makes for a lazy Indian."

"This is going to burn." The doctor poured the wound full of tincture of iodine. "It'll kill the little bit of infection trying to build. About healing, you'll be prone to spells of blacking out, and maybe even losing your balance. It'll be a few weeks before you're well enough to ride a horse."

Charlie sat up and swung his legs over the edge of the bed. He swooned forward. Jim and the doctor caught him before he fell to the floor. Charlie blinked his eyes as he lay back. "The whole room is spinning round and round, and I ain't even had a drop of whiskey."

The doctor poured water in a basin and washed his hands. He looked at Jim. "That'll be a dollar." He hesitated. "Folks hereabouts aren't partial to Indians, even the good ones. If you and your friend need a place to bed down, I have a spare room in the back. Heed my word—until he heals, a blow to your friend's head could make a difference in how much longer he lives."

Jim reached into his pocket and laid a dollar on the table. "We'll be obliged to take you up on the room, Doc." He helped Charlie from the bed and down the stairs. Once settled in the room, Jim lit a lantern. He spotted a woodstove and filled it with kindling to heat the room.

"Charlie, you take it easy while I go check on the women. I'll bring you a plate of food before stopping by the sheriff's office."

"You're a good friend to an ole Indian, Jim. Sorry I can't help track down the Dobbses."

Jim patted the man on the shoulder. "I've spent most of my life ridin' alone. This time's no different." He offered a smile. "Besides, I know a certain young lady who doesn't think you're old."

"Cora Beth has come to mean much to me in these last few days." Charlie, too, smiled as he closed his eyes.

Jim went across the street. A good hour had passed since their arrival in Medicine Lodge. Inside the boarding house, he inquired about the ladies. A few moments later, all of the women appeared.

"I know it's a mite late for visiting," Jim said, "but I figured you wouldn't mind." He directed his attention to Millie Collins. "The horses are taken care of. Did you get settled all right?"

She nodded. "We're comfortable, had a bath and ate supper. Cora Beth was getting ready to take a tray to you and Charlie."

"Mighty thoughtful of you, ma'am. Charlie is in one of the doctor's spare rooms. It's below his office. The door is unlocked."

Cora Beth said, "What about you, Jim?"

"Don't fret about me. I'll eat after tending to some business."

Ada Mae stepped forward, her arms crossed over her breast. "You going to tell the sheriff about Johnny?"

Jim shrugged. "Maybe. Miz Collins, there's a telegraph in town, if you've a mind to contact your brother-in-law." He smiled and took her hand in his. "Good luck to you."

"Wait, Jim, are you leaving us?"

"I've delayed my business long enough. If all goes as planned, I'll pull out in a day or two. Just wanted to wish you luck in case our paths don't cross before I leave."

"You, too," Millie said, with tears dampening her cheeks.

****

Jim shook hands with the sheriff. "Good to see you again, Carl."

Sheriff Carl Witherspoon, a lean rawboned man in his fifties, offered Jim a cup of coffee. He used the toe of his boot to shove a chair forward. "Little out of your territory, Jim. What brings you this far north?"

Jim wasted no time detailing the attack on the women, and their losses. "I'm certain Johnny Joe Moody is one of the outlaws."

Witherspoon opened a desk drawer and pulled out a stack of Wanted posters. He flipped through until he pulled out one and shoved it toward Jim.

"Yep, that's him all right. John J. Moody."

The sheriff reared back his chair and locked his hands behind his head. "What else, Jim? Escorting a bunch of women, and finding a small-timer like Moody isn't reason enough to bring a United States Deputy Marshal all the way to Kansas."

Jim swirled the remains of the coffee before draining the cup. Agitated, he stood to pace back and forth across the office space. Anguish and anger caused his voice to crack at times while he related what the Dobbs brothers had done to Joe and Tessa.

His voice was as sharp as the click of a trigger when he spoke. "If I have to chase them to hell and back, I'll find them, and when I do there'll be hell to pay."

"Can't say as I blame you, Jim. I never heard of the Dobbses and don't even know if they're in the territory, but you can count on my help. Makes no nevermind to me how you bring 'em in—slung on a saddle or in handcuffs. Either way, if they're in my jurisdiction, I'll see to the hanging."

"One last thing, Carl." Jim asked the sheriff to help Millie Collins send her telegram and to see to their care. "If you can talk them into wintering in Medicine Lodge, I'd appreciate it. And one last thing. Cherokee Charlie Ashwin is a good man. See to it folks treat him decent."

Jim strode to the door and opened it. The frosty air was a contrast to the warmth of the room. "I'll ask Ed Lauder if he'll hire Charlie. According to the doctor, it'll take a while for Charlie to heal proper-like."

"And I'll keep my eyes and ears open. I'll pass along whatever I hear. Best to you, Jim."

Jim hunched his shoulders against the cold. Long strides took him to the livery. He called Ed's name.

"In here, Jim."

"Ed, you come across anyone with a string of geldings with notched ears...and maybe a moon-eyed appaloosa mare?"

The old man seemed thoughtful. "No...no, I'd remember, for sure." He snapped his fingers. "Say, didn't your pa-in-law brand his hosses by notching their ears?" He slapped his thigh. "How the hell is old Joe Hennessey, anyhow?"

The traveling, the lack of sleep, the need for a solid

meal was taking its toll on Jim. More so, the telling and reliving of the tragic end to the lives of his wife and father-in-law was exhausting, but he did it once more, for Ed.

"Dagnabit, Jim. I'm sorry as I can be. Let me tell you one thing. If I spot any of those yahoos, you'll be the first to know. Now, take my *ad*-vice and get some shuteye. You look 'bout ready to fall out. I'll bring you a tray of food. You just go on over to Doc's and settle in. Oh, yeah, and don't worry 'bout your friend. Soon as he's up and 'bout, I'll put him to work and pay a fair wage."

Chapter Thirteen

Ed Lauder scuttled down the whorehouse steps, crossed the street to the back room below the doctor's office, and tapped lightly on Jim's door. Identifying himself to the grunt from within, he said, "Jim, open up. It's me, Ed."

Jim slipped the bolt and opened the door. He had a .44 Colt in his hand. "It's late."

"I said you'd be the first to know. Feller with blinkey eyes is over to Nell's Heavenly Palace. She's waiting on you, Jim. This feller's got a knife, and he's slobbering drunk."

"You tell anyone else about this, Ed?"

"Nope, just happened to be over there for my midweek back-scrubbing when I spotted this feller. Nell was 'bout to go get Carl when I told her you was in town."

Jerking his pants on over his winter underwear, Jim said, "Saddle my horse and bring him around back."

When the old man left, Jim lit the lantern on the bedside table. Moving quickly, he dressed, strapped on his gun, and grabbed his saddlebags.

Charlie roused. "He's here, ain't he?"

"Yeah, the one called Blinkey."

"When I'm able, I'll catch up with you. Maybe I haven't lost all my tracking skills."

"Suit yourself."

Jim settled his hat low over his face. Wearing a heavy winter coat, a scarf, and gloves, the sawed-off shotgun strapped to his side, and the holstered .44 Colt, he stepped out of the room and into the dark alley.

Ed Lauder stood holding the reins to the long-legged bay gelding. "Good luck, to you, Jim."

Answering with a nod, Jim collected the reins and led the horse down the alley to the main street. He kept to the darker shadows close to the buildings.

A gust of cold wind carrying a few flakes of grainy snow swirled around him. He turned the collar of his heavy wool coat up around his ears. At this time of night, on this kind of night, the dark streets were deserted save for a few horses tethered to the hitching rail in front of the whorehouse.

He tied the horse next to a shivering sorrel with a notched ear. He gave the animal a pat on the neck, then took the rifle from the sorrel's saddle scabbard. He ejected the cartridges, gripped the barrel, and smashed the butt against a tree, breaking the stock, before he flung it away into a patch of frozen weeds. He checked to make sure the saddlebags contained no weapons, then stealthily mounted the steps, entered the back door, and stepped into the dark hallway.

Nell Evans appeared like an apparition. She placed a finger to her lips, then pointed to the first door on the right.

Jim nodded, then waved her away. A dim light shone beneath the door. The groans and gasps of a climaxing rut reached his ears. He tried the doorknob, found it unlocked, and nudged it open an inch at a time. He feared the squeak of hinges might announce his arrival, but squeaks in the bedsprings obscured the sound. There in the light of a sooty table lamp, two bodies on a bed bounced beneath the covers. Or at least the top body was bouncing. The body on the bottom wasn't doing much, and her face reflected only a sort of long-suffering disgust as Blinkey Dobbs panted into the throes of orgasm.

Then, with one climatic groan, he collapsed on top of the whore. When she caught sight of Jim creeping into the lamplight, his shotgun pointed at the bed, her eyes widened. He warned her by putting a finger to his lips as he advanced so quietly that Blinkey Dobbs, his face sunk into a pillow, didn't realize Jim was in the room until he felt the cold muzzle of the shotgun press against the nape of his neck.

The man tensed and abruptly flung himself onto the other side of the bed—and found himself looking down the double barrels of a sawed-off greener.

"Get up," Jim growled.

Blinkey Dobbs cowered away from the weapon. The first sound that dribbled from his mouth was a whine: "Who...who're you?"

"My wife's name was Tessa Cloud Woman Sawyer. Remember her?"

Blinkey Dobbs vigorously indicated the name meant nothing to him, as if Jim might be mollified by the denial. "N-never heard of no such woman."

"Then maybe you know to do what you're told. Get up." He motioned to the girl. "Leave."

She grabbed the bed sheet, wrapping it around herself as she ran into the brothel owner's arms.

Blinkey Dobbs skittered out of bed. After turning up the lamp, Jim retrieved a skinning knife, still inside its scabbard, and stuffed it into a coat pocket. He used the toe of his boot to sift through the pile of clothes on the floor.

Standing with his hands in front of his private parts, Blinkey's eyes worked at a furious pace. He said, "What're you gonna do?"

Jim tossed the pants, shirt, and long underwear to the man. "Get dressed."

Grimly silent, Jim noticed the closer Blinkey got to getting completely dressed, the more he regained his composure, and by the time he pulled on his boots, he was combative. Drunkenly slurring his words, he said, "You'll never…whatever you're gonna do, you'll never get away with this. Better think twice about who you're messing with. I got three brothers, and all of 'em are meaner than rattlesnakes on a hot day."

"Get your coat on."

Growing even more cocky, Blinkey balked. He even dared bluster a little. "Now, you listen, pilgrim—"

Holding the shotgun in both hands, Jim slammed the barrel into Blinkey's gut. The sledgehammer blow doubled him over. With all his wind expelled in a cry of pain, the boy fell to his knees and clutched his chest in convulsive efforts to regain his breath. With his gloved hand, Jim twisted the kid's long, greasy hair and jerked his head upward so he could glare into a pair of widened eyes.

His voice low and harsh, Jim warned, "From now on you're going to be living from minute to minute, and the minute you give me any trouble, I'll use that skinning knife of yours to rip your guts out." He shook Blinkey's head. "Got that in your head, *pilgrim*?"

Blinkey made a few affirmative noises. As he turned loose the long hair, Jim gave the man's head a contemptuous shove.

"Don't make me say it again. Get your coat on."

Blinkey obeyed, with all the promptness fear and pain would allow. He groaned a small protest when Jim removed a pair of handcuffs from his coat pocket and cuffed his hands behind his back. After slamming Blinkey's hat onto his head, he nudged him toward the door with the shotgun's twin barrels.

He ushered the outlaw into the night and helped him struggle into the saddle of the sorrel. Holding the reins, Jim mounted his bay gelding and, leading the sorrel, galloped through the icy, crackling weeds of the trash-strewn vacant lot, angling to intersect with the road leading out of Medicine Lodge toward an old abandoned homesteader's shack he'd used on other occasions when tracking criminals.

Riding head-on into the cold northern wind, the two men hunched forward in their saddles so the brims of their hats could protect their faces against the occasional swirls of ice-crystal snow. The horses resisted running into the wind, but Jim kept them going at a pace that would bring them to the shack before daybreak.

There were no roads, nor any homesteads or settlements, and on a late November day as cold and dark as this one, no cowboys, trappers, or hunting parties looking for game were likely to be on the trail. Even so, Jim kept to the cover of the leafless cottonwoods and brush thickets as much as possible, and at noon, with a sickly pale sun filtering through a sky of dark gray wind-driven snow clouds, he stopped in a grove of cottonwoods.

Blinkey's legs buckled when Jim pulled him from

the saddle. "I'm too sore and stiff to stand, and I'm freezing." His teeth chattered as he pleaded, "Build a fire."

After unlocking the cuffs, Jim half dragged him to a nearby sapling, then snapped the opened cuff around the tree. Blinkey jerked against the sapling, whining curses under his breath.

"Build a fire. Can't you build a fire? Gawl-dangit, I'm freezing my ass off."

Jim ignored the grumbling. "No fires."

"What the hell, no fires?"

He untied the slicker from behind the boy's saddle and tossed it to him. "You heard me."

He removed the bridles from the horses and tethered them on long lines to a couple of sturdy oaks. Then he removed some jerky from one of his saddlebags. He offered a strip to Blinkey.

Wrapped in his blanket, Jim sat huddled against the trunk of a tree and gnawed on the strips of cold hard beef as he surveyed the area. It was unlikely the brothers would come hunting Blinkey, thinking he was still in town. Even so, he didn't plan to be caught off guard.

Blinkey crouched down at the base of the sapling. "Say, looky here, what's this all about?"

Ignoring the whining, Jim continued to gnaw the jerky until the boy stood and kicked dirt in Jim's direction. "Dammit to hell, what d'you want with me?"

"You're going to tell me where to find your three brothers."

For a moment, Blinkey was speechless. Then he sputtered, "What? What brothers?"

"The ones named Bufford, Fourney, and Ollie.

Them that helped you hang an old man named Joe Hennessey. He was my father-in-law. And them who helped you rape and murder my wife, and killed the child inside her. Those brothers."

Blinkey appeared flabbergasted. "What? *Me*? What the hell you talking about? No...no, you've got the wrong man. I don't know about any brothers."

When Jim didn't answer, the boy seemed relieved, almost to the point of laughter. "So all that back at Nell's place was a big mistake. I'm glad we got this cleared up. How 'bout removing these cuffs and letting me go?"

Jim pulled the blanket tighter around his shoulders and snuggled into it. He closed his eyes for a quick nap, while Blinkey continued to protest his innocence, until Jim said, "Nope, wasn't a mistake. Besides, you already said you had three brothers, or don't you recall?"

"Well, yeah, that was a mistake. I-I lied."

Jim harrumphed. "Better get some sleep. Gonna be a long night."

Blinkey lapsed into silence.

The clouds parted, allowing a moonbeam to shine directly on Blinkey. "I ain't never seen the moon so bright. It almost hurts my eyes."

"My wife was a Comanche spirit woman. She's watching you."

"Aaw, you're full of shit. Ain't no such thing."

Jim closed his eyes and fell into a shallow sleep. At dawn, he roused the boy and once again clamped his wrists together before putting him on his horse. This time he allowed Blinkey to keep his hands in front so he could hold on to the saddle horn.

They left the woods shortly after the snow started

falling. Jim, in the lead, picked his way along the trail in the darkness and blinding snow flurries. Driven by a moaning wind, the snowflakes piled up in drifts against logs and thickets of dark leafless trees.

Blinkey yelled, "That moaning is getting on my nerves."

"Her name was Tessa Cloud Woman Sawyer. It's her moans you're hearing."

"I ain't as dumb as you think I am. I know you're jest trying to spook me."

They rode all day and into the night. The snow stopped after midnight. The half moon emerged from behind the scudding clouds to shine and twinkle on the white blanketed earth.

When Blinkey toppled out of the saddle, Jim wheeled the horses around and rode back to where he sprawled in the snow.

"Get up."

The boy pleaded, "I can't go no farther. You can't make me."

Jim dismounted and pulled Blinkey's own skinning knife from the pocket of his snow-crusted coat. He put the tip of it under the boy's chin. "You've picked your place to die, then, have you?"

"No. Please. Help me. I-I'll…"

Jim picked up Blinkey's hat, shoved it on his head again, and helped him mount.

Just before sunup, they entered the mountains. The weakening horses staggered and plunged through snowdrifts. Twice more Blinkey fell out of the saddle and Jim helped him remount.

A bit before sundown they reached an arroyo where there was a spring and an old cabin built by homesteaders, later used by wild horse hunters and then outlaws. Jim half helped, half dragged Blinkey into the cabin and then locked his hands around the oak center pole that held up the cabin's smoke-blackened log rafters. The boy collapsed on the dirt floor, shivering and moaning, while Jim banked a fire in the old iron stove. Afterwards, he went outside to unsaddle the horses and tether them inside a lean-to attached to the cabin.

Within an hour he had a lantern burning in the cabin and a pot of stew simmering on the stove. The stew had come out of a can from the supplies Lettie Edwards had packed for him.

Sitting on a bench, and between mouthfuls of food, Jim said, "Boy, my name is Jim Sawyer. I'm a Deputy United States Marshal. You picked the wrong man's wife to murder."

Blinkey glared at Jim. "You'll never get away with holding me against my will. I know my rights."

Jim ignored him. When they both had finished their meal, Jim rolled himself a cigarette and puffed on it while he finished his second cup of coffee.

"Say, lawman, I could use a smoke."

Jim got up and crossed to where Blinkey sat on the dirt floor and offered him the half-smoked cigarette. As Jim leaned down, the boy hawked a wad and spit in his face. "Take that, you bastard."

Jim calmly removed the handkerchief from his back pocket and wiped the spittle from his face. It was time to get down to business. He unlocked one of the handcuffs and pulled Blinkey to his feet, then jerked his arms behind him and once again handcuffed his wrists together. He then crossed to where he had dropped the saddles, got his lariat from the latigo strap, and, knocking the boy's hat off, dropped the slipknot over his head.

"What? You...you're crazy."

Blinkey's voice was cut off when Jim tossed the coil of rope over one of the smoke-blackened rafters and pulled it taut. To keep from being strangled, the boy backed under the rope, and Jim kept pulling until Blinkey had to stand on the tips of his toes to keep from being choked. Then Jim tied the loose end of the rope around the center pole, leaving the boy half hanging, half standing, squirming, making strangled gagging sounds, edging toward panic.

"How old are you, boy?"

The words came out on a choke. "Twenty-f-five."

"Consider yourself some kind of stud horse who likes to carve up women while he rides them?"

"I don't know what you mean."

"Don't make no never mind. Because you're going to tell me where to find your worthless brothers, or eventually you won't be able to stand on your toes anymore and you'll hang yourself. I'm in no hurry. Got all night."

Jim settled in a corner. He rolled another cigarette, lit the end, and filled his lungs before blowing out the smoke. "My wife died an agonizing death. You made sure of that when you slashed her body."

"I ain't telling you where my brothers are. We Dobbses don't rat each other out."

"So, you're admitting you're one of the Dobbses. That's a start."

Blinkey dropped all pretense of innocence. "I'll die before I tell you where to find them."

"Suit yourself." Jim crushed the spent cigarette butt against the dirt floor. He pulled the hat down low on his forehead to shade his eyes. "Agonizing way to die. Suffocation is slow. Gives you plenty of time to think about…things."

Blinkey groaned, doing a little dance on the tips of his toes to keep his balance. Anytime he let himself relax as much as half an inch, the noose cut into his windpipe, cutting off his words as he declared, "I ain't talking."

Without looking up, Jim said, "Tell me where they are, and I'll let you go. You can hightail it to Mexico. They'll never find you."

"You'd let me get away?"

"Tell me what I want to know, and I'll put you on your horse and give you a head start."

"But I don't know this country, and it's snowing. What kind of chance is that?"

"Better than the one you gave my wife."

Blinkey sagged, his eyes bulging with fear. "Please, I got to…I got to take a piss. Let me down."

Jim moved to the stove to warm his hands.

"I'm begging you. I'm about to piss my pants."

"When my wife cried out, did you show her mercy?"

Blinkey writhed, moaned, and cursed. Tears trickled down his face as urine stained the crotch of his pants and soaked downward to puddle at his unsteady feet.

Jim deliberated his next move. He drew the knife from its buckskin sheath and held it up. "This what they call an Arkansas toothpick?"

"Yeah, what of it?"

"This the one you used to slice my wife's arms and legs, and across her breasts?"

Blinkey whined. "We didn't mean anything by it. Jest havin' a bit of fun and got carried away. That's all."

Jim's tone held a grim finality. He pointed the knife toward the boy. "You know what happens when a horse breeder doesn't want a stallion passing on imperfect traits to a pure blood line?"

The boy cowered away from the knife. "No! You wouldn't do that. It ain't human. No, no!" he screeched. The noose tightened, and his horrified face turned a bluish-white color before he managed to get his toes back on the floor and relieve the weight of his body. By then Jim had the boy's pants and underwear down around his trembling knees, exposing his genitals.

"I-I'm calling your bluff. You're a deputy marshal. Ain't there rules against torture?"

Jim grabbed hold of the boy's codsack and slipped the sharpened blade under the flaccid flesh.

Blinkey's breath came in gasps. "Oh, god, d-don't. I-I'll tell ya. They're camped about twenty miles from town, on the river. We sold a string of horses to a Kiowa hunting party."

Jim removed the knife. "How long your brothers plan to stay?"

Tears dripped from Blinkey's eyes and mucus from his nose. "Can't say for sure, but they won't leave without me."

"Did you sell the appaloosa mare?"

The boy seemed surprised that Jim knew about the horse. "Nah, Bufford plans to keep her for himself. That is if he can ever tame her. She's a wild one."

"My wife raised that mare from a foal. Dancer doesn't have a mean bone in her body."

A grunt left Blinkey's lips. "We must not be talkin' 'bout the same horse. Bufford said she's what they call a leopard appaloosa 'cause the spots cover her body. Kinda brown-like spots." He wheezed out a laugh. "She's a mean 'un, all right. Took a plug out of Fourney's shoulder, and tried to stomp the shit out of Ollie. Would've killed him iff'n Burford hadn't taken a tree limb to her. Gave that bitch the beatin' she deserved. Yeah, she's a killer, all right."

Jim's body shivered with anger. "I'd say Dancer is right smart when it comes to judging men."

Blinkey made feeble movements with his arms. He pleaded, "I-I done told you what you wanted to know. Lemme down."

Jim stepped to the center pole and jerked the rope loose. Blinkey collapsed on the dirt floor. With his pants and underwear bunched around his knees, he writhed in the puddle of urine, sobbing, trying to massage his cramping legs with his handcuffed hands.

"My legs are hurtin' somethin' fierce. Take the cuffs off, please."

"Nope. Can you write, boy?"

"A little. Didn't care much for schoolin'."

"Stop sniveling and make yourself decent."

Jim reached inside his saddlebag and pulled out a pencil and a tablet. He held it toward Blinkey. "Write out your confession. Write it all out. What each brother did to my wife, and to my father-in-law. Then sign your name."

For more than an hour he watched the boy labor over the confession, sometimes sounding out the words he couldn't spell, until Blinkey finally shoved the tablet forward. "I've writ down everything I can remember. You gonna live up to your word and let me go?"

Jim removed the lariat from Blinkey's neck and unlocked the handcuffs. The boy used both hands to massage life back into his legs.

"Listen here, lawman, which way is Mexico? If my brothers find out what I've done, they'll strip the hide off'n me."

Jim's smile never wavered as he moved forward with a slow deliberate step. "Due south, boy. 'Course, you'll have to look out for scalp hunters. Long hair like yours ought to bring a fair price."

He helped the boy from the floor. He placed an arm under his shoulders to give him support while he limped outside to where the horses stood. Jim cinched up the sorrel's saddle, and replaced the headpiece. And when Blinkey couldn't lift his leg to the stirrup, Jim hauled the boy astride the horse.

"I ain't worried much 'bout Fourney and Ollie, but brother or no brother, Bufford, he's crazy mean. Even when he's not drinkin'."

"We all have our crosses to bear." Jim's voice hitched in his throat. "Some of our crosses are greater than others."

The boy's eyes flittered up and down. "How 'bout sharing some of them canned goods with me? I ain't got much money."

Jim hissed a breath between his teeth. "You're testing my patience, boy. Time's running out."

"I'd rather go to jail than face Bufford." Blinkey tried to swing his leg over the saddle's cantle. A spasm caused him to yowl and drop back into the seat.

"You're gonna kill me, ain't you. That's why you're lettin' me go. Gonna shoot me in the back."

Jim slapped the sorrel's rump, sending the startled horse plunging through the snow. He called out, "I'm no back shooter, boy."

Chapter Fourteen

Jim waited a few minutes, listening to the horse's muffled hoof beats fading into the night, before he returned to the cabin. Inside, he added a few sticks to the dwindling fire. He blew out the lantern and rolled into his blanket, imagining tomorrow, wondering how long it would take Blinkey to find his way back to Medicine Lodge. The boy was too much of a coward to strike out on his own. Take away the skinning knife and the protection of his brothers, and Blinkey Dobbs was nothing more than a sniveling punk.

From far across the frozen prairie came the yipping and howling of a coyote, and from somewhere another coyote answered. Jim closed his eyes and listened to the wind whistling around the cabin. A sorrowful sound...weeping. "Don't worry, Tessa. I didn't let him go. He'll ride back to his brothers and brag about humping the whore at Nell's place. He might even exaggerate about how he carved on her. I'll take 'em down, Tessa, or die trying."

My soul is weary. My spirit cannot rest...cannot rest.

Jim wasn't sure if he'd actually heard Tessa's voice or if it was the wind playing tricks with his hearing.

The next morning was cold and gray. When he rode out to pick up Blinkey's tracks, he found him no more than a mile from the cabin. The boy lay face down in the snow, frozen stiff. Jim turned the body over and was surprised to see claw marks covering the boy's face and neck, and the front of his coat ripped to shreds. Jim searched the area and was puzzled to find only hoof prints and boot prints. Yet, from all appearances, Blinkey had suffered an attack by a mountain lion.

It appeared that whatever attacked the boy had spooked the horse. Jim mounted up and followed the hoof prints. With no shovel, he had no way of burying the body.

The sorrel hadn't gone far, standing with its rump turned toward the stinging wind. Jim grabbed the reins and led the horse back to where the body lay, removed the slicker from the saddlebags and wrapped Blinkey inside it, slung him over the saddle, and secured the hands and legs to the stirrups.

Jim unbuckled the flap to his saddlebag and pulled out the tablet and pencil stub. He wrote a detailed accounting of how he'd found the body.

A movement off to his right captured his attention. A wisp of white disappeared among the trees. He trudged to the spot and found nothing. A gust of wind toppled his hat to the ground. Each time he bent to retrieve it, the wind rolled it across the snow.

"Tessa, did you do this to the boy?"

Was it a woman's laughter he heard, or the spring waters gurgling over stones? A breeze tumbled the hat to settle at his feet. He set it firmly on his head. Setting the toe of his boot in the stirrup, he swung into the saddle and turned his horse toward Medicine Lodge. In spite of the brisk chill, he was certain warm arms caressed him. A sigh...a moan.

A cold smile touched Jim's lips. "Three more, Tessa."

He glanced at the sky. It had cleared now and was a bright, brilliant blue stretching from horizon to horizon.

****

Saturday, before noon, Jim rode down an alley. He hauled up at the back entrance to the sheriff's office, left the horses, and walked around to the front and inside.

Carl Witherspoon sat hunched over his desk, flipping through a stack of Wanted posters. He looked up. "Coffee's hot."

Jim reached into his coat pocket to remove the tablet and tossed it on the desk. "Got a body out back. Think you'd better take a gander."

"Whose?"

"Kid by the name of Blinkey Dobbs."

"I heard about the incident at Nell's. You take this feller down?"

"Didn't have to. Looks like a mountain lion got him." Jim nodded toward the tablet. "It's all in my report."

Carl pushed away from the desk. He snatched his coat and hat and led the way through the jail's rear entrance. Standing next to the sorrel, the sheriff grabbed a handful of lank hair and lifted the head to inspect the kid's face. "Gawd almighty. There ain't much left to identify him. I'll read your report while you take him over to the undertaker's. Tell him the county will pay for the burying."

Jim slung the boy's scant belongings next to the door. "You folks having problems with mountain lions in this part of the country?"

The silver-haired sheriff scrubbed a hand over his chin whiskers. "Haven't heard any complaints. Ole man Soukis runs a couple hundred head of sheep at his place. If there were mountain lions around, he'd have let me know."

Jim pulled the tobacco pouch from his pocket. He offered it toward the sheriff, who declined. The hairs on the back of Jim's neck prickled as he thought about Tessa and the way the wind had whispered and moaned around the cabin. "Maybe the cat was just passing through and the kid got in its way. Only explanation I can think of."

The sheriff cleared his throat, frowning. "By the way, Jim. The night after you left, Nell came to the office. She was pretty shaken up. Seems a fat fellow with flabby jaws and wearing bib overalls came looking for his brother. Said the boy had a problem keeping his pecker in his pants, and when he disappeared the fat man figured the boy had headed for the nearest whorehouse. Nell told the man the boy had taken his pleasure with one of her girls, then left. This fellow put a fist to her face, blacked her eye, busted her lip, and called her a liar. Said the boy never showed up back at the camp. He told her if she didn't tell him what he wanted to know, he'd hang her and all the girls and then burn the place to the ground. Mean sombitch."

Jim paused while he considered the complexity of the problem. "She put a name to the sodbuster?"

"Yeah, Bufford Dobbs."

"And I reckon she told him about me and what happened to the kid?"

"You'd be right again, Jim. Except she told him

you had ridden south with the boy."

Jim's face showed his anger. He wasn't in the mood for a long discussion. "Did he...did Dobbs ride south?"

"The next night, a fat man and two other fellows rode through the center of town, around midnight. They were yelling and shooting up the place. Threw some lighted torches at buildings. I got off a few shots. Didn't see any of them falter. But they were headed south. Since none of the town's people were hurt, I didn't figure there was any need to give chase."

Jim shivered. Not from the cold. A searing rage filled him. "Reckon I'll head south."

He gathered the reins to both horses and worked to keep his voice indifferent. "How's the women, and Charlie?"

"Your friend is up and about. He's sleeping at the livery. 'Fraid the news for the women isn't so good."

A concerned curiosity struck Jim. "How so?"

"Telegram came through yesterday." Carl tsked. "Sometimes tinhorns ought not to chase dreams. According to the sheriff in Elko County, Mrs. Collins' brother-in-law was the victim of a land scandal. Seems when he went to demand his money back, there was an argument, with Mr. Collins ending up on the wrong side of the bullet."

"Dead?"

"As a doornail."

"Damn. Did the women say what their plans are now?"

The sheriff shrugged. "For certain they're not going to Colorado."

Jim concurred. "After leaving the undertaker's, I'll

drop by the hotel to check on the ladies."

"When you finish your business, c'mon back to the office. May have a few questions about the victim."

Jim nodded. "Keep the coffee hot."

He led the horses down the dirt street. Curiosity seekers emerged from doorways and gathered on the boardwalks to gawk. A stray dog ran snapping and snarling at the bay gelding's heels. The horse hunched and lashed out with a rear leg. The blow sent the cur yelping off with its tail tucked between its legs.

Once he had finished his business with the undertaker, Jim made his way to the livery stable. He spotted Charlie pitching hay to horse-lined stalls.

He clasped hands with Cherokee. "How's the head?"

"Still get woozy. Who did you bring in draped across the saddle?"

"Blinkey Dobbs." Jim briefly explained his encounter with the kid.

"You put a bullet in him?"

Jim answered with a shrug. "After the kid spilled his guts about where his brothers were camped, I let him go. Strangest thing, Charlie. Late that night I swore I heard Tessa's voice. Maybe it was the wind playing tricks with my mind. All I know is, I let the boy go, thinking he'd lead me to Bufford. The next morning, I found him clawed to shreds and frozen stiff, but there were no cat tracks to be found. None."

A small indulgent smile played at the corner of Charlie's lips. "It wasn't the wind, my friend. Cloud Woman died before she had time to complete her circle of life. Her spirit can't rest."

A long silence stretched between the two men

before Jim said, "That's exactly what I heard in the wind—*My spirit cannot rest.*"

A rush of warm air swirled around the two men as they walked down the boardwalk to the café.

Charlie grinned and clapped Jim on the shoulder. "She's with you now."

Jim glanced over his shoulder as he opened the café door and beckoned Charlie inside.

During the meal, Charlie apprised Jim of the women's situation.

"Cora Beth and her mother are gonna stay here and open a boardin' house. Ada Mae ain't happy. She's all for goin' back to Alabama, even after her ma explained there weren't nothin' for 'em there."

"Yep, she's headstrong. My guess is the girl will run off with the first drifter that sweet-talks her." Jim drained his coffee cup. "What about you, Charlie...and Cora Beth?"

The Cherokee was thoughtful a minute. "Doc says I'll have dizzy spells for a while."

"And...Cora Beth?"

Jim watched Charlie's face shutter to a mask of stone. "When you're ready to ride out, count me in."

"It's a simple question, Charlie."

The chuckle was bitter and harsh. "I'm a breed...not white...not red. Cora Beth deserves better. That answer your question?"

Reflective, Jim studied the man sitting across from him. "Thought you were a man, Charles Ashwin. Guess I was wrong." Jim scowled, but he wasn't about to argue further.

He was conditioned to finding flaws in others. As a Deputy United States Marshal, knowing what was in his opponents' minds quickened his own reactions. He had also learned to find out what men on the run valued most. And then he would take it away. It was the way of lawmen, yet those lessons had spilled over into his personal relationships as well. Sometimes he found it impossible to separate the two.

His tone of voice didn't suggest any argument when he explained all the sheriff had related about Bufford Dobbs' attack on Nell and then shooting up the town. "I'll be riding hard and fast, Charlie. If you can't keep up, I won't wait for you."

Charlie met Jim's unflinching stare. "I'm not asking for any favors and don't expect any."

It became awkward with the two of them trying to stare each other down. The chair legs scraped against the wooden floor as Jim shoved away from the table. "We'll need ammunition, and food. After stocking up, we'll bed down at the livery. No sense paying for a room when I plan to pull out before daybreak. You need anything from the doctor?"

"He gave me some headache powders. Reckon I could use a few more packets, and I'd like to say goodbye to Cora Beth."

Jim stuffed his hands into his pockets. "Give the ladies my regards, and express my regrets for not stopping by. Sheriff said he had a few questions for me about Blinkey Dobbs. Afterward, I'll drop by the general store for supplies."

Darkness was descending, and with it came a curtain of light snow. Jim smiled at the weather. The cold meant the Dobbs brothers might not travel any great distance before seeking a warm place to hole up. He hoped it wasn't at the expense of any innocent victims.

After satisfying the sheriff's questions, Jim made his way to the livery. He palavered a bit with Ed Lauder before finding an empty stall. He removed his saddle from the sawhorse and set it on a patch of fresh hay to use as a pillow. Wrapped in the blanket, he settled down to plan his strategy once he caught up with the brothers.

For a long time he lay, his hands behind his head, looking up at the rafters. A wolf howled in the hush of night, setting off a rash of barking from the town's stray dogs. A man's voice yelled out, "Shaddup!"

Jim's mind shifted to Tessa, to his last look at her standing in the ranch yard, in the predawn light. She wore a white nightgown. The scooped neck showed the swell of her breasts. There was a wide yoke of delicate embroidery around the neckline, with threads of red and yellow and green that she had meticulously worked into a border of springtime flowers. She was as exquisite and as feminine as the flowers on her gown. He wondered what her last thoughts were as she waved goodbye. It etched a picture on his mind that he knew he could never forget.

He didn't remember falling asleep until someone with a distinct southern accent shook his shoulder and called his name. "Jim...Jim, wake up. It's me, Cora Beth."

He sat up with a start, ready to pull the trigger on the shotgun. "Cora Beth?"

"It's Charlie, Jim. A fever has took hold of him. We were sitting in the parlor, drinking coffee, when the chills gripped him so hard he near fell off the settee. Ma and I managed to get him over to the doctor. Charlie said he's sorry as he can be to let you down."

"Stroke of rotten luck," Jim said, for lack of something better to say. He was silent for a long breath. "You should go back to the hotel and get some rest."

Her voice was soft, and tinged with worry. "Will you come back to Medicine Lodge?"

"Can't answer that, ma'am. Depends on how far away my business takes me."

She stood and pulled the shawl tighter around her shoulders, as if warding off a chill. "You know, Charlie feels honor-bound to keep you safe. I hope he didn't breech any confidences by telling us about your wife. He said that in a way you saved his life. He also said to tell you he believes the Great Spirit led you to him."

Jim felt his brows rise. "Even though my wife was part Comanche, I don't put much stock in that spirit stuff. Tell Charlie to keep his powder dry. He'll know what I mean."

Cora Beth stared at Jim, looking confused. With a curt nod, she gathered her skirts and walked away.

Chapter Fifteen

Jim rode for three days, stopping long enough to rest his horse, to snatch a few hours of sleep, and to satisfy his hunger by eating a little sliced roast beef and biscuits he had bought at the cafe. He spent hours hunched in the saddle, a canvas poncho wrapped around his heavy coat to help ward off the biting cold.

He used the time to wonder about Bufford Dobbs and his brothers. Usually a family had one bad seed to cause them shame. He found it unusual that all four of the men he hunted were cut from the same cloth of meanness. He wondered about their parentage. Had these men brought their mother heart-rending grief? Had the man who sired them reveled in his sons' insanity? And surely it was a form of madness that drove them to carry out such extreme acts of violence—especially against women.

The pre-dawn November morning boasted frigid temperatures, led by a howling wind that gripped the countryside. Jim rode along the snaking trail, allowing the gelding to pick its way. Faint light began to show along the horizon. It wouldn't be long until daylight, he reasoned. He was gambling on Bufford Dobbs' turn of mind, and felt certain he was right. It was cold. Damned cold. The men would find a place to hunker down. No sane human who cared two whits about his horse or his own neck would risk moving along on such dangerous footing in the dark of night, he reasoned, even if these weren't sane men.

Around midmorning, with the sky clearing and no signs of renegades anywhere along his back trail, Jim spotted a hollow, well off the path, and drew to a halt. The bay was in need of a few minutes' rest and a handful of grain, and Jim felt the need for something more substantial than the roast beef and biscuits he'd had earlier.

Walking across the crest of one of the hills that encircled the hollow, he made doubly certain he'd not overlooked any riders in the area and then returned to where the gelding waited, poured a small amount of sweet feed into the horse's nosebag, and put it in place before seeing to his own needs.

In short order, he had gathered enough dry twigs to build a fire and in ample time had a pot of water heating, balanced on a flat rock, and ready for the ground coffee.

He ate quickly, consuming a can of heated beans, the last of his biscuits, a can of peaches, and two cups of coffee. The meal might have to last him until dark— or perhaps later, if he discovered the Dobbs gang anywhere in the vicinity.

When the meal was finished, he stored the utensils in one of the grub sacks, removed the nosebag from the gelding and returned it to his saddlebags, then once again climbed a hill to search for signs of campfire smoke or mounted riders.

There was still no sign, and that set up a faint worry within him. He would feel much better if he knew where Dobbs and his two crazy brothers were. It was far too easy to blunder into them, traveling blind.

He didn't waste time laboring over this fact. He'd move on, get his bearings when he entered Indian Territory, and then, depending on where Dobbs was, decide which way to go. There was a slim possibility the men had taken a wrong trail, which would account for them not being seen. Headed south, he figured they would ride to Texas, then on to Mexico.

Jim surveyed his surroundings. In less than an hour he would cross the border back into Oklahoma. Instinct brought him to an abrupt halt. He tilted his head to listen. The sound grew louder. The steady shushing-crunch of horses moving across snow. Jim dismounted. He clutched the reins in one hand and crouched lower, the shotgun in his right hand. He didn't want it to come down to bloodshed with Dobbs or the brothers. As a lawman, he wanted to bring these men to stand in front of a judge; as a grieving husband, he wanted to watch while a hangman placed a noose around each of their necks. To watch them dangle as the trapdoor fell from under their feet. These were men who committed wanton murder. Still, if push came to shove, he would defend himself.

Jim hunched lower. He was in an ideal position to spring an ambush if he so desired, and the thought did enter his mind. He brushed it away. Ambush wasn't his style, never was, in all his years as a lawman. He thought about the number of men he'd killed over the years. Killing was never easy, even in self-defense. He needed courage to face these devils.

His thoughts came to a full stop. He cut his eyes to the left. No doubt the sound was made by the shod hoof of a horse coming in contact with rock.

A rush of adrenalin heightened Jim's anticipation

when he spotted the dimly silhouetted riders in the next moment. A small raiding party of Apache, whose attitudes toward whites was well known. He hardened the line of his jaw, and a fury raced through his veins when he spotted fresh scalps dangling from one of the rider's scalp belt. The blonde hair brought to mind the last time he'd spoken to Katie Em, and had watched her ride away, blonde braids flapping beneath her hat. Guilt squeezed his heart. Just like Tessa, another woman, perhaps two, had lost their lives to heartless bastards.

Two Apache led one horse each. No doubt stolen from the homestead they had raided. The braves were traveling at a fairly fast pace. Jim placed his hat on the ground as he peered around a tree, and he stayed hidden until the riders disappeared into a cedar grove. When he left his protective hiding place, he didn't bother stepping into the stirrup. Instead he grabbed the saddle horn and swung into the seat. He gigged the gelding forward. "Time to get the hell out of here." He said the words more for himself, but the horse flicked its ears as if understanding the urgency.

Near sundown, Jim found himself on the northern bank of the frozen Canadian River. The snow had piled high, making travel difficult. It had taken him eight hours to cover twelve miles, and the sky was threatening more snow. He decided both he and the bay gelding needed a break. Surveying the area for a likely place to spend the night, he spotted the opening of a cave about halfway up the side of a bluff.

He left the gelding tethered to a leafless cottonwood tree. Jim's first attempts to climb the stone plate proved fruitless. His leather-soled boots couldn't get traction on the damp, slick surface. He cursed the weakness in his left arm. It took two more attempts before he made his way up the rock track to the cave's opening. In the last light of the sinking sun he saw the remains of recent campfires near the entrance, and there was a cache of firewood piled near one of the recently used firepits. Jim placed his hand over the pile of gray ash. Cold. To make doubly certain, he pulled the glove from his hand and used his fingers to scoop below the bottom of the cinders. No heat. The cave hadn't been used for a while. It was safe enough.

Though there was ample room for the horse, knowing the effort it took to pull himself up to the entrance, Jim knew he'd need to leave the gelding tethered to the tree, though he worried about leaving the animal to weather the cold. He gathered enough wood for a fire and, using his knife, peeled away strips of dried bark to act as kindling. Striking a match against a rock, he set the flame to one of the thin strips, then another and another until he had sufficient fire to ignite the stacked wood.

Once he had the blaze going, he descended to the bottom of the track. He removed the saddlebags and draped them over his shoulder. He untied the canvas slicker from his saddle and then, removing the saddle, used the oilskin to cover the horse from withers to rump. He set the saddle back in place, leaving the cinch strap loose.

Filling the nosebag with oats, he positioned it over the bay's head. He gave the animal a pat and said, "It's the best I can do for you, Red. Hope it's enough."

The horse responded with a huff and a toss of its head.

An hour later, after filling his own belly with a

much needed meal, Jim drained the last of his coffee. He scooped sand to clean the grease from the small cast iron frying pan, then rewrapped it in oilskin and repacked the grub sack to make ready for tomorrow's departure.

He tossed two more logs on the fire. Settling against the saddle, Jim drew the blanket tight around his chest. He placed his hands behind his head. Thoughts filled him. Thoughts of Charlie, Millie Collins and her daughters, Katie Em, Lettie and Hank, Joe…and Tessa.

He didn't resist when his eyes closed. He stirred in his sleep, and felt as if he were in an exotic dream. Someone whispered his name. The sound of it, spoken softly, sent a quiver of response through his body.

The aroma of lilacs filled him. Tessa's favorite scent. He opened his eyes. Her ebony hair caught the night wind and unfurled as she faced him. Through the haze of sleep he looked up at her, so wildly beautiful there in the moonlight.

One pale hand reached out to him. He caught and held it for an instant. The sapphire eyes that gazed down at him glittered with unshed tears.

A heavy mantle of sadness draped over him. "I miss you, Tessa."

Her lips moved in broken fragments. "The loss…of our child haunts me. I cannot…rest."

Grim outrage fired that special sense of honor and justice deep inside of him. "It's all right, Tessa. If it takes me a lifetime, I will find the men who took you and the baby away from me."

Then, suddenly, she was in his arms. He held her tight, telling her without words how much he loved her. Her own arms encircled his rib cage, binding him close.

His senses drank in the miracle of her closeness, the fresh rainwater scent of her skin, and the sound of her heart hammering against his ear. Love for this woman glowed, throbbed, ached inside him, making it all the more painful that their time together on earth had ended too soon.

She sighed. "Punish them, Jim. These men are like rabid wolves who kill for the joy of killing. Dangerous men."

His arms tightened around her, lingering for the space of a breath.

Their fingers clung for a moment, then separated. "Don't go, Tessa. Don't leave me."

For a moment longer, she paused, staring at him. "I am always with you. Be well, my husband. I will keep you safe."

He sat gazing after her as she melted away. He glanced about. The only sound was the tiny, crackling fire. Gulping back the ache in his throat, he lay curled in a ball and closed his eyes. Darkness flowed around him like cool water, alive and with the prickling sensation of danger. His mind churned with questions.

Light streamed through the cave's gaping entrance. Jim awakened without any memory of having gone to sleep.

Chapter Sixteen

Fourney Dobbs whined, "It's danged cold, Bufford. How come we can't find us a town to hole up in? You don't never let us go to a town. Why's that, Bufford? Jes' 'cause you're the oldest don't make you the smartest."

Ollie's lips pulled back over his yellowed buckteeth. "Yeah, who made you the boss anyhow, Bufford?"

Bufford Dobbs removed the twig from his mouth and pointed it toward Ollie. "For one thing, I'm the oldest, which automatically makes me the boss. Second, you see what happened when that halfwit brother of our'n disobeyed my orders about not going to town. He did anyhow. Look what that slut did. She let some jackleg march right in and take Blinkey."

Bufford hawked a wad and spat in the fire, causing the flames to sizzle. "We ain't found him or the varmint that took him. For all we know, Blinkey's laying in a cold grave out in the middle of nowhere. Nope, we ain't going to a town."

Fourney stood. He hitched up his britches. "I say we mount up right now and go find the sumbitch and give him what for."

Bufford also stood. He removed his slouch hat and beat it across the younger man's face, head, and shoulders. "You stupid twit. Aint that what we're doing—tryin' to pick up the trail of that kidnapping jackleg?"

Ollie jumped to his feet. He crouched low, and struggled to whip the old Dragoon Colt from the holster hanging beneath his coat. "Look at me," he shouted. "I done got my iron out, and I'm gonna shoot him dead. Dead. Dead. Dead!"

Bufford slammed the hat back on his balding pate. He asked with a sneer, "Who you gonna kill, stupid? Show me."

Ollie's buckteeth emitted a whistle when he sucked in a breath and blew it out. His voice rose an octave. "I...ah...well, didn't that floozy say his name was Jim somethin' or other?"

"Sawyer. His name is Jim Sawyer. And why don'tcha talk a little louder, Ollie. Let every Comanche—hell, the whole damned Indian nation—know where we're camped." Bufford fisted his hands on his hips. Clearly exasperated, he kicked the fire, sending glowing red sparks to dance and die in the air.

Bufford puffed out his chest and rose to his full height. "Ma named us all Dobbs, but Bufford Dobbs, senior, was *my* pappy. Being the who-ore she was, it didn't make no never mind who she laid up with, long as they had a dime to throw her way. 'Cept for my pa, half the time she didn't even know those buckra's names."

Smugly triumphant, Fourney defended his parentage. "Aaw, Bufford, that ain't no way to talk about Ma. She told me my daddy was a rich rancher. You can't be rich if'n you're an idiot. You gotta have smarts to run a ranch."

"If he was so rich, then how come you were born

in a house of ill-repute and raised by a bunch of pox-infected prostitutes? Answer me that, Fourney."

The boy scooted closer to the fire. He wrapped his arms around his drawn-up knees, and used them to cushion his forehead. "Still ain't no way to talk about Ma. She weren't no who-ore. She was a soiled dove."

Bufford sat on the cold ground and laid a beefy calloused hand on the fifteen-year-old's shoulder. "I keep forgettin' you was only five when she died. 'Course, by then she'd done lost her beauty. Sometimes I look at you and see a little bit of her." He glanced over to where Ollie sat sulking. "Ollie's pa must've been an ugly sumbitch, what with them buckteeth and that matted straw hair. Kinda reminds me of a scarecrow I saw onct."

Fourney looked up at his brother. "Tell me again why we had to leave Kentucky?"

Dobbs reached both hands toward the fire. He rubbed them together as if trying to garner more warmth. "'Cause Ollie and Blinkey had their way with Cousin Killean's daughter. Would've been all right if'n Blinkey hadn't carved up her face."

The kid looked at Bufford as if trying to comprehend it all. He nodded. "I know it's a terrible thing to say about a brother, but I hope Blinkey is dead. He onct said I was too purty to be a boy. He threatened to carve up my face. When I pissed my pants, he laughed and called me a nancy boy. I ain't one of them, honest, I ain't, Bufford."

In a rare moment of compassion, Bufford patted the boy on the shoulder. "Should've left you in Kentucky. You're a might too squeamish when it comes to killin'. But don't you worry, Fourney. You proved you were a man back when we had fun with that pretty l'il Comanche gal. You know—where we stole them notch-eared horses."

Bufford stretched the kinks from his knees and walked off into the night. When he returned, he held a bottle in his hand. "How 'bout a snort of Kentucky 'shine to warm up our innards? We got some plannin' to do."

The brothers gathered around the fire, each one taking a turn to swallow a generous tug of gullet-scorching moonshine. Ollie and Fourney listened as Bufford laid out his plan of attack if they caught up to Jim Sawyer.

****

The brothers led the animals for the first few yards, hearing as they did the sounds of riders closing on the camp. Shouts went up, and Bufford realized the Indians had discovered the body of their tribe member. When he and his brothers were well clear of their campsite, they swung up into their saddles and, staying in the pine grove, put the horses to a lope.

They were now following a due-south course in hopes of losing the Indians and running across Jim Sawyer. By daylight, they had crossed the Red River into Oklahoma. The area was wild and forsaken.

Ollie yelled out, "Bufford, why you 'spose those Indians are after us? It weren't us who killed their brother. Any idjit can see we don't use a bow and arrow. At this rate, we'll all be scalped before we even find this Sawyer feller. Hellfire, we don't even know what he looks like."

Bufford pointed. "It ain't us they're after. Looks like they're turning away. As for Sawyer, he'll make himself known to us."

About midmorning the brothers halted beside a creek, built a low fire, and brewed up some coffee, using the small, blackened pot from Fourney's grub sack. Breakfast was warmed beans and fried bread made from flour and water, washed down by the strong, thick brew.

Bufford took a final swallow of the coffee and glanced at the sky. The weather had cleared and now was a brilliant blue stretching from horizon to horizon.

Getting to his feet, Bufford stretched, then pulled the brim of his hat lower to shade his eyes. "Don't look now, but we've got us a lone rider. I spotted him yestiddy. Can't figure why he's dogging us."

Ollie raised a hand to shade his eyes. "Where?" He stretched his arm forward and pointed. "Yeah, looky yonder. I see 'im."

Bufford landed a solid punch to his brother's shoulder. "I swear sometimes I don't think you're wrapped too tight, Ollie. Didn't I say not to be obvious?"

"No, sirree, you said, 'Don't look now.' "

"Damn, it means the same thing." Bufford snorted his disgust. "Fourney, get the supplies on the horses. It's time we move out."

Fourney grabbed the grub sack and looped the strap over his saddle horn. "Supplies are low, Bufford. We ain't had no meat in so long I'm pure salivatin' for a plateful of bacon fried the way Ma used to do. Can't we find us a town?"

Ollie joined his younger brother's lament. "Yeah, Bufford. I'd like a nice warm beer to wash down a plate of store-bought food."

"You remember what happened in Twin Forks. We got ourselves all likkered up. Blinkey cut the tits off a whore; and you, Ollie, you went crazy and broke up the saloon, and then I had to shoot that fool sheriff to keep him from putting a rope around you and Blinkey's necks." Bufford raised his fist, his voice a menacing growl. "No towns."

Fourney's voice held its usual whine. "There's that old Indian's shack. I 'spect with the beatin' we gave him, the only thing we'd find is his skeleton. Why can't we ride out the winter there? We could shoot us a deer or two for meat. And...and...I could ride to town for other supplies. Honest, Bufford, you can trust me to not bring any attention to myself."

Ollie danced around. "Yeah, Bufford. Whadda you say? Huh...huh?"

"That's heading back toward Kansas. Lest you've forgotten, that woman Nell said Sawyer was riding south. *South!*" Bufford shouted. "Get it in your thick skulls, we ain't going back to where we just come from."

He looked up and again spotted the dimly silhouetted rider. He appeared to be studying their movements for several moments before he rode off to his left. This worried Bufford. "Let's get a move on."

Fourney grumbled, "Talking to you is like talking to the wind. Ain't right. We're your brothers...not...not your slaves."

Bufford's irritation was recognizable. "You want to strike on your own, go ahead. Git on outta here. Five miles down the road me and Ollie will find you with an arrow in your back and that mop of brown hair hanging from an Indian's scalp belt. Is that what you want, little brother?"

Fourney, recognizing the futility of protesting, said nothing. He took a firm grip on the appaloosa mare's lead rope and climbed aboard his own horse.

The mare reared up and pawed the air. She bared her teeth as she lunged toward the boy.

Ollie, seeing Fourney was in danger of the appaloosa's front hooves, grabbed a piece of firewood and flung it at the horse. "Settle down, crow bait, or I'll slit your gawl-dang throat."

The mare squealed and made a run toward Ollie, and Fourney wrapped the rope around the saddle horn. He spurred his gelding into action to back the mare off his brother.

Bufford yelled, "I'll break her spirit or die trying."

Ollie's hands trembled as he climbed aboard his horse. "Give her a chance, and she'll stomp the puddin' right out of you."

The trio struck due south across the snow-covered grass flats, stopping early for the night in a place close to water. Conversation between the brothers remained almost nonexistent. Being a man who liked his own company, the grim silence did not bother Bufford.

As they gathered around a meager fire, Fourney ventured to break the silence. "Do you know where we are, Bufford?"

It was true, he'd didn't know where they were. He wasn't about to admit he'd lost his bearings. "Expect I do," Bufford replied, irritated as always by the brothers' questioning his decisions. "Can't be more than a couple of days to the Oklahoma border."

"You know what I'm thinking, Bufford?" Fourney pushed a little harder.

"I suppose you're going to tell us, whether I give a rat's ass or not."

"I'm thinking this Sawyer fellow will head to a town. Maybe he's gonna take Blinkey to jail."

"Listen, stupid. Medicine Lodge had a sheriff and a jail. If he was going to do that, he would have done it there. Besides, what reason would Sawyer have for taking Blinkey to prison? There ain't no bounty on him."

Fourney avoided Bufford's eyes. "I-I been thinking. You know that man we hanged, the one we stole the notch-eared horses from? Maybe them folks was Sawyer's family. Maybe the rider that's doggin' us is Sawyer. Maybe he's done killed Blinkey, and we just don't know it. I figure this Sawyer is behind us, not ahead of us."

Bufford considered the boy's reasoning. He also considered that with half a chance and a different environment, Fourney might actually be smart. He'd never been to school, yet he could read and even write his name. Maybe his pa had been a rich rancher. Too bad Fourney would never know a better life.

"I ain't sayin' I'm agreeing with you, little brother. But, I ain't disagreein', neither. If it is Sawyer, then we need to rethink our plan. Here's what I got in mind—"

Afterward, Fourney sat with his arms around his legs as he watched a million stars twinkling in the clear, cold sky. His voice was soft, almost reverent when he spoke. "When this is over, I'm leaving. Striking out on my own."

Bufford scowled at the boy's statement. "Striking out on your own. Just like that. Where you gonna go?"

Fourney stammered his reply. "All this killing, and

for what? I don't have the stomach for it like you and Blinkey, and even Ollie. It don't matter where I go as long as it's far, far away where no one has ever heard the name Fourney Dobbs. I-I might even take one of them aliases."

"So you're suddenly gettin' all high and mighty righteous on us, are you, little brother? For a fact, I'd say that's right dandy of you."

Ollie came to the defense of his younger brother. "Aaw, don't make fun of him, Bufford. He's still a wet-behind-the-ears kid."

Anger rode the edge of Bufford's voice. "And to top it off, you're ashamed of your name? What in the name of Hades do you plan to call yourself?"

Fourney appeared thoughtful. "Ma's name was Primrose Miles. Her pappy's name was Obadiah Miles. He was a preacher man. His was an honorable name, and I want to become an honorable man." Fourney's voice cracked with tension. "I figure since he's dead, he won't mind me taking his name."

Both Bufford and Ollie looked intently at their baby sibling. It was Ollie who finally spoke. "Dang, Fourney, I never knowed Ma had a name. How'd you know all this?"

"When she was sick, I used to sit with her. She talked a lot about her life and her ma and pa. She made me promise to make something of myself. I'm gonna keep my promise as best I can."

Ollie's high-pitched squeak bespoke his agitation. "You can't jest up and leave your brothers, Fourney. 'Tain't right. You gotta stick by us like we've done with you. Ain't that so, Bufford?"

Bufford shifted his gaze between the two younger

brothers. He didn't answer.

A sharp retort sprang from Fourney's lips. "I'm most of sixteen, and I'm my own man. I'm leavin', and you can't stop me."

Bufford reached inside his saddlebag and removed the bottle. He used his teeth to pull out the cork. "All this syrupy nattering makes me want to puke. I need a tug of likker to settle my innards."

When he finished, he passed the bottle to Ollie, who passed it to Fourney. The kid chugged down the fiery liquid, then lay back to stare up at the stars. He whispered, "Soon as we kill this Sawyer fellow, I plan to keep my promise, Ma."

Chapter Seventeen

The alcohol fueled Bufford's inbred anger. The more he drank, the more his temper flared. He considered Fourney's declaration of becoming an honorable man, of abandoning the Dobbs name.

Life wasn't fair.

What had life ever given him? A pa who was an abusive drunken sot who beat his wife, then expected her to gratefully spread her legs while he rutted and grunted like a hog wallowing in slop. When she lay bruised and battered, the man had turned his fists on a boy too young to defend himself.

Bufford lifted the bottle to his lips. Empty. He flung the container into the dark. He lay back. The night seemed to hover over him like a suffocating blanket. He remembered lying on the floor next to his mother's bed, in a mixture of terror and wonder, the first time he'd watched his pa and ma humping, with her begging the man all the time to stop hurting her. And when she would lie spent and lifeless, he remembered the feeling of intense pain when that monster, with his putrid breath and beefy hands, took away a little boy's innocence. His innocence. Bufford tried to think back to when he had become the image of his father, a man he hated so much that at the age of eight he took an axe and split the devil's head open the same way he'd split a piece of cordwood.

Images floated in and out of his mind. Bufford barely remembered Obadiah Miles. What he did remember was the preacher man spouting that the frail woman was no longer his daughter, that she had defied his word to run off with a devil, and devils always spawned fiends. Bufford had hid behind his mother's skirt when the old man pointed a gnarled finger toward him.

With a little boy in tow, Primrose Miles had drifted from town to town in search of work until all that was left was a series of whorehouses to call home. Four sons, by four different men. He was fifteen when she died. Used up and wasted at the age of thirty, she no longer resembled a beautiful flower. The realization that he had lived thirty years and accomplished nothing important in his life created a strange feeling, like a tight band wrapped around his chest. He lay gasping for breath.

And now...well, there was no point in looking back. No point in wondering what it would have been like if life had given him a different set of circumstances. Aware that he was drifting perilously close to regret, Bufford gave himself a mental shake. He had made his own choices, and he would have to live with the consequences.

He shifted restlessly, as if trying to dislodge the memories pressing down on him. He thought about his kid brother's intention to strike out on his own. The chuckle building in his chest burst from his throat in a series of phlegmy coughs, and then he hardened his mouth into a straight line.

Yeah, Fourney, you go ahead and dream your dreams, boy. In the end you'll wind up in a hole with someone shovelin' dirt over your face, just like the rest of us.

Bufford rolled to his side and propped on an elbow to stare at the appaloosa mare. In his inebriated state it took a moment to bring her into focus. It seemed a beam of light sparkled across her moon eye. She stood there in all her radiance, daring him to approach her.

He struggled to rise, falling to his knees. He pointed and said, "Stop lookin' at me with that evil eye of your'n. Darin' me. I know what you're doin'. Darin' me."

He pushed to his feet and staggered toward the horse. "I'll show you who's boss."

As he neared, the appaloosa raised her head. She pawed the ground and snorted to make her agitation known.

"Ain't a woman nor a horse I can't ride."

The mare flattened her ears against her head. She bared her teeth and lunged forward. The tether halted her within inches of Bufford, while he reeled backwards, landing hard on his butt.

He hesitated a fraction of a second. "Ollie, Fourney, get your sorry asses up. I'm gonna ride this she-devil even if she kills me."

Ollie mewled, "It's too dang cold. 'Sides, you're drunker'n a skunk. That she-devil will stomp all of us to death."

Bufford yelled, again, "Get up, Fourney. She cottons to you. See if you can get a saddle on her."

"Aw, Bufford. I was just getting' warm. Do like Ollie says and leave the horse alone. 'Sides, it's dark."

Bufford's voice grew impatient. "Ain't cold. I got enough Kentucky 'shine in me to light a fire." He waved his arms about. "Sorry sumbitches. I hope you freeze your sweetbreads off."

He reached down and snatched a stout limb from the campfire. The end smoldered red. "Mebbe onct I put my brand on her, she'll know who she belongs to. Show me a little respect, too. I deserve respect."

Ollie's mocking cackle filled the campsite. "When she splits your head open, reckon me and Fourney'll have to figure a way to dig through the snow so's we can bury you. You know any respectful words we can say over our brother, Fourney?"

Bufford whirled around. A wild fury flared like a grassfire inside him. He waved the burning limb back and forth, and tiny sparks flared and floated through the air to die. He staggered forward. "Gonna show you who's boss."

The mare reared, pawing the air, lashing out with her hooves. Bufford knew what was coming. He was too close to back off. On impulse, he threw the branch. The mare squealed when the piece of wood struck her chest.

The earth seemed to vibrate when her front feet hit the ground. Again, she lunged, this time breaking the rope that bound her. Her scream filled the area, echoed through the night. She reared again and on hind legs walked toward Bufford.

Instinctively he braced himself, for it was going to hurt. His hand went to his holster. The slowness of being intoxicated was evident to him. His eyes widened, and then the force of the hooves striking his breastbone drove him backward and down to the ground. There was a moment of utter silence.

Still silence.

The ghostly image of a woman descended from the appaloosa's body. The iridescent illumination hovered over Bufford. She raised an arm and extended a finger to touch his chest, her voice bitter, her laughter harsh. "The Great Father Spirit knows your face and the face of your brothers. Their time on this earth is measured."

The apparition swirled to where Ollie and Fourney sat huddled in their blankets. Ollie said, in a high-pitched, shaky voice, "B-B-Bufford...what the hell's going on?"

The spirit once again flew toward the rotund man with a bulbous nose. "*Your* time has not yet come. *You* are last."

In spite of the frigid air, hot sweat pooled beneath Bufford's armpits. He swallowed down the acrid bile threatening to spew from his mouth. "Who are you? What do you want from us?"

She gave a mirthless laugh. "I am the one who cursed you. I know your face."

"W-where's our brother, Blinkey?"

Laughter seemed to reverberate in and among the trees. In the blink of an eye, the apparition changed from a beautiful Comanche woman to a snarling cougar. A large paw swiped down the front of Bufford's coat. The sound of rending cloth reached his ears and searing pain filled his senses. As quickly as the big cat's image appeared it was just as quickly replaced with the ghostly lady. "The spirit soldiers took him. He lives no more."

Bufford blinked to clear his vision, lowering his glance. When he looked up, only the night greeted him.

The appaloosa mare stood quiet, her head lowered. The rope around her neck was fastened to the tether line. Bufford ran his hands down the front of his coat. The cloth was intact. He patted his chest, his fingers searching for the wet stickiness of blood from the powerful cat's horrific claw marks.

Nothing.

He reasoned that the last batch of Kentucky moonshine must've been tainted. He'd heard of bad whiskey causing hallucinations. A tiredness ran through him. He was very unsure of what he'd witnessed. He sleeved away the light film of perspiration on his forehead. He needed to sit down.

Ollie crawled on his hands and knees to where his brother sat. "Bufford...what just happened?"

It was dark, but his eyes had accustomed themselves to it. "I don't know what you mean, Ollie."

Fourney joined his brothers, his breath coming in hard gasps. "Blinkey's dead. The g-ghost said so."

Bufford's glance swiveled from brother to brother and saw the fear evident in their eyes. Hell, he was scared, too. He touched the gun butt resting in its holster, as though he found reassurance in it.

"There ain't no such thing as ghosts. You didn't see nothin'. We just got a bad batch of likker, that's all. Now, git on over by the fire and catch some shuteye."

He lay back, pulling the blanket over his head. The spirit's words seemed to whisper a reminder in his ears, *I am the one who cursed you. I know your face. Your time has not yet come. You are last.*

Clasping his hands together to keep them from trembling, Bufford remembered the old man they had hung, and the Comanche girl...how she had kept her gaze on him even as she lay dying.

Chapter Eighteen

Jim had slept little during the night. His mind was too busy trying to sort out whether he'd dreamed Tessa had visited him or if he'd actually been in the presence of her spirit. In fact, he found the awareness of her sensually arousing. He'd been swept up in the force of her affection. In the aftermath, she had whispered, *Forgive me for leaving you, Jim.*

There is nothing to forgive. Oh, Tessa, if only you knew how much I miss holding you, loving you. I miss— you.

His heart had hammered as she settled next to him, her body yearning. His lips met hers, so smooth, so perfect...

A chord struck deep in his soul, one that felt familiar and so achingly true that all he could think was...she was here, with him.

A deep sigh escaped his lips as Tessa nestled in his arms. The moist juncture between his thighs throbbed. He was certain her legs parted, her body soft and welcoming. He inhaled deeply, smelling the lilac scent once more. Knowing her, loving her, wanting more of her, as he'd never wanted any woman before. His lips caressed hers, teasing, exploring, tasting, until a fire was built inside him.

The knowledge of her seeped into his bones, ensnaring him. How could he bear life without this woman—his Cloud Woman? The thought shook him to the core.

I love you, Tessa.

I feel as if I am alive... Her voice trailed off.

She pulled away. Her tone desolate. *I am sorry. I must go now. Do not fear what befalls you.*

Is this a warning, Tessa?

The men you seek are evil. They must pay for killing our child.

He nodded, his heart aching. It didn't surprise him that he felt his life would never be the same. The loss was too great.

A warmness enveloped him, like a soothing bath. *You will love again, Jim. And there will be children. Your life is long to live.*

He was certain she wept at the declaration, and he had noted how fragile she had seemed at that moment as he watched her essence fade into a spiraling wisp, and then she was gone.

He didn't know which emotion was the strongest— the lovemaking that had shaken him to the core, or the anger of not finding the men who had taken Tessa from him.

The leaden sky outside the cave promised more snow. Jim walked from the entrance to the fire pit. He turned the coffeepot upside down and emptied the dregs. Dying embers hissed and sizzled from the moisture. He used a fresh stick of wood to scatter the gray ashes. Satisfied the fire was out, he left the warm interior and, digging his boot heels into the moist dirt, managed to get to the bottom of the precipice without losing his balance.

A whicker from the bay gelding greeted him. Jim

rubbed a gloved hand down the horse's neck. A dusting of snow had settled on the saddle, making Jim glad he'd used the oilcloth to cover the horse during the night. The animal seemed no worse for the weather, and Jim slipped the nosebag over its head.

The crunch of teeth grinding oats and the twitter of birds filled the dismal morning while Jim bunched the slicker into a tight roll. After securing the saddlebags and the oilskin, he tightened the cinch strap. When the grinding stopped, he removed the feedbag from the horse's head and stowed it away.

"Don't know about you, Big Red, but I have a feeling today is the day we meet up with the Dobbs brothers."

The muscled gelding answered with a toss of its head and a grunt. Jim laughed. Stepping into the stirrup, he settled in the saddle.

Horse and rider moved like a speck across the empty immensity of land, across brown, brittle grass flats, through fringes of shaded spruce. Here Jim halted, his eyes noting the hide of his horse with the thin coating of sweat. In his nostrils was the strong pitchy smell of spruce mingling with the hot scent of horse. He looked across the cold morning haze of the plain and beyond, toward Oklahoma…home.

He was cold from the frigid breeze, and desired a cup of strong black coffee laced with a shot of bourbon. He yearned for a comfortable bed, a juicy steak, and conversation with someone other than his horse. A thick stubble of dark brown whiskers covered his lean, muscled jaw. His blue eyes were brooding as they searched the landscape for some sign of the men he hunted.

An edge of irritation rose in Jim's voice. "Where the hell are they, Red?"

Tessa had told him today was the day to find the brothers. Perhaps it really was a dream. Perhaps last night had been a figment of his imagination. He tried to deride himself out of his irritability but somehow failed. It seemed to grow rather than diminish, for behind him now were two grueling months of chasing Kentucky sodbusters—cold-hearted murderers.

Knowing his horse was weary, Jim allowed the animal to walk. Light faded from the sky and the grays of dusk fell across the land. Half a dozen deer, browsing in a field, raised their heads to stare at him, then bounded off out of sight into the forest.

There was a peace in this, the last of the day, and slowly Jim's anger faded. He rubbed his bewhiskered jaw ruefully. Gradually the faint light of dusk was gone, and the first of the stars winked out above the towering rims of the plains. He thought of Tessa, and regretted all the times he had put his job before their marriage. She had begged him to stop marshaling to take up ranching full time. He'd put her off by saying, "in time." The time had never come, and now it was too late.

His eye spotted a glimmer in the distance, and he squinted through the pale darkness. There was a campfire out there. He had an inexplicable feeling that something ugly was about to happen. He puzzled about that for a moment.

Gigging the horse forward, Jim knew an urgency that could not be denied. After a mile or two, a hum of voices reached him. There was something amiss— something he sensed without being able to name.

He knew something was wrong the minute he rode to the outer edge of the camp. Dread settled over his heart. The first indication he'd ridden into an ambush was from his horse. A snort, ears pricked up, a toss of the head indicated other horses were nearby. And then Jim heard from somewhere behind him the faint wind-muffled metallic *click-click* of a gun being cocked. Instantly he drew his own revolver and jerked around in the saddle to fire at a glimmer of what he saw in a thicket of trees near the creek.

He spotted the flash too late. A resounding blast followed. The bay gelding screamed in pain. The horse reared. Jim kicked his foot from the stirrup and rolled free of the horse's weight as it folded beneath him.

A voice rasped. "Why you doggin' us, mister—what'd we ever do to you?"

Crouched with his gun drawn, Jim squinted hopelessly through the darkness trying to locate the voice.

Another voice called out, "We gotcha covered. If you don't want blood leakin' out of you, you'd best toss that hog-leg toward the fire."

Jim obeyed.

"Step into the light so we can see who you are."

Again, Jim obeyed.

A paunchy man with unshaven jowls—his baggy, grease-stained pants held up by suspenders, and his red-and-black plaid coat missing a few buttons—spoke. He seemed to talk through a throat that needed clearing, and he sported a shaggy growth of coppery beard, small jaundiced eyes, a big nose reddened with ruptured capillaries, and a balding head. He held a rifle pointed at Jim's chest. "My brother asked you a question, mister. I'd suggest you answer him."

Jim cut his eyes toward a bucktoothed man wearing a sweat-stained, tattered slouch hat. Scrawny. Younger than the heavier man. This one wore a long black canvas coat that hung loose on his slight build.

Every muscle, every nerve in Jim's body was wound tighter than a fiddle string. Working to calm his voice, he exaggerated his drawl. "I ain't nobody special. Just a cowpoke looking to hire on a ranch in Oklahoma so's to ride out the winter. Don't mean you fellers no harm. Saw your campfire and was hoping you'd be neighborly enough to share a plate of grub and a cup of coffee.

"But I'm here to tell you, I don't take kindly to you throwin' down on me, then killin' my horse, so I'll just take that appaloosa mare yonder as a fair swap for the blooded quarter horse you shot out from under me."

A boy with a shock of curly black hair stepped into the light. "Don't you give the mare to him, Bufford. She's special. Even if she does hate your guts."

"Shut up, Fourney. You talk too much."

Jim watched the interaction between the three brothers. Tessa had been right. He'd found Bufford and Fourney Dobbs. He reckoned the man sucking on buckteeth was Ollie Dobbs. He regretted not having the sawed-off shotgun strapped to his side. Wearing it had proved a nuisance when straddling a saddle.

His next action was controlled by motivation. Live or die trying to live long enough to bring these bastards to justice. He whistled, then called her name. "Dancer."

The appaloosa's ears flicked forward. She looked in his direction. Jim had helped Tessa bring this mare into the world. He counted on her knowing him.

She reared backwards against the short rope holding her to the tether line. Her frantic scream rent the night.

Jim leaped across the fire. Suddenly the three men surged forward. Ollie seized Jim by the coattails. Bufford's beefy fist struck him behind the ear. Hands clawed him. They yanked him back, and all seemed to be hitting him at once in unplanned frenzy. He tried to whirl and face them, but one of his arms was held by the kid named Fourney, while Bufford kept beating at his face with both hands.

Jim bent convulsively and straightened like a whip. His fist struck the kid's head and the boy went wild. Kicking, kneeing, he swarmed over Jim, his fists flying in a frenzied windmill fashion, some striking, some missing. In an instant blood was streaming from Jim's nose. His eyes felt puffy and numb. He managed to bring his boot up. He kicked savagely, and left Ollie hugging his belly.

Bufford waded into the fray. One of his boots caught Jim in the groin and pain spread agonizingly. Jim noted the manic smile, and Bufford's eyes reminded him of cold bits of stone. Ollie and Fourney continued yelling, "Kill the sumbitch. Beat him 'til he can't stand up."

Jim fought as he'd never fought in his life, yanking and jerking at the restraining clutches on his arms, jackknifing his body convulsively when that failed.

Twice he tore loose and rolled on the ground, but each time the brothers were on him again, smothering him, bearing him back to the ground with the weight of their numbers.

Jim still fought like a Comanche warrior, kicking,

arching his body and butting them with his head. But he was growing weak, and he felt the strength draining from his left arm. The brothers were too many, and, although he inflicted hurts upon each of them, the hurts they inflicted upon him were greater.

Bufford held him down, kneeing him in the small of the back. The blows didn't hurt so much now. His head reeled and felt very light. His body was almost without sensation. Jim heaved a deep sigh before falling unconscious.

****

Bufford bent from the waist to gag. He sucked in great gulps of air to clear his head. Ollie lay on the ground moaning. He hugged his arms around his waist. "Dang, that pisser sure had some fight in him. Thought we was never gonna take him down."

Bufford finally had enough air in his lungs to speak. "Fourney, go get his saddlebags. He don't look like no ordinary cowpoke to me. Didn't fight like one, neither."

The kid limped off into the dark. It didn't take long for him to return holding the sawed-off shotgun. "Look here what I got. I found it. It's mine."

Bufford sneered at the boy. The kid's face was red and beginning to bruise where Jim's fists had left their marks. He saw the hot eagerness in the young face. "Consider it a birthday present."

Ollie said, "I hope you found some food in one of them saddlebags."

Fourney tossed the leather pouches and a canvas bag to his brother. Ollie's fingers trembled as he opened the sack. He cackled. "Hot damn. Bacon. Beans. One tater. Flour. Peaches, and real coffee. No more boiled tree bark. We gonna have a feast tonight."

While Ollie used a knife to open a can of beans, he said, "Hey, Bufford, what you got planned for that sumbitch?"

The rotund man finished tying the knot around Jim's wrists, and then around his ankles. "I got a plan, don't you worry 'bout that. While you fix us a meal, I'm gonna search our friend to see if he's who he says he is."

Bufford used his skinning knife to snip the buttons from Jim's coat. He opened it wide. Again, he used the knife to slice away the leather straps from the vest covering Jim's chest. Bufford folded the tanned hide back. There was steel in his voice when he spoke. "Well, looky here, brothers." He held the badge forward. "We got us a genu-wine United States Deputy Marshal."

"Aw, shit, Bufford. We can't be killin' no lawman."

"Shut your hole, Ollie. I ain't stupid, you know. I got a plan working around inside my head. Now, you just hurry up with the food." Bufford's stomach let out a timely squeezing growl. "What's writ on that piece of paper you're a-holding, Fourney?"

The boy looked up. Fear showed in his dark eyes. He held it forward. "It's a picture, Bufford...of...of—"

Bufford snatched the tintype away without allowing his brother to finish speaking. He looked at the two men dressed in Sunday finery. The older man was the one they'd hanged. The younger image was of the man they had just beaten within an inch of his life. But it was the face of the Indian girl that caused icy fingers of fear to slither up and down his spine. Her eyes...her accusing eyes looked straight into his.

Fourney interrupted Bufford's musing. "There's writing on the back. You want me to read it?"

Bufford's mouth was grim when he handed the picture over to his brother. In the halting voice of a beginning reader, Fourney stumbled over the words. "Jim Saw-yer, Joe Hen-nes-see." He sounded out Tessa's full name, then met Bufford's gaze with a worried frown. "We done killed a lawman's wife. This ain't good, Bufford. Whatever you got planned better be extra smart."

"Don't you worry, little brother. By the time anyone finds Deputy Sawyer, we'll be long gone, and they'll think a band of Kiowa tortured him. Since Sawyer'll be dead, won't nobody know any different. 'Sides, we need to avenge brother Blinkey's murder."

Ollie called out, "Vittles are ready. Maybe we'd better lickety-split our tails to Mexico. I hear tell lawmen don't go down there."

Bufford dipped a spoon into the iron skillet. He shoveled beans into his mouth. Between chews, he said, "For once you make a lot of sense, Ollie."

Fourney helped himself to the food. "I don't care where we go, but I'm takin' the mare. You hear, Bufford?"

Bufford placed his face close to Fourney's beardless cheeks, his upper lip twisted into a snarl. "Don't be gettin' too big for your britches, boy. I'm still the oldest, and I still give the orders. You don't take what's not yours. The mare is mine."

The evening air quivered with squeaks and chirps as a myriad of night creatures awakened to the moonlight. Sated from a long overdue meal, Bufford refilled his cup with coffee. "You boys ready to hear what I got planned for Deputy Sawyer?"

Chapter Nineteen

Jim stood in the center of the desolate camp, his hands roped together and tied behind his back to a leafless cottonwood tree. His expression remained devoid of emotion as he stared straight ahead, outwardly ignoring his enemy.

He had the oddest, most overpowering inclination to laugh. Instead, anger welled in his chest. He shook his head to clear his thinking. Piled atop the hurts of last night, the hurts of today were becoming unbearable. There was not a square inch of his body that didn't ache. Blood still dripped from his nose and from the long gash where the scar on his cheekbone had opened. Blood matted his bearded stubble and spotted the front of his upper body.

His heavy coat, chambray shirt, pants, socks, boots—even his long underwear—had been removed and piled on the frozen ground in front of him. The Dobbs' intent was clear. Jim would die. While his eager audience watched, Jim could look at his clothing while he slowly froze to death.

Three men stood in front of him. Revolvers drawn to give them courage, they circled and jeered, yelling insults as they stomped their boot-clad feet in an effort to ward off the frigid temperature. Yet each brother kept a safe distance, as if fearing their prisoner might decide to break free of his bonds and attack.

"What'll we do if he shucks off them ropes, Bufford?"

The stocky man grinned. "Ollie, you worry too much. Only place he's goin' is straight to hell."

Bufford expelled a loud and energetic guffaw, slapping his knee with gusto. "You get it? Hell?"

The puzzled expressions on Fourney and Ollie's faces caused him to yank the hat from his head and beat it over his brothers' heads and shoulders. "Hell! It's hot in hell, dumbasses." Bufford pointed to Jim. "He's naked as a jaybird. It's damned cold. He'll wish he was in hell to warm up while he's freezing his balls off. Now d'you get it?"

Fourney wrapped his arms around his body as he danced a jig and offered a half-hearted laugh. "Bufford's making a joke, Ollie."

The bucktoothed man again shrugged his shoulders. "Yeah, if you say so. Don't see nothing funny 'bout standing around watching a naked man freeze to death. Can't we just get on our horses and do like he was gonna do—find a ranch to hire on, to ride out the winter in a warm bunkhouse, with food? My old nag is near done in, and I'm tired of sleepin' on the cold ground."

Bufford pulled his thick eyebrows together in a furrowed line. "Ollie, I swear you have mush for brains. He's a lawman. He was tellin' a lie to throw us off track."

A feeling of unease settled in Jim's mind as he continued o watch the three brothers. He'd faced down many an outlaw and had lived to tell about it. He now faced the fact that if a miracle didn't happen he wouldn't live to see another sunrise. Instinct told him

Bufford's oversized ego wouldn't allow him to leave. For a reason known only to this deranged halfwit, Bufford expected him to beg for mercy. To whimper for a quick end.

Jim chastened himself to stand proud. To keep from shivering he sought a place in his mind to think about Tessa, and the days they had swum naked in the creek, then dried their bodies in the warm sunshine while they made love. His mind shifted to the night of the fire. He recalled the scorching heat as he raced to the house when he thought Tessa was inside. He concentrated on the hate he had for these men when he'd held her abused and mutilated body in his arms. He would not give his enemy the satisfaction of watching him suffer a slow death.

Ollie tossed another branch on the fire. He stood close, holding his hands over the blaze to catch the heat. "He ain't acting like a man who's gonna die."

"Yeah, Bufford, he ain't even shivering." The chattering of Fourney's teeth was audible even to Jim. "I'm jiggered, he don't even have goose bumps. It ain't natural."

Jim was at least a head taller than any of the three brothers. He stood with his long powerful legs braced apart, his stance suggesting he was capable of killing them all—if he became so inclined.

"How long we gonna wait around, Bufford?"

Bufford rose to his feet, dusting the back of his pants. He pulled a handkerchief from his back pocket and dabbed at the cut on his lip, a gift from Jim in last night's foray. "I'm sick of your whinin', Fourney. You're so all-fired determined to strike out on your own to be an honorable man, well, be honorable and fix some grub. I'm hungry."

The day wore on. Darkness descended, and with it came a curtain of light snow. The two younger brothers continued to complain about the weather in earnest. "Ain't no need for us to freeze to death right along with him," one muttered.

The other complained, "He won't die for hours yet."

Bufford refused to admit the cold was beginning to irritate him, too. His unease had grown, as well. "Hellfire, I was sure Sawyer would be broke down and screamin' for mercy by now."

Fourney stamped his feet. "Yeah, look at him. I got on two pairs of socks and boots, and my feet are stingin' cold." He pointed at Jim's feet. "He's barefoot and hasn't moved or shifted balance once since you tied him up. You know what I'm thinking, Ollie?"

Ollie wiped his dripping nose across the sleeve of his jacket. "Yeah, it ain't natural. I remember what that ghostie woman said a few days ago. I don't want to die, Bufford. She said it, didn't she, Fourney? Didn't you hear her say we was gonna die?"

Bufford cursed his brothers' superstitious nature and gave the order to throw more wood on the fire. He went over and checked the ropes around Jim's ankles and wrists to see if the bonds were secure. He then came to stand directly in front of his captive. "You're just a man, and you'll die soon. Come mornin', we'll ride away from here and let the wolves feed on your carcass. If some pilgrim does happen by, no one can put our names or faces to you."

He gathered spittle in his mouth and spat it in Jim's face, hoping this new insult would gain a reaction.

Jim's eyes met those of his enemy. What Bufford saw there was enough to cause him to swallow loudly. He muttered something to himself, then turned toward the safety of his brothers and the campfire.

Jim flexed his hands, again and again, trying to force the numbness from his fingers. There was little feeling in his feet, a bad sign, he knew, even as he accepted that nothing short of a miracle could save him now.

Jim longed to rub the ache in his shoulder. After three months, the jagged pink skin was still stiff and unforgiving, a wound that would have killed most men. Mercifully, his brain had blotted out the pain of the initial injury. How he wished Tessa had been the one to stitch him back together then, rather than the town doctor. A competent man, nonetheless a drunk, and never gentle.

A fierce gust of wind gathered snow from the ground and swirled it like a dust devil. The scent of lilacs reached him. When he inhaled the light fragrance, he decided the freezing temperature had certainly muddled his mind. Lilacs in the middle of winter, in the middle of a bleak forest? He shook his head. The logical part of his mind knew he was hallucinating.

He closed his eyes and allowed his head to droop forward until his chin touched his chest. The appaloosa mare loosed a shrill whinny. The sound jerked Jim alert. He looked toward the mare. She stood in a halo of moonlight, where he could effortlessly capture her gaze. He thought her eyes were as blue as the sky above on the clearest of days. Tessa's eyes were blue...she had Tessa's eyes.

He reminded himself that this was a horse.

Magnificent though she was, he couldn't afford to fantasize, even as he felt himself becoming mesmerized by her bewitchingly innocent stare.

Querulous voices drew his attention away from the mare and toward the three men huddled around the campfire. He tried to suppress the groan as he watched them argue about who had swallowed more of the whiskey than the other. A weakness caused his knees to buckle. He shook his head numbly, waiting for the sensation to pass. There was growing in him an altogether new kind of anger that was cold and steady and dangerous. It was not the irritable anger of yesterday, nor the burning rage he'd felt toward the brothers during their fight. It was something altogether different.

"I won't die, Tessa. Not like this. Not stripped of my dignity. Not before I avenge what they took away from me…from both of us."

"Who the hell you talkin' to, lawman?"

Jim hadn't realized he'd spoken aloud until Bufford's raspy voice called out to him. The outlaw struggled to stand and then stumbled forward. He placed the bottle of whiskey to Jim's lips, even tilted it so that a bit of the vinegary liquor dribbled down his chin and stung one of the many lacerations on his neck and chest. And though he desired to lap up the fiery liquid, he managed to still his tongue.

Bufford laughed and jerked the bottle away to close his own mouth over the neck and gulp long until he gasped for air. He sleeved away the moisture from his lips. "You know, lawman, that she-devil yonder is…is…" In his drunken state, he seemed lost for words. A hiccup followed. "Tonight's the night. I'm gonna break that split-tail's spirit. Show her Bufford Dobbs is boss."

He reached beneath his heavy coat and unbuckled his gunbelt. He slid the holster free and tossed it to Ollie. "Hold on to this while I take the mare to school."

Ollie looked at Fourney. Both men shrugged. Even if the brothers were too stupid to grasp Bufford's meaning, Jim knew the man meant to punish the mare.

As he lunged against the ropes that held him tight against the tree, the horse whinnied and lunged against the tethers that held her.

He let himself feel nothing, not the throbbing in his head or the rope burns chafing his wrists and ankles. Fourney and Ollie stood, stumbling over each other, giggling like drunken fools.

Bufford raised his arm and twirled the belt over his head. He lashed it forward, striking the mare hard on the shoulder. She screamed and flung her head from side to side. She backed away, tugging hard on her restraints.

The resounding smacks of belt against the mare's flesh caused blood to ooze inside his mouth as Jim clamped his teeth together. Bufford threw the belt aside and pulled a knife from beneath his coat. Jim strained forward until it felt as if the corded veins in his neck would burst, as if his arms would pull from their sockets. "You bastard! You dirty, stinking, murdering bastard!"

Jim raised his head toward the heavens and called out, "Great Spirit, I call on you to avenge Cloud Woman's death and protect Dancer."

The sky closed over, turning from gray to black as thunder rumbled. Pounding hooves vibrated across the plains as all the men looked to the dark clouds and then toward the appaloosa. The mare reared, breaking the bonds that held her.

Jim's heart leapt as he watched spirit warriors astride their ghostly steeds gallop through the trees along the edge of the open plain, their horses blowing and snorting. Arrows rained down. The snow-covered ground appeared to run red with blood.

Ollie and Fourney stood back to back, twisting and turning in a crazy dance. Fourney's voice climbed to the octave of hysteria. "Ollie, I peed my pants."

A spirit warrior raced forward, a spear pointed toward Ollie's chest, and the frightened man yelled as he fumbled to pull the pistol free from its holster. "You ain't real. None of this is real. There ain't no such thing as ghosts."

He twisted around, pointed, and fired. The bullet struck Fourney in the chest. A quizzical look on his face, the boy fell backwards into a patch of snow. In a panic, Ollie used his left hand to fan the trigger, as he turned in a complete circle, firing blindly.

Jim cringed as a bullet struck just above his head, sending splinters of wood into his hair. He feared for the appaloosa as she pranced and spun in circles to escape the volley of bullets. Her sleek muscles quivered. He yelled, "Run, Dancer. Get out of here."

A cold shock of sweat broke out over him as the mare reared. He blinked not once, but several times when a woman, enraged and fearless, her skin as pale as death, emerged from the appaloosa's white-and-gray leopard coat.

Dressed in a flowing white gown, her face was framed with hair the color of a raven's wing. A jolt of white hot energy tracked through him. "Tessa!"

He wanted to reach out to her, touch her, hold her in his arms. Her nearness gave him comfort. If possible he would have smiled, but his lips were chapped and cracking. His whole body ached, his legs and arms heavy as lead weights. It took every ounce of strength he had to keep breathing.

Ollie screamed, "She's done made me kill my own brother! For God's sake, Bufford, cut the deputy loose, and maybe the ghosties will leave us alone."

Jim shook his head in disbelief when he spotted Bufford cowering behind a spruce. In a wild panic, Ollie cried out, "Bufford, where are you?"

Jim's voice came out in a croak. "He's deserted you, Ollie. Cut me loose. Let me take you in. I'll see the law goes easy on you."

Ollie snatched Bufford's knife from the ground. "You're a lowdown tit-suckin' coward, Bufford. Me and you is quits." With the knife lifted in the air, he sprinted toward Jim.

He was so overwhelmed by the mad mayhem Jim was certain fever ruled his mind when Tessa became one with the mare. The appaloosa squealed. She reared, a hoof coming down hard on Ollie's head. The blow that cracked his skull sounded like a gunshot. Ollie folded like a rag doll, never knowing what had killed him.

The air crackled with tension. Violence had been done here tonight. Violence compounded by hatred and fear. It was as deadly as the curling lip and silent snarl of a cougar before she leaps. Then there was silence, a silence so vast it was as terrifying as the spirit warriors and their fierce, snorting horses.

Bufford Dobbs left the safety of his hiding place. He crawled forward on his hands and knees and raised his head to look at Jim. "She cursed us. If I let you go, do you think she'll have mercy on me?"

Jim had always known Tessa had a gift, though he hadn't been aware how dangerous and powerful it was. A power untapped and undisciplined, but a power, nonetheless. "You murdered her child. A mother scorned, alive or dead, might not want to show forgiveness."

Bufford rose to his knees. He shoved his hands forward to show he bore no weapons. His voice sounded incredulous. "You lie, lawman. There weren't no child. Me and my brothers might be a lot of things, but we ain't baby killers."

In an instant, ringed in a halo of light, Tessa's spirit appeared in the dark, shadowy clearing. Jim swore he saw tears clinging to her eyelashes. "She carried the child in her womb." He seethed, the veins at his temples throbbing. "My wife was a free spirit when she lived. In death, she is a force you don't want to reckon with. I suggest you cut me loose, and maybe she'll spare your life."

Dobbs scuttled forward. He worked the knife under the ropes and sawed until the bonds around Jim's wrists and ankles fell to the ground. His legs unable to bear his weight, he collapsed, but feeling was quick to return to his feet. It felt like a thousand needles being thrust into his soles with an intensity that caused beads of perspiration to pop out on his forehead. "I'm not going to kill you, Dobbs. Not now. But know this: I will hunt you to the ends of the earth until you get so tired of running you'll beg me to put a bullet in you."

Dobbs scrambled to his feet, staring at Jim with a puzzled expression on his face. "Tell her to stay away. I'm leaving. Look at me. See? I'm leaving now."

He turned, slipping on the slushy snow, and ran to where three horses stood tied. Grabbing a saddle, he slung it over Fourney's horse and cinched it up. The gelding was younger and more sturdy than his own or Ollie's. Then, with a deftness that belied his hulk, Dobbs vaulted into the saddle.

As Bufford spurred the horse from the campsite, Jim could have sworn he saw Tessa wink before she disappeared like a wisp of smoke. The logical part of his mind knew exactly what he'd seen. Every detail was accurate in his mind, but misleading, too. He was certain his mind had played tricks on him. He actually shook his head in denial. And then her voice reached him and he knew what he had seen wasn't a figment of his imagination.

Take him to the place…where evil lives.

Jim clutched his garments to his chest with one hand, letting the heavy boots dangle from his fingertips. In the glow of the bonfire he quickly donned the clothing. "Come to me, Tessa. I need you."

He heard a faint whisper and quickly raised his head. The half moon gave the snow an eerie glow and outlined the woman he had loved and lost. She took hold of his hand, and settled next to him. Then she did the one thing he had not expected. She kissed him, a passionate kiss that tasted of wild strawberries, a kiss so filled with desire and longing Jim felt the ache in his loins flare like a newly stoked fire.

She pulled away. *I must go. But my heart will stay with you.*

Time stopped, and Jim grappled with the urge to pull her lips back to his, to hold her prisoner in his arms. She was lifted by a gentle wind, and the last thing he remembered was seeing a wisp of white and inhaling the sweet scent of lilacs.

Chapter Twenty

Jim was almost sick with hunger. Thankful for the blazing fire, his hands trembled as he scooped snow into the coffeepot and set it on a flat rock to heat. He glanced about until he spotted his grub sack sticking out from under Fourney's stiffened corpse. With each step his feet still felt as if he were walking on shards of glass. He pulled the canvas bag free. The lightness of its weight told him the men had nearly depleted his already meager food supply. As much as he wanted to dog Bufford Dobbs, to wear the man's fortitude down to the point of begging for a bullet, Jim decided to put an end to both their misery. He would pick up Dobbs' tracks, then force him to switch trails, steering the man toward his own personal hell. The place Tessa had requested. The place where evil lived.

Jim heaved a ragged sigh. When it was over, he would go home to decide if he wanted to accept Hank's offer to pin on a marshal's badge.

He spooned in enough ground coffee for two cups, then opened a can of hash and dumped it into the small iron skillet to heat. A can of peaches rounded out the meal. Strength flowing through his body, he gathered his saddle blanket around him and lay back. Alone, beside the fire, he was tired, and felt adrift. Not at all like the man who had rejoiced when first learning he was to become a father. Not at all like the lawman who brought outlaws to justice. His body protested when he shifted to his side. It wasn't only his physical injuries that caused him pain.

The appaloosa mare came to stand over him. Her breath warm on his face, he reached up to stroke her velvety muzzle. She whickered and blew, then lipped the top of his head. Chills wafted over Jim. Tessa used to run her fingers through his hair when they lay together.

"Go to sleep, Dancer. We've got a long hard ride ahead of us. Together, we've got a man to kill."

As if understanding his words, the mare squealed and pawed the ground before moving off into the shadows. Jim didn't know how he knew, but he could trust she wouldn't wander off.

He thought about the first night he had shared with Tessa. He needed her now. He wanted to bury his face between her breasts. To inhale her womanly scent. He missed her. He missed having her sleep by his side. The blood coursed through his veins at a gallop as he imagined how she had lain naked, her head back, inviting him to layer searing kisses down her neck. She had protested when his lips abandoned hers.

He would lift on an elbow to search her eyes as his hand grazed her face, his touch tender and exploring, as if he were trying to memorize how she looked and how she felt. Even now, he recalled every inch of her body.

His chest tightened. He could hardly breathe. The very thought of never loving her again stole the air from his lungs. He remembered the strength in her voice when she had proudly pronounced that to be the mother of his son or daughter would bring her great joy. She had opened her legs and urged him to enter her. She'd smiled and run her hand to rest on his chest for a moment before she trailed her fingertips down his belly to close around his throbbing manhood, the torture of her touch divine, too sweet to be real.

He moaned, a deep animal-like wail of anguish. Her name was on his lips when sleep, blessed sleep came to him.

Shivering awakened Jim. Tossing another piece of wood on the fire, he coughed until he gagged. He'd passed two days on the cold hard ground, not caring whether he lived or died but devising ways to kill Bufford Dobbs, who had taken the only thing in life worth having—the woman he loved. He turned his neck to flex the aching muscles.

The rope burn across his neck had healed, but the anger in his soul continued to fester. He was too exhausted and too sick to move. Even in his weakened state, he needed to gather more wood for the fire. He tossed one of the few sturdy sticks on the graying ash. It seemed the heat was warmer than he wanted. Gathering his coat and the blanket closer to his chest, he poured tepid water from the kettle into the cup. His cache of ground coffee gone, only two cans of stew remained of his food supply.

While sliding the tip of the knife around the top of the tin can, the blade slipped and nicked his hand. He cursed and wiped the blood on a pants leg. His stomach growled as he waited for the meager fare to heat. Maybe tomorrow he'd feel strong enough to saddle the mare and ride out.

The first spoonful of food settled hard, causing him to retch. Knowing he needed to regain his strength, he forced himself to finish the can's contents. Exhaustion rode him hard.

He thought of Tessa, her gentle curves and the look of exquisite pleasure on her face while he had soaped her firm young breasts. Even in his weakened state the vision of her was enough to drive him to distraction.

"Tessa," he called, aware that his voice was a hoarse whisper, though it rang in his ears like a hammer on an anvil. "Tessa."

He listened. But only the wind answered.

The cramps in his stomach drew his knees to his chest. His gut rolled. His insides churned. He needed to answer the call of nature, but when he pushed from the ground, his legs buckled under his own weight. He raised a limp hand to wipe the puke from his chin.

The appaloosa came to stand over him. For two nights he had listened to her throaty whinnies and watched her bunch her hind legs to lash out, sending a pair of wolves whimpering and slinking off into the night. He was too puny to give the mare the attention she sought. Weakened by the ague, he could not diagnose his own illness.

Jim's skin burned hot, and his head throbbed. He squinted against the dim but painful morning light. Someone touched his forehead, a gentle breath against his cheek.

A woman! Tessa.

No. The scent that lingered in his nose was too earthy, and too masculine, not at all like the subtle sweetness of Tessa's perfume. Images raced through his mind.

A hand lifted his head. A spoon of warm coffee laced with brandy pressed between his lips. He was grateful for the square brown face and hazel eyes that seemed to loom out of the fog around him. He wondered if the angel of darkness had come for him.

His breathing whistled inside his lungs. Regret fogged his fever-racked body. He would die without having avenged the deaths of Joe and Tessa.

****

The mare whinnied. Her shrill call echoed across the clearing. Jim squinted his eyes. A low voice rumbled from the opposite side of the campfire. "'Bout time you rejoined the living."

Jim rubbed his eyes. He yawned. "How long have I slept?"

"Not sure. I've been with you for three days."

Jim groaned and tried to lift his legs, the effort draining his breath. He fell back. "I'm mighty glad to see you, Charlie."

"Shot a rabbit last night. Got a stew bubbling. You hungry?"

"Yes." He winced and rubbed the scar on his left shoulder. It was the first time he noticed that beneath the layer of blankets he was naked as the day he was born. Jim moaned and closed his eyes.

"The fever nearly killed you. But I see it's not the first time you've been close to death. How'd you come by that wicked scar?"

Jim ignored the question. "What happened to my clothes?"

Cherokee Charlie wrinkled his nose. "They were rank where you'd soiled yourself. Plus you were burning with the fever. Undressed you, rubbed you down with snow, got some broth into you, and washed your clothes in the stream."

Jim nodded. He lifted his body to look around.

"There were two dead men."

"Yep, I buried them. 'Pears you've got a lot to explain."

Accepting a plate of rabbit stew, Jim cautiously filled his mouth. When his stomach didn't rebel, he savored each morsel. In between bites, he explained about the beating he'd taken from the Dobbses, the way they had stripped him naked and staked him out in the frigid cold. He also explained about Tessa's spirit and how he'd seen her and the mare merge as one, and the strange circumstances of Ollie and Fourney's deaths. "I don't know, Charlie. Maybe I was delusional."

The Indian reached over and filled Jim's cup with coffee. "In my world, we believe restless spirits roam the earth. Sometimes they take the form of animals. Could be a cougar, a buffalo"—he looked over the rim of his cup—"or an appaloosa mare."

Though Jim welcomed the comment, he mused over it. "She wants revenge, Charlie, and I do, too."

The Cherokee nodded. He pointed a spoon toward Jim. "The way she died, and the baby, too, I can understand why her spirit can't rest."

Jim agreed. "What brought you here, Charlie? How'd you find me?"

Charlie seemed to drift to another place for a moment. "I'm an Indian. We Indians are supposed to be good trackers." He laughed a little at his joke, then grew serious. "I couldn't stay in Medicine Lodge."

"What about Cora Beth and her mother, and Ada Mae?"

"Ada Mae did as we expected. She run off with a whiskey drummer. Miss Millie and Cora Beth…they're good."

"Did they open up a boarding house?"

Charlie stretched his arms over his head. "No. They said something about Medicine Lodge didn't feel right to them."

No longer a man on the brink of death, Jim ladled his plate with the remaining stew. "Why couldn't you stay, Charlie? I thought you and Cora Beth might have feelings for each other."

Charlie appeared to struggle with the subject. Jim waited. A thin wind gave him a shudder.

Charlie swirled his cup, drained the contents, then set the cup aside. "When I took a wife, I didn't know about love. I just knew a man needed the comfort of a woman. I'm not sure what I feel for Cora Beth. Whatever it is, it hurts like hell." He pointed to his heart. "She's a good woman, Jim."

An awkward silence fell across the fire. The flames crackled, burning orange and blue. Jim studied the craggy face, the sad eyes. He waited.

Charlie's hands balled into fists. Anguish filled his voice. "In the world we live in, people don't look down their noses when a white man takes an Indian wife. But when a white woman is escorted by a half-breed, it's a different story. My feelings run too deep for Cora Beth to have folks shunning her because of me. There's no future for us in Medicine Lodge or any other town. It was best I ride away before she got hurt."

Jim nodded his understanding. "If there was a place where the two of you could live together and be happy, would you go back for her?"

"Damnation, Jim. There ain't no such place. There's no sense talking about it anymore."

He met Charlie's glare. "I feel your pain, my

friend. But I can offer you a place, and with a guarantee not a single living soul will ever show or voice any prejudice."

Charlie harrumphed. "There ain't no such place."

Jim coughed. Not the bone-rattling croupy sound he'd suffered a few days ago. "I've told you about how my father-in-law raised Tessa as his own. No one dared call her a half-breed. What I'm getting at, Charlie, is this. My good friend Hank Edwards is on the down side of sixty. He's used up and too worn out to continue marshaling. He's offered me the badge. Until now, I had intended to drift once I put an end to Bufford Dobbs' sorry life.

"You're a mustanger, Charlie. I have a ranch that needs rebuilding and a man who knows horses to run it. Now, Lettie, that's Hank's wife, owns a boarding house. She wants to sell it so she and Hank can move to California where the winters aren't so cold. It's the best I can offer."

The brown-skinned man stood. "I've got me some thinking to do, Jim. Come morning, I'll give you my answer, but I'm not promising anything."

A slow sly smile spread across Jim's face. "It's all a man can expect. Now where's my clothes?"

****

A full moon lit the forest in hues of dusky blue and green by the time Jim opened his heavy-lidded eyes. He lifted his hand to feel the mare's velvet muzzle nuzzling the top of his hand. The great horse nudged him on the cheek. Jim tried to focus his blurred vision. He could barely make out Charlie's form sitting cross-legged next to the fire.

"That's some horse, Jim. She's sure devoted to

you."

"There's no amount of money can buy Dancer from me." Jim wobbled as he stood. "Guess I'm still not as strong as I thought."

"Give it another day, friend. Dobbs doesn't know the country. He's probably out there wandering around in circles. We'll find him."

Jim walked a distance from the camp to take care of personal needs. Returning, he settled by the fire and poured himself a cup of coffee. He had always believed himself to be a practical man. He knew he was stubborn, set in his ways, too, but didn't look at either of those as flaws in his character. As a lawman it was imperative he maintain discipline. He kept his voice rich and commanding. "About Dobbs. There is no *we*, Charlie. He's mine to find and mine to bring to justice. I appreciate your offer."

Charlie grinned, his fine white teeth shining in the darkness. "Odd the way them two bush-busters met their ends. I reckon Cloud Woman's spirit has something special planned for Bufford. Reckon I can respect the way you want to go it alone."

Charlie rolled over on his pallet to face away from the fire.

Jim rummaged around inside one of the saddlebags to remove his journal and pencil. Using the firelight, he recorded the circumstances of his capture, the deaths of Ollie and Fourney, and Bufford's escape. He noted his illness, and how Cherokee Charlie Ashwin had nursed him back to health. He deliberately left out the parts about Tessa and her spirit and her part in the deaths. Anyone reading that would surely think he'd imbibed too much rotgut whiskey.

****

Jim had saddled the appaloosa and was ready to ride before the full light of dawn reached the sky. Charlie sat astride his pinto. "I have considered your offer, my friend. It is a worthy proposition. If I accept, how will I make it known that I am not some dirty Indian trying to claim squatter's rights?"

Jim reached a gloved hand into a side coat pocket. He withdrew a folded document, a page torn from his journal. "Give this to Hank Edwards. It says we're partners—you and me."

Charlie unfolded the paper. His eyes widened as he scanned the missive, then, folding it, he slipped it beneath his poncho. "You honor me with your words. No man has ever done so much."

It took all of Jim's determination not to smile. "What about Cora Beth and her mother?"

His lips pursed in thought, Charlie said, "I have lain awake most of the night thinking about what you said. It is true, the woman has found her way into my heart, and it is heavy without her. When we part ways, your path takes you toward Bufford Dobbs. My path travels back to Medicine Lodge. If she will have me, Cora Beth and I will meet you in Texhoma." A crooked grin rested on his lips. "And most likely her mother will be with us."

The two men moved their horses closer together and reached out to grasp hands in a strong symbol of friendship. For a few moments they sat there, motionless, until Charlie broke the silence. "I will pray for the Great Spirit to give you courage to face the devil, my friend."

The richness of the Cherokee's voice had a

calming effect on Jim. "If this turns out bad and Bufford takes me down instead, I'll send Dancer home. She knows the way. The only thing I ask is that you never sell her, or let anyone ride her. Her name is Spirit Dancer. Honor the freedom she has earned."

"Do not fear, Jim. No harm will come to you. It is Dobbs who needs to make peace with his maker." Charlie reached his hand toward the appaloosa. "Wha-ho, Spirit Dancer, bring our friend home safely."

Slightly uncomfortable with the sentimentality, Jim smiled. He nodded, and gigged the mare in the direction he'd seen Dobbs take the night he'd run for his life.

Chapter Twenty-One

It didn't matter that Bufford Dobbs had a week's head start on Jim. The weather had held, with no new snow. He urged the mare into a lope. No wind roiled the ground's almost ankle-deep powdery crystals. A wintry haze lay across the plains and gave the land the appearance of glass. The sky was cloudless and a clear blue. A good day for tracking down a killer.

Except for a solitary stag cutting diagonally across his line of vision, Jim was alone. He surveyed the scene ahead of him. A strange, light feeling in his head and a steady, implacable anger in his heart made his mission an even more visceral necessity for him.

He cut toward Wild Horse Creek. The mare reared. She crow-hopped and danced in a circle. Though he'd never ridden the appaloosa, he'd never known her to act unpredictable. He withdrew that thought, and almost laughed aloud when recalling the mysterious amalgamation between a spirit woman and a horse named Spirit Dancer. "What ails you, Dancer?"

Even when he kicked her sides to urge her in the southerly direction she stretched her neck forward, tugging the reins as if insisting they ride easterly. As he fought the mare to gain obedience, a gust of wind knocked his hat from his head.

"Hellfire." He dismounted, allowing the reins to ground-tie the horse. He walked a few paces and bent to lift the hat. A breeze turned the hat on its brim, rolling it like a wheel just out of Jim's reach. He grinned to himself, recalling the way the wind had knocked his hat from his head on another occasion—an occasion that led him to discover the hoof prints of horses stolen from his ranch, that eventually led him to the Dobbs brothers.

"Okay, Tessa, you can stop playing games. If you want me to ride east, then east it is."

The wind settled. He lifted the hat from the ground, brushed snow from it, and snugged it on his head. The mare loosed a whinny that, to Jim, sounded distinctly like laughter.

He grumbled to himself as he toed a boot into the stirrup and swung into the saddle. "I swear I'm a candidate for the madhouse. Standing out here in the middle of nowhere, the wind playing tricks with my hat, a horse that's laughing at me, and me—talking to nobody. Damn…damn it to hell."

He extended his hand forward as if he were offering an invitation, his voice bemused. "Lead the way, Dancer. It appears I'm just along for the ride."

The mare tossed her head up and down and let loose a little squeal. She broke into a gallop, heading east.

After an hour of keeping a steady pace, a strange feeling of depression settled over Jim. What was it that caused men to commit unspeakable violence? And when it was finished did these men suffer any remorse? He knew the answer to both questions. Bufford Dobbs and his brothers had expressed no regret, no sorrow, over any of their actions.

He reined in slightly, then slacked the reins and rode on. At the end of the day, he found shelter in a grove of oak trees. After seeing to Dancer's needs, he settled down to build a fire. Thankful for the stock of food Charlie had given him, Jim put the coffee on and prepared a light meal of bread slathered with wild strawberry jam. After days of not eating, his stomach wasn't ready for anything heavy. He enjoyed a cigarette with his cup of coffee.

He banked the fire to last through the night, then hunkered inside his heavy jacket, with the blanket around him for added comfort.

Tomorrow. Tomorrow, he reasoned, he would begin seeing signs that would lead him to Bufford Dobbs.

He pulled the hat down over his face, and as the fringes of sleep visited him, a woman's voice whispered, *The place where evil lives.*

Expelling a breathy sigh, Jim's face twisted into consternation. He did not need to look for hoof prints or broken twigs. He knew why the horse insisted on traveling east. He knew exactly where to find his enemy.

****

Jim followed the narrow trail, a zigzag thread that wound through the dark fringes of spruce trees. The clouds darkened, adding to the gloominess where he traveled. A flake of snow left a spot of cold as it melted against his cheek. More flakes drifted down and left him squinting to see through the white veil.

The mare quivered beneath him. She blew and snorted, alerting Jim to her nervousness. She sank fetlock-deep into the snow. Jim deliberately reined her to a stop. Sitting tall, he shifted his gaze to locate the object of the appaloosa's unease. By his stance, he was saying, *You'll never get a better chance, Bufford. If you're going to shoot, pull the trigger now.*

But no shot came. Seconds ran on and became minutes, and at last Jim touched heels to the horse's sides, and he sighed with enormous relief.

He did not delude himself that Bufford wasn't nearby. He spotted the mushrooming of smoke from a rifle before he heard the shot. He tried to fling himself sideways out of the saddle, knowing even as he did that it was probably too late.

The bullet struck behind him, and a spray of dirt and snow fanned out like a fountain. Jim lay flat on his belly, his face pressed against the snow-covered earth. Another report reached him, flat and wicked and deadly, while the spray raised by the first bullet was still settling down.

A chill slithered down his spine as he realized what path the bullet must have taken to hit behind him. It had to have been aimed directly at his chest, and it could not have missed by more than a few inches.

Cautiously he raised his head. "Give it up, Bufford. This is one fight you won't win."

"Go to hell, lawman." Violent cursing followed, with Bufford screaming at his horse to come back. "You sorry bag of bones, get back here."

Jim surmised that Bufford had neglected to tie the animal before he decided to start taking potshots at him. The animal galloped past. Another shot rang out, a sound like that of a flat board striking a horse's rump. Jim, flat on his belly, pressed himself to the ground.

The brown horse stumbled, regained its balance, and ran like a fire had been set to its tail, sending clods of dirty slush from its hooves. The horse continued on as if it had lost its mind with fear.

Jim's shoulders shook with laughter. He decided to taunt the man. "Lost your horse, Bufford. Hope you're wearing a good pair of walking boots."

The rifle roared again, and this time the bullet tore away a chunk of sod not six inches from Jim's head. "My Aunt Fannie couldn't hit the broad side of a barn, but she has you beat."

He lay still, his arms hugging his head. He hoped there was enough distance between him and Dobbs' rifle. The waiting seemed hours instead of a few short minutes. The rifle kept barking, and the bullets kept striking near, each time flinging up a shower of dirty snow and each time whining off into the distant countryside.

"Keep firing like that, Bufford, and you'll run out of bullets."

The rifle barked again and Jim felt a tug at the crown of his hat, which miraculously stayed on his head. Jim removed his hat, and rolled over and over, to seek shelter behind a large oak tree. For several moments, he sat with his back against the broad trunk, dragging air into his lungs in great sighing gasps.

"Where are you, lawman?"

Jim glanced around. He didn't see the mare. His heart lurched, and he worried a bullet might have taken her down. He didn't whistle for fear Dancer would expose herself to danger if she answered his call.

"I'm here, Bufford. You might as well start running. I'll give you an hour's head start."

"Go to hell."

Jim started counting loud enough for the man to hear. "One...two...three...Time's wasting, Dobbs.

Four...five. Either run or take one of my bullets. I guarantee I won't miss. Six...Give it up. A Winchester only holds thirteen shells. By my count, you're out of ammo."

The sound of boots thumping against the ground brought a sneering grin to Jim's lips. He waited until the shy sun faded from the sky before leaving the safety of cover. He pursed his lips and emitted a long, sharp whistle. The mare answered with a high-pitched whinny.

He heard the sound of her hooves before he watched her emerge from the dark shadows of the oak grove. She came to him. He held her jaws between his hands and spoke softly. "Not much longer, girl. It'll soon be over, and then we can go home."

The mare brushed her massive head against his chest.

As he hoisted into the saddle a thought came to Jim—every lawman needs a loyal horse, a rifle, and a woman. He sighed deep and long. He only had the horse, and a revolver.

The last thing he saw before he set out after Dobbs was a wisp of white. Lifted by the gentle wind, it fluttered and then disappeared. His heart quickened. He narrowed his eyes, searching, wanting to see more.

Sweet Tessa. She had a temper as fierce as a winter storm, a smile that would brighten the darkest day, and laughter that sounded like tinkling bells. His heart ached. Spirit or woman, he missed her.

With a mutter of disgust, Jim touched a heel to the mare's side, urging her forward. "Time's up, Dobbs. Get ready to make peace with your maker."

Chapter Twenty-Two

Black-shadowed thickets, spreading ever onward. Snow hung like invading tendrils from gnarled branches and sent small droplets plummeting to the ground. Now and again the pale moon pierced the broken, scudding clouds and, with its silvered light, created an unearthly landscape of dark shapes rising from a luminous haze. A decrepit wooden structure sat alone, hugged by a cluster of trees.

An abandoned hovel now, the shack had been built perhaps fifty years ago by trappers and had been used as a line-shack for cowhands, and later as a hideout for outlaws.

For most of the day snow fell and pelted the earth, but as night settled, the driving storm and erratic winds subsided. The countryside grew quiet in hushed relief. The very air seemed to hang in breathless suspense. Even the impatient appaloosa stood quiet as Jim gazed at the cabin down below.

A squeak intruded on the silence. The sound ended almost as quickly as it began. A bush twitched unnaturally by the front door. From Jim's vantage point he watched a shadowy form cautiously emerge from behind the shrub. A waiting hush prevailed as the phantom carefully surveyed the area; then, like a large, winged bat, the darkly cloaked figure entered the dwelling.

A welling filled Jim's chest. He didn't suppress the smile that drifted across his face when he spotted the flash of fire from inside the cabin. The mare's ears flicked forward when Jim whispered, "We're here, Tessa. Rattlesnake Junction."

The moon cast dancing shadows across the snow, and when the wind sighed, Jim was certain he heard Tessa say, *He's the last one.*

It was only a matter of time; Jim settled down to wait.

****

Bufford Dobbs squinted in the dark, trying to focus on his surroundings. Exhausted beyond measure, his chattering teeth broke the silence. After miles of being dogged by Jim Sawyer, Dobbs was foot weary, his skin chilled to the bone. He looked forward to a warm fire, drying his wet clothing, and sleep. Yes, uninterrupted sleep. After his horse had deserted him, Dobbs had walked for hours, with Sawyer always one step behind him.

Once Dobbs spotted the shack, he ran, sinking into drifts of snow, stumbling, getting up, fighting his way toward shelter. The weight of his wet coat dragged him down, tempting him to shrug it off. Mentally weary, he clung tight to the saddlebag slung over his shoulder. He huffed, "Damn you, Sawyer. I ain't goin' down like my brothers. You ain't drivin' me 'til I drop." And then he yelled, "I'll see you in hell first. You hear me, Sawyer? I'll see you in hell."

Bufford squatted behind a bush. He called out, "Hullo, the cabin." He waited. When no response came, and when he determined the shack was abandoned, he left his hiding place, shoved against the door, and entered.

He collapsed on the floor, shivering and moaning. Relief came when he spotted the stone fireplace. Desperate for heat, he used a sliver of moonlight to guide him as he scooped up leaves that had blown in underneath the door. Placing the leaves inside the rough-rock fireplace, he bunched them into a nest.

His fingers trembled as he removed the last bullet from his gunbelt. Numb with cold, he cursed when he almost dropped the slug, catching it before it hit the floor. He clenched his hands and blew on them. The warmth from his breath offering temporary respite from the cold. He reached into his pocket and withdrew a penknife. He used the open blade to remove the cap from the shell. A three-legged chair lay on its side. He picked it up and smashed it against the floor, breaking the dry-rotted wood into kindling. When he was satisfied with laying the wood, he carefully emptied the gunpowder over the makings, and with his lone match struck the sulfur head against a rock.

Sparks splashed outward until a sudden blaze flared to life in the flash and continued to glow as Dobbs lit the kindling. He squatted, reaching his hands forward to soak up the meager heat. Still trembling from the cold, he stripped down to his long underwear.

As the flame grew, a soft glow cast shadows around the room. Dobbs yawned and scratched between his legs where the material from his long underwear had wadded and bunched, and had galled him.

He walked to the window and peered out. "I see you, you sumbitch. Sittin' up there on that she-devil horse of your'n. I hope you freeze your gawl-danged balls off."

Dobbs did a little slew-foot shuffle. He smacked his hands together in glee and cackled, a maniacal sound that filled the small space. Fumbling with the clasp on his saddlebag, he removed a half-empty bottle of rotgut. Clamping his teeth on the cork, he gave a tug, then spat the plug into the fire. Upending the bottle, he glugged until not a drop remained, and then he tossed the bottle against the wall.

Wiping his mouth across the sleeve of the soiled underwear, he staggered to the lone cot. He stretched on the bed, breathing out a long sigh of relief.

Warmed by the fireplace and the heat from the whiskey as he was, exhaustion rode him hard. His eyes fluttered, and then he allowed the sweet essence of sleep to envelop him.

A deathlike stillness followed, and the lonely shack seemed to moan in sorrow for its impending doom. While jewel-bright snowdrops fell like tears from the rotting eaves, a low, confused murmur began to drift from the dwelling. Soft cries, distressed whimpers, and the mad screams of a demented soul shredded the light with haunting, mindless sounds. The distant moon hid its face behind a thick cloud and continued on its arch across the sky, heedless of time.

The heat from the fireplace had awakened a nest of hissing serpents. From between the rocks of the fireplace, the ceiling beams, an old spittoon, and holes in the straw-ticked mattress, snakes slithered with blind obedience along their prelaid paths, bright flashes marking their arrival. Their agitated tongues reached out to taste the sleeping man's scent.

Bufford Dobbs lifted his hand to flick the annoyance that touched his face. He shifted to relieve the weight on his chest. It was the sound, the buzzing, that disturbed his sleep. He mumbled incoherently, "Leave me be."

The movement between his legs, over the top of his balding head, over his shoulders, and the slithering of something inside his boot caused him to sit up. He blinked, trying to bring the room into focus. A chill spread through his veins and iced downward to his nether parts, threatening to release his bowels. "What the hell?"

Horror washed over him in waves when he realized his blanket of warmth radiated from a mass of slithering bodies. He grabbed the head of one large monster and flung it across the room. Dobbs jerked from the cot, landing on his hands and knees. The soft glow from the fireplace brought him level with a squirming throng of ebony-eyed rattlesnakes. The attacks were rapid, bringing searing hot pain from multiple bites to his hands, his legs, and the top of his head. He forced himself to stand, and then he ran to the door, the power of his yank felling it from the hinges.

As a ray of moonlight shifted across the horizon, Jim Sawyer sat astride the appaloosa on a hill overlooking the shack. Dobbs yelled, "I'm bit! I'm bit all over. Have mercy, Sawyer. You gotta help me."

His low moans turned to high-pitched shrieks of fear and deep-chested cries of outrage as he slogged through the snow to reach Jim.

"What kind of devil place is this, Sawyer?"

Jim answered in bemusement. "My wife calls it the place where evil sleeps. Folks who know these parts call it Rattlesnake Junction."

A snake head pushed through the neck of the long-sleeved shirt. Dobbs screamed again as the rattler sank its fangs deep into him. He reached up and jerked the serpent from the roll of flab around his neck and flung it toward Jim.

Dobbs dropped to his knees, his arms outstretched as he begged, "Gawd almighty! You knowed it all along, didn't you? That's why you dogged me here." He swiped a trembling hand across his mouth. "Shoot me. Don't let me suffer."

Extreme anger mottled Jim's face as he stared at the man. "You mean like my wife suffered at the filthy hands of you and your brothers?"

"Your wife? Oh, yeah, the Comanche gal. It weren't nothin' personal. Me and the boys was jest havin' ourselves a bit of fun."

A coldness congealed around Jim's heart. His limbs quivered with rage. "I'm going to sit here and watch you, Dobbs...watch you writhe in pain as the poison eats its way through your veins and to your brain. You'll froth at the mouth like a mad dog, and inch by inch you'll feel the life drain from your body."

Dobbs struggled to his feet. He stretched his arms and hands forward as he stumbled toward the appaloosa. Jim backed the mare out of the man's reach.

Jim raised a brow sharply as he gave Dobbs a meaningful stare. Abject horror reflected in Dobbs' eyes . He choked and spewed a yellowish foam. "Ain't a lawman s'posed to show mercy? Put a bullet in me. I'm beggin' you."

Jim surmised it wouldn't be long now. "A man's only reward is how well he chooses to live his life and how well he chooses to die. How much mercy did you show my father-in-law, my wife, my unborn child, and

God knows how many other of your victims? You deserve to burn in hell for the torture you and your demented brothers gave them."

Dobbs nodded, as if accepting the explanation. "Then let the devil take me."

He collapsed to his knees, his arms spread wide. The words he tried to speak never departed his lips as he fell face down into the snow.

Jim stepped out of the saddle. He toed his boot under Dobbs' chest and with a swift thrust flipped the man on his back. Dobbs showed no sign of life as a rattler slithered across his chest and onto the snow.

Jim unholstered his revolver. Smoke spiraled from the barrel as he fired. "That's two less snakes to worry about."

A mystical light emanated from the darkened sky and cast an eerie ice-blue glow. Jim gathered the collar of his jacket against the cold's sharp bite. Wind kicked up, and like a dust devil, snow whirled and danced over the dead man's body.

A groan followed by a crack as sharp as a rifle's bark caused the mare to squeal and back away. Jim barely had time to grab the reins and gather his wits as a tree branch burdened with snow broke, dumping its icy contents over Dobbs. Only the tips of his boots remained visible.

Jim cocked his head to one side. He was certain he heard laughter. After all he had experienced, he no longer questioned whether or not it was his imagination playing tricks on him. A part of him wanted to join Tessa in her jubilation. Instead, a peace he hadn't felt in a long time filled him. He looked up and smiled at the brightest of the twinkling stars. "It's done, Tessa. You and Joe can rest easy, now."

He considered what he should do about the body. With no shovel and the ground burdened with snow, burying Dobbs was out of the question. He thought about taking the body and placing it inside the cabin. A fitting place for a snake, among snakes. Or he could wrap the corpse inside the oilskin slicker and deliver it to Hank as evidence. Jim reasoned it was a long cold ride to Texhoma, and there was no sense in burdening the mare with both his weight and the weight of a dead man.

"What would you have me do, Tessa?"

The wind stirred. The scent of lilacs wafted around Jim. He closed his eyes and inhaled deeply. She was here.

Open your eyes, Jim.

He obeyed. She stood before him, in her gown of white, iridescent, hair flowing. He ached to hold her, to make love to her one more time.

My time is over. I am at peace, now. My spirit can rest.

"No, Tessa. Stay."

My heart aches as does yours. Do not be sad, my love.

The aura faded into nothingness. Jim was certain he heard, *Time to leave this place of evil. Never return.*

"Tessa, what about Dobbs?"

Like a wisp of wind, the words drifted away. *He…is…no…more.*

He knew she was right. Bufford and his brothers were no more, and leaving carrion for the scavengers was a fitting end.

Jim gave the appaloosa mare an affectionate pat

before swinging into the saddle. "C'mon, Dancer. It's time to go home."

Chapter Twenty-Three

Dark pink and purple streaks coated the edges of the early morning sky. The faint lowing of cattle drifted up from distant grazing lands and the gentle chirping of birds filled the air around Jim. He watched the dawn greet the horizon with a golden yawn over the distant hills that rimmed the snow-covered valley.

He had seen this sight at least a thousand times. Dreamed of it thousands more since he had been gone. A shiver raced up his spine and trembled across his shoulders. He heaved a shuddering sigh, knowing that returning to the ranch wouldn't be easy.

He reached the main road and slowed his tired mount to a walk. There was no hurry. The town was still asleep. For a long moment he gazed down the road, weighing the wisdom of returning to this place.

A warm contentment—a sweet sense of peace and freedom he had never thought to feel again—settled in his soul as he rode down the slushy road that led to the marshal's office.

He'd trailed the Dobbs brothers for three months. It seemed longer. Saddle weary, he rode past the church which doubled as the schoolhouse. Except since the widow Jackson had taken ill the town was without a schoolmarm. He passed the widow's house and noticed the picket fence was no longer falling down, and someone had given it a new coat of whitewash.

As he rode down the building-lined road, Jim struggled to focus his thoughts. Through the morning's dawning glow, he spotted Hank Edwards standing on the front porch of the marshal's office. A grin bunched the wrinkles on the old man's leathery face. His lifted his coffee cup in a salute. "Well, as I live and breathe, boy, you are a sight for these ole eyes. Light down off that cayuse. Lettie'll skin my hide if I don't bring you over to the boarding house so she can fix you breakfast."

Jim swung down from the saddle. He stretched and rubbed his backside. Stepping forward, he gripped hands with the marshal and relished the welcome home. "Good to see you, too, Hank. I could surely eat a stack of Lettie's flapjacks, a couple of fried eggs, and bacon. Lots of crisp bacon. A bath and a soft bed will do me, too."

He tied the mare to the hitching post. "Maybe we should go inside and let me give you my report before breakfast."

Hank flung out the coffee dregs that had settled in the bottom of the tin mug. He hooked the handle on a porch post nail, his face serious. "Had a Cherokee visit me a few weeks back, by the name of Charlie Ashwin. He had quite a story to tell, all about how you and him hooked up, about the raid on those wagons, and how you rescued the women. He also gave me the report you sent, and told me lots more, too. Good man, this Charlie Ashwin.

"I figure whatever else you have to tell me about Bufford Dobbs can wait. Besides, you look pert near done in. Reckon it's been a long hard ride."

He patted Jim on the shoulder.

Jim swallowed hard, his Adam's apple sliding up and down his throat. He squinted against the glare of the morning sun and tugged the brim of his hat down lower.

"No argument there, Hank." Jim gathered the reins. "Mind if we stop off at the livery? Dancer deserves a good rubdown and an extra measure of oats."

"You go ahead, Jim. I'll meet you at the boarding house. Ain't had my breakfast yet. But a little forewarning—you know how Lettie likes to give hugs. Plus there's two other ladies who'll be proud to see you."

Jim had a suspicion as to who the two women were, especially if Charlie had come to Texhoma. "I noticed the fence on the widow Jackson's house. Somebody fix it?"

"Yep, your friend Charlie. The old gal went to meet her maker a day or two after you lit out. A few weeks ago, the town council hired a new schoolteacher by the name of Cora Beth Collins. She bought the widow's house, and her ma bought the boarding house. Lettie and me, well, we were just waitin' for you to come home so I can hang up my badge."

A smile broadened Jim's face. This meant Charlie had brought the women and that he planned to stay. "I reckon this means you and Lettie are still bent on heading to California?"

Hank waved as he parted from Jim and marched across the road toward the boarding house. "Yep, that's the general idea."

Jim arched his brow and stared at his friend's prepared readiness. "You once told me that a man's gotta do what a man's gotta do. That's for certain, but next to Joe and Tessa, you and Lettie are 'bout the only people I can call family."

With a look of contrition, Hank shrugged his shoulders and spread his arms and hands wide before crossing the road and entering the building.

After seeing to Dancer's needs, Jim bunched his hands inside his coat pockets and sprinted across the wide road and up the steps to the boarding house's veranda. Before entering, he stamped his boots good and hard to knock off any mud. Lettie was a woman with a kind soul and a generosity beyond measure, but she could wither the staunchest man's fortitude with a frown if he tracked dirt on her polished oakwood floors.

A bell tinkled when he opened the door. They stood there, lined up, grinning from ear-to-ear—Lettie, Millie, and Cora Beth. Hank sat off to the side in a parlor chair. Heat flared in Jim's stubbled cheeks. Damn, he wished women wouldn't make such a fuss. Nonetheless, he opened his arms wide, accepting first Lettie's hug. She then stood aside and, using the corner of her starched white apron, wiped tears from her eyes. Next came Millie, and then Cora Beth.

All their voices blended together reminded Jim of a gaggle of excited gabbling geese. His heart swelled, and he laughed out loud. "Thank you, ladies. This is a perfect welcome home."

Perfect except for two special people missing from his life. Determined not to spoil the women's coddling, he pushed the gloom aside. "Is that bacon I smell?"

Lettie said, "Got bath water heating. By the time we've filled you full as a happy tick, the water will be ready, and we'll fix you a tub. I've already got the bed turned down for you." She paused and, grinning wide, said, "Land a-goshen, I've plumb forgot that Miz Collins and her daughter own the boarding house now."

Millie Collins quickly added, "Oh, Lettie, I told you to call me Millie, and you just fret over Jim as much as you want. Cora Beth and I owe him our lives."

Jim's smile widened, carving deep lines along the sides of his mouth. "Though I can't say I deserve all this fuss, I do appreciate the attention."

He allowed Cora Beth to take his hand and lead him toward the kitchen. "Charlie usually rides in for lunch. With today being Saturday, he'll take breakfast with us. I expect him any minute. He'll be mighty glad to know you're here, and safe. He told us a little about the men you sought."

A visible shudder wracked over the young woman. "I hope you've righted the grievous wrong that was perpetrated against you."

Jim released her hand. He removed his hat and coat and hung them on the coat rack in the hallway next to the kitchen door.

Lettie said, "Sit yourself down, and I'll pour you and Hank a cup of coffee." While she busied herself helping Millie Collins and Cora Beth, she chattered away. "About two months ago, a young woman came riding in. Pretty little thing. Said she knew you from a long time ago, and your paths had recently crossed. She didn't go into any details, and I didn't ask. 'Tweren't none of my business."

Lettie stopped long enough to catch her breath, pour a batch of pancake batter on the griddle, and then take a sip of coffee from her own mug. "She said you told her to come to me if she needed help making a change to her life."

Except for the clattering of the utensils and the spattering of bacon in the frying pan, the kitchen filled with an abrupt silence.

An odd feeling gnawed at the pit of Jim's stomach. Exhaustion tugged at him, and he wasn't in the mood for playing guessing games. "She have a name?"

At that moment, a soft voice spoke. An almost shy voice. "Good morning, Marshal Sawyer."

He hadn't expected to cross paths with Katie Em again. True, the last time he'd had a conversation with the girl who rode with outlaws was in an outhouse with a dividing wall between them. He did recall mentioning that if she wished to change the direction of her life, she should seek out Lettie.

He came to his feet and stepped forward for a better look. "Ka...ti...?" he began, and then halted. This wasn't the same girl he'd seen almost three months ago. The one dressed in bib overalls, with a pistol strapped around her waist and wearing a coat two sizes too big for such a small frame. The features were similar, but more refined. "You're not Katie Em?"

A wry smile curved the younger woman's lips. "Perhaps in another lifetime." She stretched her hand forward. "Pleased to make your acquaintance, sir. My name is Kathryn Emerson. I am visiting my aunt and uncle." She cut her eyes toward Lettie and Hank. "Marshal Hank Edwards and Lettie."

A diminutive blush rising to her cheeks, Katie gathered her skirt, bowed her head slightly, and offered a curtsey.

Shaking his head in mute dismay, Jim sought Lettie for an explanation. She gathered a stack of pancakes from the griddle to put on a plate while Cora Beth and

Millie conveniently busied themselves setting the table.

The cheery-faced woman cleared her throat and hastened to speak. "That's right, Jim. Kathryn is our niece. Hank and I are her only living relatives, you see, and, ah…well…she plans to go on to California with Hank and me."

A light frown touched Lettie's forehead as she stared at her husband. "Ain't that right, Hank?"

Jim almost held his breath and waited for the old marshal's reaction to this bold statement. He wondered what kind of game was being played. Other than a slight tensing of the lean jaw, he saw no real change in the marshal's expression and came to the conclusion that either Hank hadn't heard his wife or had misunderstood her statement.

He carefully studied the oval face staring back at him. His eyes followed the slim, straight line of the young woman's nose downward to the full, pink lips, and the creamy perfection of her skin. Soft brown brows swept upward in a delicate arc above thickly fringed black lashes, while the eyes were a deep smoky blue and as lively as a sky before a storm. A thick blonde braid draped over one shoulder. She wore a matronly, navy-blue dress that accented her narrow waistline. The high-necked bodice, adorned with a white lace collar, was darted at the bustline, drawing his attention to the full swell of her rising and falling bosom. He inhaled her womanly scent. The blood pounded in his veins, nearly overwhelming him. Jim caught himself, realizing he had stepped forward with a hand outstretched and ready to caress Kathryn's cheek. For a moment it seemed their gazes fused. Then with some disgust for his own lack of self-control, he clamped his hands together and moved to grab his coffee mug from the table.

With the time he'd spent away from home before Tessa's death, and the months chasing down the Dobbs brothers, nearly a year had passed since he'd been with a woman. He drank deep as he forced his mind to take control of his lustful thoughts. A pang of anguish stabbed him for his disloyalty to Tessa's memory.

In a quiet resolve, Jim shifted his look toward Lettie. "Well, Hank?"

The marshal uncrossed his long legs and stood. He reached under his hat and scratched. "What Lettie means to say is that we all need a change of scenery. You, better than most, know how it is, Jim. Much as I'd like to live out the rest of my days in Texhoma, there will always be some jackleg I put behind bars or some dead outlaw's relative come looking to settle a score. Don't matter that I'm a whole lotta long in the tooth, and my eyesight ain't so good anymore. Once a person sets out for blood, nothing will satisfy 'em until the deed is done.

"Me and Lettie just want to live out the rest of our days without me having to look over my shoulder. Kathryn has her own reasons for wanting to start a new life. If she decides to travel with us, we'll be mighty proud to have her come along. Now, all this long-windedness has stirred up my appetite. You reckon we can eat before the food gets cold?"

A brisk wind filled the kitchen when the back door opened and closed. Charlie walked straight to Jim and grabbed his hand. "Wha-ho, my friend. I am happy to see you have returned. When you are ready, we have much to talk about."

Chapter Twenty-Four

His stomach filled with an excellent meal, and his head reeling from more talk than he'd heard in several weeks, Jim breathed a sigh of relief when he shut the bedroom door and turned the key in the lock. He unbuckled his gun belt and laid it across the bed, hung his hat on the bedpost. Shrugging out of his vest and shirt, he looked forward to an all-over bath. Sliding out of his jeans, stiff from too many days without washing, he kicked them aside. Next came the boots and socks. He tested the temperature before easing into the portable bathtub until the steaming water covered the thick mat of hair on his chest.

He had just closed his eyes and allowed the water's warmth to seep into his bones, when a light thud brought him to full alert. A clicking sound followed, and then the door opened. The key lay on the floor. He immediately regretted not having his .44 caliber within instant reach. His body tensed, his hands on the sides of the tub, ready to leap for his weapon.

As he forced his mind to take control, he found himself staring at Kathryn Emerson. Haloed by morning sunlight streaming through the window, she reminded him of a picture he'd once seen of a Grecian goddess. Gradually a different concern overtook him. He glanced around for a towel to cover his nakedness. Spotting nothing, he used his hands to cover the growing length of his manhood.

Their eyes met. Her cheeks pinked, and Jim slid deeper into the water. She gasped. "Oh, I thought you had joined Charlie for a smoke. I-I'll leave the towels on the bed. S-sorry."

Jim willed Kathryn not to look into the tub as she moved away from the bed. His lustful manhood grew thick and demanding until he feared it would escape the confines of his hands. He resisted the urge to grab the darn thing and pump it until sweet relief washed over him.

Her hand was on the doorknob when he called her name. "Katie?"

A moment of silence ensued. There was no trace of the old Katie Em, neither in speech nor in manner of dress. Her face flared with color when she turned to him.

"Katie Em is dead, Marshall Sawyer. That gun-toting outlaw girl who could barely read or write her name no longer exists. She is buried in a grave next to her ma. On a wooden cross is etched *Katie Em.*"

He fixed her with a steely look. "What about Ruben?"

In complete honesty, she said, "In death he gave new life to his sister. It was the most unselfish thing my brother ever did for me. I buried him and spoke words over him. And unless you tell, there is no one to truly know who lies beneath that pile of dirt on an old abandoned homestead.

"I was born Kathryn Emerson. No one ever knew me by that name. Cora Beth is teaching me to read, and to speak proper—properly. But if I remain in the territories, there will always be someone who will recognize Katie Em. That is why it is important for me to go to California. I intend to take advantage of a new life—the gift from my brother."

The unmistakable trembling at the corners of her mouth didn't help Jim's composure. She gave him a weary smile. "Do you understand, Marshal?"

His heart swelled with pride for her. "It's a pleasure meeting you, Miss Emerson. You'll pardon me if I don't stand up, but perhaps you'd like to join me for an afternoon carriage ride. Later in the week?"

"Perhaps." With a last glance at his face, she left the room, softly closing the door behind her.

****

Kathryn rushed down the hall and to the back stairs. She grabbed her heavy coat and, with head held high and her heart aching with something she couldn't define even to herself, left the boarding house. She took pleasure from walking outside. There at least she felt alive, the wind stinging her cheeks, the bare branches of trees starkly outlined against the gray sky.

The graveyard situated on a hill outside of town possessed a unique beauty with its sprawling ancient oak trees. But it possessed something else besides, a special magic that seemed to draw her there.

She couldn't exactly put her finger on what that magic was, only that her spirit felt soothed and comforted when she walked there. She always found a stillness of mind as she stood beneath one particular oak tree, her thoughts drifting away into nothing, like wind-blown clouds crossing the sky. Peace. Heavenly peace that she longed for, a balm for her bruised soul.

She had often felt like one of the raw biscuits Lettie slipped into the oven and patiently let bake, watching all the while to make sure the dough came out according to plan. Kathryn covered her face with her hands, and her shoulders shook as she cried silent tears of regret for the direction of her life and for hope of a new beginning.

Try as she might, she gave in to the smile tugging at her lips. She was no simple-minded girl to ogle a man, especially a lawman sitting in a bathtub. She had stared at the wide expanse of Jim Sawyer's well-muscled chest, down to where his torso tapered to a lean waist. She had noted how his broad shoulders flexed, the hard flesh of his arms rippled. She had fought to keep her jaw from dropping.

True, she'd seen men before, but she had never seen such a well-built man. She remembered something her mother had always said: "Dress a boar in fancy clothes and he's still a mud-grunting hog." Kathryn could not deny that Jim was a very handsome boar.

She closed her eyes in mortification. Since the age of fifteen, when she'd cut the heart out of the man who had violently stolen her virginity, she had cloaked herself in protective armor, allowing no man to touch her, and lusting after no man.

She held in a groan of frustration. These new feelings were completely foreign to her. She had sensed Jim's leashed desire. The knowledge of it sent a dangerous, foolish swirl of longing, thick and demanding, to settle in the pit of her womanly core.

And then she shook herself loose from the emotional turmoil, realizing she had to return to the boarding house and to her chores.

****

Jim nestled in the downy quilt. It felt good to lie on

a soft mattress that cushioned his body, with a pillow instead of a saddle to support his head. He drew in a long deep breath and let his shoulders relax. He wasn't sure if guilt would come knocking again, but he knew how much he blamed himself for Tessa and Joe's death. It was finished. He'd found their killers, and the men had been brought to justice without the firing of a bullet. He forced down the blame that rose in his chest with engulfing intent. Tessa meant everything to him. But then Kathryn had unexpectedly walked into his life. He wasn't certain what these new feelings meant, and he had nothing to offer her, in any case.

He blew out a weighty sigh and rolled over to punch the pillow before settling on his belly. His eyes closed and he drifted into the ether-realms of a dream.

The sweet scent of lilacs wafted over him. He opened his arms to welcome Tessa. Beating with lust, he took her lips with his own in a rush of breaths.

Possessing, sliding, seeking, his lips glided over her moist mouth. A soft press here. A nibble there. He curved his arms about her middle, hands at the small of her back, pressing her even closer.

His next kiss was deeper, hungrier. He felt like a man starved, and she was his banquet. Suddenly he floated in hazy pleasure. She responded to the demand of his kiss, matching his insistent rhythm. Yet he kept the pressure light enough that she might yearn for more. The tips of her breasts stiffened against his chest, through the translucent nightgown she wore.

He encompassed each breast with calloused palms. Never wanting to cause her pain, he regretted the roughness which abraded her soft flesh. She panted beneath him, her mouth pressed to his as if asking for more.

"Tessa," he whispered as he trailed kisses from the corner of her mouth to the sensitive spot behind her ear. "Show me your spirit."

The dream changed. She broke away from his embrace and drifted to the other side of the room, the essence of lilacs trailing after her. Her chest heaved as if she were gulping in large breaths of air.

He knew she wept.

Jim, we were happy, and I cherished each moment we shared together, but our lives are no more. You have avenged me and Papa. My time on earth is finished. You must let me go. I belong with the spirits of my people. Guard the appaloosa.

Somehow he knew he was angry, and knowing this made him angrier. *No, Tessa. I need you. I don't want to let you go.*

She seemed to tremble. *My spirit will always remain in your heart. It is now your time to live. It is time for you to open your eyes and open your heart. To see what is before you. A new journey awaits, my love. In death as in life, I give you much happiness. Guard the appaloosa.*

When he was with her, emotions seemed more vivid. And then she was gone.

He rolled to his back, and rubbed his hand over his forehead, trying to reconcile the possibility of never seeing her again. *Don't leave, Tessa. Stay a little longer.*

He inhaled the delicate aroma of lilacs, and though he didn't see her, he knew she was near. He sighed heavily, and then a small smile formed on his lips when she appeared.

He closed his eyes for a moment at the enticing image she created. Her essence faded, and he tried to concentrate on her barely audible words. *You will see me in the clouds. My touch will be a breeze rifling your hair or stroking your cheek. You will hear my songs in the wind. Oh...my wonderful husband...do not call again, for I...am...no...more.*

A knot formed in his throat. Perhaps it was best to let Tessa go. Body and mind warred. He grabbed the pillow and punched at the injustice.

He hated it.

His eyes fluttered open. He sat up and glanced around the room. Squeezing his eyes shut, and then reopening them, he questioned his sanity. Had he dreamed Tessa, or had he really conjured her spirit, and what had she meant by saying a new journey awaited him?

Chapter Twenty-Five

Christmas had come and gone, with very little celebration. Jim spent his days between the marshal's office and helping Charlie build a new corral and barn to hold the horses they had rounded up and brought back to the ranch.

Jim felt he was living in limbo. The world he had known with Joe and Tessa seemed a million miles away, but his new life didn't seem any more real. He went through his duties as Texhoma's new marshal as a matter of rote, taking little pleasure in them as he filled out paperwork and trained two new deputies.

The days marched by, one drifting into another, all the same without any respite from the cold weather or the tedium of being cooped up in an office. He almost prayed for a bank robbery, or a request from the home office to go on a manhunt. Even a good fist fight would do.

He hefted on his jacket, pulling leather gloves over his hands. "Ezra, I'm going for a walk. Mind the office."

The young deputy leaned against the broom. "When I pinned on this badge, I didn't expect part of the job was sweeping floors. Sure do wish we'd see some kind of action."

Jim quirked a smile at the lad. "Right now, outlaws are holed up for the winter, but don't worry, time will come soon enough when your belly will beg for something more than beef jerky and cold beans from a can, and you'll be so saddle weary that pushing a broom will feel like a luxury."

"Yeah, well, maybe. Say, Marshal Sawyer, what's it like, killing a man?"

Jim situated the new tan hat on his head. He mulled the young deputy's question. "Taking another human's life, even if he's the most vicious critter with two legs, is in no way easy. Leaves you with a feeling you never quite get over. Like everything else, killing comes with the job."

To lighten the seriousness of his answer, Jim pointed to a place next to the potbelly stove. "Missed a spot over there."

The deputy snorted his disgust, which left Jim chuckling as he walked out into the cold. He stared across the road, frowning at the hard knot that suddenly tightened his gut. There was no sign of her, but his body hummed with the feel of her presence. His blood raced with apprehension as he thought about Kathryn. He swallowed the dryness that hovered, unwelcome, in his throat, and he shook off the odd feeling.

Hank exited the boarding house. Jim lifted a hand and waved. "Cold enough for you?"

The old marshal hunched his shoulder against the brisk breeze. "Lettie's got a fresh pot of coffee brewing, and Kathryn's baking up some apple pies for supper."

"I've had coffee. Thought I'd take a walk."

Hank came to stand next to Jim. "You know, Jim, I'll surely be glad when March gets here. Then we're California bound."

"Yep. Where you off to this morning, Hank?"

"Oh, thought I'd ride out to see if I can give Charlie a hand. Don't rightly know what to do with myself now that I'm not marshaling anymore."

Jim looked up and down the slushy road. All was quiet. A couple of horses stood hitched in front of the saloon. A wagon sat parked in front of the general store. Shop doors were closed against the wintry weather, and dark smoke spiraled from chimneys. "Doesn't look like much will happen today. I might ride out to the ranch after lunch to see who is beating who in checkers."

Hank pshawed. He pulled a handkerchief from his pocket, blew hard to clear his nose. "Ain't none of my business, but I'm making it my business, only because you're like a son to me." He stopped for a second as if to collect his thoughts. "There's a little lady over to the boarding house who is as moon-eyed as a newborn calf over you. If you'd take the blinders off, you'd see how Kathryn looks at you. Now, don't get me wrong, I s'pect she doesn't know her own feelings toward you. If she does, then she's hiding 'em pretty well. Take my advice and invite her for a buggy ride. Let nature take its natural course. I'm sure you get my drift."

Anger flushed through Jim. It raged like a heated furnace, and the emotion stymied him. He respected Hank and valued the old man's friendship. "I'm the marshal, which means I'm staying in Texhoma, Hank. You know about Kathryn's past. She can't expect to have any kind of quality life if she remains in the territories. You know it, I know it, and most of all she knows it. I'm not about to dally with her emotions. Besides, she deserves more than I can give her. Gone for weeks and sometimes months on a manhunt. Never knowing when or if I'll return home. And"—his heart hitched as he recalled the night he rode in to find his house in flames, and his family dead—"a woman needs a man who can protect her. I couldn't do it with Tessa, and it'd be no different with Kathryn. Not all of us can be as lucky as you and Lettie."

He touched the brim of his hat to signal the conversation was over. "Think I'll take my walk now."

Hank bunched his lips into a sly smile. "You're a stubborn jackass, Jim. Remind me of myself thirty years ago. Just one more thing...you could give up marshaling, and come to California with us." He ended with a waggle of his eyebrows.

Jim stood for nearly a minute before he made a vague sound of contempt and stared as if Hank's words meant nothing. He resisted the urge to tell the old man to mind his own business. Protests formed in his mind as he turned to walk toward the graveyard.

****

Kathryn perched on tiptoes, peering over the kitchen sink and out the window. Jim stood in the middle of the street conversing with Hank. From the scowl on Jim's face and the grim line of his mouth, she surmised the conversation wasn't to his liking.

She thought back two months to when she'd ridden into town and gone straight to the boarding house. After explaining her story about knowing Jim, and about her life, she'd been amazed that instead of passing judgment Lettie had offered her the position of maid, but Lettie had also firmly gone over a set of rules. Kathryn didn't fault the older woman's strictness. Especially since she was kind enough to offer free room and board in addition to the job.

"Kathryn?"

Startled, her heart pounded at being caught staring out the window, and at the handsome town marshal. And, heaven help her, she wanted him to kiss her. Warmth rose in her cheeks. She blinked, then took several breaths. "The pies have about fifteen more minutes to bake, Lettie."

"Fiddlesticks, I'm not worried about the pies. What does concern me is the way you keep mooning over Jim Sawyer. Where's your gumption, girl? A vixen can't catch a rooster unless she goes after him."

Kathryn glanced toward the window where the morning sun beamed its brilliance. "I have no business being attracted to him. He's not leaving Texhoma, and I'm not staying. Besides, I don't think I can compete with a dead woman's spirit."

Lettie placed her hands on rounded hips and eyed Kathryn with a challenge. "I was with him the night he found Tessa. It wasn't a pretty sight. It's a fair assumption that it will take him a while to heal, both from the loss of loving her and the tragedy of finding her the way he did."

She hesitated, but then her voice brooked no argument. "If you ask me, you're both a couple of stubborn fools. You for not going after that tall, handsome drink of water, and him for not seeing the real you.

"When I was a bit older than yourself, I wanted Hank Edwards and went after him with a vengeance. True, I was a saloon gal with a reputation, but I'd put all that behind me and, like you're doing now, worked real hard to build a new life. I'd stopped calling myself Lola Albright and became just plain ole Lettie Askew. The real me. Same as you're no longer Katie Em. Now get yourself out of this kitchen and invite Marshal Jim Sawyer to join you in a stroll down to the creek. And while you're there, tell him how you feel. Bless my sweet bones, girl, kissing a man doesn't take near the courage as robbing a bank."

Kathryn swallowed at the seriousness of Lettie's words. "What about the pies?"

Lettie arched a brow, her dark brown eyes sparkling with amusement. "Haven't you heard a word I've said? Shoo, get on out of here. I'll watch the dang pies."

Kathryn giggled like a school girl. She grabbed her coat and was shrugging into it when she spotted two horsemen rein to a stop in front of Jim and Hank.

Melancholy dimmed the excitement building inside her. She hung the coat back on the rack. "Not today, Lettie. Looks like Charlie and another man have business with Jim."

Lettie folded her arms around the girl, patting her on her on the back. "There's always tomorrow. Just don't give up on your feelings for Jim. I'll finish in here. Why don't you go for a walk, do some thinking."

Instead, Kathryn trudged up the stairs to her room. She lay on the bed, one arm flung over her eyes. The circle of her thoughts was of sheer confusion. She tried to unravel the tangle of her feelings and her logic— each telling her something different.

She had helped rob banks and stagecoaches, she'd killed a man, and wounded a few. She'd faced down the meanest of killers, cut bullets out of members of the different gangs she'd ridden with, and all without fear.

What, by ginger, is wrong with me? Jim is more than a lawman—he's warm and considerate, kind, and he treats me like a lady. I enjoy listening to his and Hank's conversations. He's a man of consequence and honesty.

Do I love him?

The truth hit her like a kick in the head.

She could think of no other reason why her heart soared when Jim smiled. No other reason came to mind as to why she ached when he didn't come to the boarding house for supper, and why her whole being lit up with joy when he did come near.

Surely, these feelings meant she loved him. She admonished herself. This is no game to play, Kathryn Emerson.

For the first time in her life, she longed to feel a man's arms around her. Not any man's, but Jim's. Another wave of feelings swept across her heart. The decision to stay in Texhoma or go to California weighed heavy on her mind.

Chapter Twenty-Six

Jim entered the office. He held the door open while he greeted Charlie and the man with him. "Howdy."

Charlie nodded. "Can we speak to you in private, Jim?"

Jim's lips pressed into a firm line. "Ezra, how 'bout doing a safety check around town."

"Yessir, Marshal. Any objections to me stopping by the boarding house for a bit of lunch?"

Jim crooked a smile as he removed his hat and hung it on the hat rack. "Safety check first. Maybe Hank will keep you company."

The old marshal grumbled, "Reckon I can take a hint. C'mon, boy, let an ole-timer show you how it's done."

As soon as the office door closed, Jim turned toward Charlie and his neighboring rancher, Bob Ellis.

Jim shifted his gaze from Charlie to the rancher and back. "Is there trouble at the ranch, Charlie?"

Bob Ellis spoke first. "No trouble. My visit is of a business nature. I asked Charlie to ride in with me, since my offer affects him, too."

Jim motioned for the men to sit as he leaned back in his own chair. He steepled his fingers together. "I'm listening."

Without hesitation, Ellis laid out his idea. "I plan to expand my cattle operation. Your six hundred acres abuts my property. Charlie explained about how you intend to continue raising horses. Thing is, Jim, even with Charlie running the place, how can you give it the attention needed when your job takes you away sometimes for months at a time?"

Jim studied the hard planes of the rancher's face. A tall, lean man in his fifties. A man who knew his business, a man who would fight to keep what he had, and fight to gain what he desired. And a man who had the money to back his ventures.

"Charlie will run the ranch when I'm gone. I've got complete confidence in him; and if need be, we'll hire a couple of hands to help out."

The quiet that settled over the office set Jim on edge. His lawman's instinct told him to expect the unexpected. He waited.

Charlie cleared his throat, the unease on his face apparent. "That's just it, Jim. What with Cora Beth ownin' a house in town, and the ten-mile drive out to the ranch and back, she prefers livin' in town when we're married. It'll be easier with her near the school, and with her mother runnin' the boarding house.

"Aw, hell, you might as well know the rest. Mr. Weidermeir is sellin' his livery stable. I've offered to buy it." Charlie harrumphed. "Who'd a thought a drunken half-breed would ever end up with a beautiful woman to marry, and ownin' his own business. You're the best friend I've ever had, Jim, and I'm sorry as I can be for lettin' you down."

Jim leaned forward and placed his arms on the desk. "A man has to look out for his best interests, Charlie. I've got no hard feelings against your decision as long as I still get to be best man at the wedding."

Charlie seemed to relax as he offered a wide grin, then just as quickly sobered. "Wouldn't have no one else."

Hank's words about giving up his job as marshal and joining him and Lettie—and Kathryn—in California resonated inside Jim's head. Past experience told him Bob Ellis was an honorable man and a good neighbor. He was also a man who could buy and sell most of the people in Oklahoma.

"I'm willing to listen to your deal, Bob. Might not give you the answer you're after, though."

"Fair enough. I'm prepared to pay ten dollars an acre. That's a hefty six thousand dollars."

Jim pushed from the chair. He flexed the numbness from the fingers on his left hand as he walked to the stove and lifted the pot. "Ezra's coffee is strong enough to melt a spoon."

At their nods, he poured two extra mugs.

Settling back in his chair, Jim lifted his long legs to rest on the corner of his wooden desk. "Nope, don't think I can sell for ten dollars an acre."

Bob Ellis grimaced as he swallowed a large gulp of the ropy brew. "Maybe, I can go fifteen, and you keep the stock. Horses of that quality will bring a hefty price from the Army."

A knot built in the pit of Jim's stomach. Not much of a gambling man, his counter-price was a long shot, and he knew it. If Ellis accepted the offer, Jim walked away a rich man. If the offer was refused, then he still owned a ranch that he didn't have the heart to pour his soul into.

"Ellis, I admire the offer. My place has prime water on it. Water that you don't have. Hundred dollars an acre, and I keep the stock. No haggling. That's my final price. Take it or leave it."

Ellis shifted his lanky frame, placing one booted foot across his leg at an odd angle. He lifted the mug to his lips and then changed his mind, setting the cup on the edge of the desk. He settled back, thrumming his fingers against the chair arm.

Only the clock's ticking broke the heavy silence, until Bob Ellis slapped his hand against his knee.

"Danged if you don't drive a hard bargain, Sawyer." He leaned forward and offered his hand to Jim. "You willing to walk with me to the bank so we can get this deal done today?"

Jim offered a smile. "What's your hurry, Ellis? Afraid I'll renege on the agreement?"

"Nope, you're too honest of a man. Truth is, my son is due in next month. He's bringing a new bride, and a prized Hereford bull and two heifers all the way from England. My wedding gift to the bride and groom is a new house on a portion of the property. I'd like to begin construction right away."

Jim's thoughts rolled one over the other. He hadn't expected Ellis to pay the price. Tamping down an uneasy excitement, he nodded his agreement to the bank meeting. "I've read about Herefords."

"Yep, I expect to improve the breed of range cattle. I might even start a beef revolution."

"I reckon if anyone can, then you're the man to do it."

Charlie stood, too. He shook hands with both Ellis and Jim. "I'm proud for you, Jim. Odd how life has changed for both of us. I think I'll mosey on over to the school and tell Cora Beth the news."

"You mind holding off a bit, Charlie? It's not a done deal until the papers are signed and the money's in my name."

Ellis clapped Jim on the back. "I like a cautious man. After the papers are signed, the first drink is on me. Charlie, how about joining us?"

The corners of Charlie's mouth tipped upward. "Make mine coffee, and it's a deal."

Worry stabbed at Jim's gut as he scrawled a note for his deputy.

Damn! What did the future hold for him, now?

****

Later that evening, conversation topics around the boarding house kitchen table switched back and forth from wedding plans to Charlie's becoming a business owner to settling in California, and then to Jim's good fortune.

Jim excused himself. "Town's quiet. Think I'll relieve Ezra and Lundy."

"I'm convinced Ezra'll make a fine deputy marshal. Not quite sure 'bout Lundy. What's your thoughts, Jim?" Hank wanted to know.

Jim finished his coffee, his voice matter-of-fact. "Ezra's got the instinct, all right. Lundy has what it takes. A bit too quick on the draw, though. I'm convinced both will make fine lawmen." He placed a hand on Hank's shoulder. "Eighteen years ago, you took a chance on a hot-headed, snot-nosed kid, and look how he turned out."

He pushed away from the table. Donning his coat and hat, he said his goodnights. Outside, he pulled the collar higher on his neck, then fisted his hands into the jacket's deep pockets. As a matter of habit, he turned to gaze at the hill. Moonlight shone down, highlighting two wooden markers. A force seemed to tug at Jim until he relented and walked toward the graveyard.

He bent to wipe snow and dried leaves from Joe and Tessa's headstones. The way the moonlight shone down reminded Jim of twin beds blanketed in white quilts.

Brushing his hands against the legs of his pants, Jim stood quiet, lost in thought. Talking to Tessa always brought him comfort.

"I don't know where to begin, Tessa. I sold the ranch to Bob Ellis today. You remember him, don't you? It wasn't my intention to part with the land. He made an offer, I countered with what I thought was a ridiculous price, never dreaming he'd take me up on it. But he did, and now I'm not sure what I should do."

He stopped to listen. Very often he felt her presence and thought he heard her sighing. Tonight nothing moved. Not even the coyotes sang their songs. It was as if the night creatures were listening, too.

"Part of me feels like I've betrayed you by selling the land; part of me knows it's time to move on with my life. It's like you said the other night, you'll always be in my heart.

"There's a woman. I've known her a long time. She was fifteen when we met. Her name is Kathryn, and she's completely different from you, Tessa, but I'm developing feelings for her. Strong feelings. I can't say yet whether it's love or lust. Maybe both.

"The thing is, Tessa, Kathryn has an outlaw past. Don't get me wrong, she's working hard for a new beginning by moving to California with Lettie and Hank come March."

Moisture seeped into his boots, and he stamped his feet to ward off the cold. The next words almost hung in his throat. Unexpected tears welled in his eyes.

"After losing you, a light went out in my life. Tracking down the Dobbses and seeing them in their graves was the only thing that kept me from laying down and dying. That's all done with, now. My heart isn't into wearing a badge anymore. I should've given it up when you and me married. I didn't, and will always live with the consequences of that decision.

"To tell you the truth, Tessa, I'm giving serious thought to turning in my badge and taking Hank up on his offer to join him and Lettie and Kathryn in California. It's a difficult decision, because it means leaving you here…alone."

The icy weight of his words stirred in Jim's chest and began to crumble. He could scarcely bear the pain.

A voice startled him. "Jim?"

His hand automatically reached for his revolver.

****

Despite the cold, Kathryn's cheeks became hot merely at the thought of what she was about to do. After Jim left the kitchen, she considered Lettie's words about taking the initiative of approaching him. But she wrestled with herself about following him to the gravesite.

She shouldn't do it. But then Lettie winked and gave an ever-so-subtle nod. The decision made, Kathryn decided to follow Jim up the hill.

His back was toward her, and she was relieved. She couldn't restrain her sigh. "Jim?"

He looked over his shoulder at her. His hat was pushed back, showing his strong profile—the square, rugged jawline, the slight crook to indicate a once-broken nose, the full yet firm mouth curving into a questioning smile.

Then she made the crucial mistake of looking into his eyes. For a moment, he didn't move, and neither did she. They just looked at each other.

She couldn't move, really. Kathryn felt like she was melting. She felt like she was nothing more than a puddle in the snow, not unlike those during a spring thaw. She was melting, melting into nothing more than a mess of slushy doubt. But she wasn't a puddle. She was an outlaw woman, preparing for a lifetime of making up for her sins, and for intruding on a grieving man's private moments.

Standing tall, Jim turned around, once again presenting her with his back.

Still, she didn't move.

She prayed for divine intervention. Unexpectedly, he turned and took a step toward her. She stepped back. She didn't dare speak for fear she would say what she was thinking instead of what she ought to say. All she could think was, *Kiss me.*

Without a word, his wrapped her in his arms, his mouth near her neck, and the warmth of his breath stole across her skin. It made her shiver. It made her desire him more.

He pushed back and looked into her eyes, and she saw his gaze drop to her mouth. She parted her lips to speak, but she didn't. His lips were so close she could feel his breath on her lips. All she had to do was lift her head a fraction of an inch for the kiss.

All the years of chastity, of fighting off unwanted advances from men whose only intentions were to satisfy their base animal desires, did not erase her own need to be held, to be touched, to be kissed, to be loved in such an earthly way. With Jim's arms around her, she felt closer to being whole.

He whispered her name. Warm hands slipped beneath her woolen cloak to caress the sides of her breasts, to slid down the length of her body, to settle around her waist, to pull her close until she felt his arousal at the apex of her legs, just as she felt an intense surge of heat and desire. And she experienced another emotion, a flash of unwanted memory, panic.

She twisted her hands together, trying to create a space between them. Her words sounded bold, though she was feeling anything but. She bit down hard on her lower lip. "I followed you tonight with every intention of seducing you. I'm sorry. I shouldn't have intruded on your privacy."

She lifted her skirts and ran down the hill, then raced up the back steps to the boarding house, down the hallway, and through the doorway of her room.

Flouncing face first on the bed, she beat her hands against the mattress. *Coward...coward... coward.*

****

Kathryn had stopped him. Stopped so close that he could almost taste her. He imagined her soft and luscious beneath him when she had placed her hands on his chest, closed her eyes, and parted her lips. He almost lost himself on the spot. She was a beautiful, bewitching woman, dangerous to his emotions.

The expression on her face had revealed that she was concerned for him. It had been a long time since anyone had looked at him that way, caring. About him. That look, to him, felt like a glass of cold water after months in the desert.

And then she had run away.

"Tell me what to do, Tessa. Am I wrong to want someone to care for me?"

The wind didn't stir. There was no subtle scent of lilacs. Nothing to indicate Tessa's spirit was near.

He couldn't help but sigh his disappointment as he walked down the hill and toward the marshal's office.

Chapter Twenty-Seven

New Year's Day arrived with the sun shining bright, and with the entire town of Texhoma turned out to celebrate Charlie and Cora Beth's wedding.

Cora Beth stood with her back facing a crowd of hopeful young women waiting to catch the bride's bouquet.

Not Kathryn.

Jim stood off to the side, watching her. Under the tutelage of Lettie and Cora Beth, Kathryn had changed to the sophisticated woman she was meant to be, dressed in a mauve gown with a white lace collar, her blonde hair pulled back into a fashionable chignon. He drank in her beauty as if he were a man dying of thirst.

Since their near kiss in the graveyard, she had tried to avoid him. But with Hank's insistent pestering, Jim had finally relented and invited her for a buggy ride to see the ranch he had once owned, and had encouraged her to pick out a horse of her choice. A belated Christmas gift, he'd said.

She'd offered him a questioning look. "I don't recall anyone ever giving me a gift, Jim. These are very expensive horses. I thought you'd sold all of them to the Army."

"Except for one or two, Charlie bought this bunch as rentals for the livery stable. Besides, a special woman should have a special horse." He lifted her hand into his. "I'm sorry no one has ever given you a gift, and it pleasures me that I'm the first."

She had gazed up at him through a mist of tears and then had taken her time to look over the small herd inside the corral. "In that case, I choose that one." She pointed toward a long-legged, blaze-faced sorrel with a blond mane and tail.

He had lassoed the gelding and walked it to Kathryn. "Excellent choice. He's already broke to saddle. All he needs now is a name."

The animal had reached out and lipped the artificial flowers on Kathryn's hat, snatching it from her head. It was the first time Jim had ever heard her laugh. The sound filled him with contentment.

Like an excited child, she had gurgled with laughter. "He's a beauty, Jim. I think I'll call him—Blaze."

Jim handed her the rope. "Blaze, meet your new owner. Miss Kathryn Emerson."

Excited female shouts and squeals rang out, bringing Jim back to the present in time to see the bridal bouquet sailing through the air, over the heads of young women standing on tiptoes, some jumping into the air with outstretched arms, only to have the bouquet land in the hands of a very surprised Kathryn.

It pleased him to watch her holding the flowers, as she stood next to Lettie. He willed her to look in his direction, and when she did, her cheeks pinked. Lettie hugged Kathryn and offered congratulations, while disappointed ladies drifted toward the barn for a dance and refreshments.

An elbow in his ribs, and Hank's voice, caused him to frown. "Well, don't just stand there, Jim. Let's escort two lovely women to the dance."

The four friends chattered as they walked toward Ashwin's Livery and Horse Sales. Jim looked up at the sign. "I'm right proud for Charlie."

Hank hooked Lettie's arm in the crook of his own. He smiled at Kathryn. "How 'bout honoring an ole codger with a dance?"

All Jim wanted to do was make love to her. And there she was, in front of him, looking luscious, and offering him a secret smile as she dipped her nose to smell the flowers.

Jim offered Kathryn his hand. "If it's all the same to you, Hank, I believe I'll claim the first waltz."

After several hours of eating, and dancing, the number of people had increased. Many of the men were descending into advanced stages of intoxication. A group in a far corner concerned Jim. With a slight nod he indicated for Ezra to join him.

"I see 'em, Marshal. Don't none of 'em look familiar. What about you?"

"Nope. Ease over to the office. You and Lundy go through the new posters, see if there's any matches."

"Yessir, Marshal. I'll hotfoot right back if there is."

"Bring Lundy with you."

By the time the young deputy returned, the men had gone. Jim walked outside on the pretense of smoking a cigarette, while watching the six mount up and ride out, allowing the dark to swallow them.

Ezra sprinted to where Jim stood. "Nothing, Marshal. We even looked through some of the older posters." He removed his hat and scratched his head. "My gut tells me just 'cause we don't have Wanted posters on those yahoos, don't mean they ain't wanted, somewhere."

"I hear you, Ezra. Go over to the saloon and situate yourself in a dark corner. If these men return, it'll be for liquor. If they don't show in a half hour, then go on home. I'll spell Lundy in about an hour."

Ezra tipped his hat. An unease filled Jim. He looked up and down the street, his eyes scanning for anything out of the ordinary. It was late. The band stopped playing and packed away their instruments. People strolled past him, calling their good nights.

A plethora of voices mingled with buggy wheels and clopping hooves filled the darkness. A smile touched Jim's lips as he recalled spotting the bride and groom escaping through a rear door.

He turned back toward the barn. Kathryn stood in the wide doorway. Candlelight haloed around her. If there were magic words, he would say them. He held forth his hand and urged her to him.

"May I have the honor of walking you home?"

Slipping her arm through his, she smiled her answer. "It was a beautiful day. Perfect in every way for Cora Beth and Charlie."

And so it went with small talk until they stood in front of the door to her room inside the boarding house.

Jim intended nothing more than a brief kiss on the cheek, after which he would say goodnight and lie in torment on a cot inside one of the jail cells in his office. But Kathryn had turned her head and captured his kiss on her lips.

He didn't resist. And how could he when the woman he'd come to cherish and long for was warm and willing in his arms?

It was a kiss worth waiting for and worth suffering

for. He cradled her head in his hand and wrapped one arm around her waist. Kathryn pressed all her luscious curves against him. He groaned into her mouth, and she, slightly unsteady on her feet, rubbed against his erection. He took a step backward so he could lean against the wall.

The woman was making him weak in the knees.

With one hand at the small of her back, he urged her against him. She was melting his resolve to remain an honorable man. His voice rasped when he spoke. "I've wanted to kiss you ever since that night at the graveyard."

She sighed and cupped his face with her hands. "I was afraid, but not anymore."

The primitive portions of his brain thought of two things: one, to open her bedroom door, and two—

Reality intruded in the form of loud voices coming up the stairs, and shrill laughter filtering up from the boarding house lobby. He broke off their kiss, and not a moment too soon. Millie Collins walked down the hall, a ring of keys in her hand, as she escorted a couple past Jim and Kathryn.

Millie raised one eyebrow, gave Jim *the look,* and managed to reduce him from a thirty-five-year-old United States Marshal to an embarrassed fifteen-year-old stealing his first kiss.

Jim squeezed Kathryn's hand. "Good night."

He walked down the back stairs into the night and drew in large gulps of cold air to cool off his heated body.

****

The next morning, a basket swinging from her arm, Kathryn hummed a tune as she stepped jauntily across the street to deliver a batch of fresh-baked cookies to the general store. She waved to several people and called them by name.

Cora Beth and Charlie stood on the front porch of their house, holding hands and talking. She spoke briefly to them.

A little bell dingled when she opened the mercantile door. "Good morning, Kathryn. My, don't those sugar cookies smell good. Ought to sell every one of them."

Kathryn smiled. "Fresh baked, and still warm from the oven."

"Say, my mister did a little too much dancing last night and threw his back out. I can't leave the store, so could I trouble you to go to the hen yard and collect eggs for me?"

Kathryn headed toward the back door of the mercantile. "Of course, Mrs. Wallace."

She made her way through the morning shadows of the back alley toward the tall, wire chicken coop. She had just reached out to lift the gate's latch when a large male hand snaked from behind, clamped over her mouth, and jerked her to a halt. Her head snapped back. Her heart stopped, and a chill ran up her spine. She stared down at the broad, dirty fingers. Her pulse raced, and spurred her full-force into action. She rammed her elbow back, connecting hard enough in the man's muscled midsection to send needles of pain jarring up her arm. A low grunt issued from her captor.

The man circled his free arm around her waist, pinning her arms tight to her sides. He hauled her against his chest. Kathryn kicked backwards, striking his shinbone. He yelped, loosening his hold enough for her to twist around as she struggled to free herself.

"Stop fighting, Katie Em. I ain't gonna hurt you unless you give me a reason." He laughed. "At least not now, I ain't gonna hurt you."

Kathryn stilled. The fear of having her past catch up to her was now a reality. She turned her head slightly, cutting her eyes to look at him and catching a glimpse of white hair beneath his hat, one clouded-over eye, and the black bandanna tied around his face—before his fingers dug like a painful vise into her cheeks and he jerked her head toward the front again.

Nausea roiled in the pit of her stomach. *Whitey Tillman.*

A cold knot fisted in her stomach. Bile rose into her throat, not only from the stale sweat of his unwashed body but also the fetid stench from the hand pressed firmly against her mouth.

He tightened his hold, crushing her ribs until tears rose to her eyes. She tried but couldn't bend her elbow enough to get her hand inside her pocket. Then, quick as a striking snake, he lowered his arm and shoved his hand inside her pocket, ripping it from her skirt. "What you got in there, Katie Em?"

He wrapped his hand around the small barrel of a derringer. Kathryn took advantage of the slackening of his grip. He cupped the gun in his palm and twisted his hand free of her clawing desperation, then pinned her arms at her sides again as he reclaimed his tight hold around her waist.

"I've tracked from hell and back trying to find you, Katie."

"My name is Kathryn. You've obviously mistaken me for someone else."

"Ah, Katie, I'm blind in one eye, but I see real good out of the other'n. In fact, I 'member the night you jabbed that stick through my eye. Took me awhile to heal over and learn how to manage. It ain't easy learning how to shoot and ride with only one good peeper." He cocked his head to one side as if to see her better. "You 'member what I said that night, Katie Em?"

She remembered all right. He'd threatened to search the ends of the earth and, when he found her, promised to cut out both her eyes.

When she didn't answer, he said, "I can't wait to find out what else you've got hiding under them skirts. Always did want to get me a taste of what was under them baggy overalls you always wore. But a fancy dress don't make you a fancy gal. Don't matter what name you're calling yourself." His warm, tobacco-stale breath brushed across her cheek. The lustful insinuation followed by a low chuckle increased the alarm coursing through her blood.

He lifted his arm higher, pressing against the underside of her breasts. "I think we'll wait until that marshal can watch what all I've got planned for you. Sashaying 'round the dance floor last night all duded up and ladylike. Even without them baggy britches and a pistol slung low on your hip, I knowed it was you."

Tremors rippled through her limbs and repulsion swirled in her stomach. Whitey Tillman lifted her off her feet and moved backward, deeper into the shadows that claimed the back alley and lay over the chicken coop.

In desperation, Kathryn parted her lips and sank her teeth into the man's palm, gagging on the salty filth that laced her tongue.

"You bitch," he growled deep in his throat, then she felt his flesh tear as he jerked his hand away.

He stepped back, grabbing his bloodied hand. Kathryn used the advantage to issue a swift and hard kick to his groin. Whitey Tillman grabbed his crotch and groaned before dropping to his knees.

"Kathryn?" Jim pushed from the store's back door and, not bothering with the steps, he jumped to the ground.

She walked into his open arm while he used his other hand to level the Colt .44 at the moaning man. His eyes narrowed with grave concern as he raked his stare over her face. "What's going on here?"

Whitey Tillman was up like a shot, one hand still clutching his groin, the other hand grappling for his revolver.

"Touch it and you're a dead man." Jim's voice brooked no nonsense.

"Kathryn!" Mrs. Wallace came running down the steps, and hurried to take Kathryn from the crook of Jim's arm. "Oh, my goodness, you're bleeding." She pulled a small handkerchief from the sleeve of her dress and dabbed it against Kathryn's mouth. "What happened?"

Kathryn's breaths came raw and hurtful as she tried to quell the trembling of her body. "I-I believe he intended to rob your store, and when I came out to collect the eggs, I must have interfered with his plan." She regretted the lie, but it wouldn't do to destroy the new image she had worked so hard to build for herself. She shifted a pleading stare between Jim and Whitey Tillman.

Jim nodded his understanding as he slapped a pair of handcuffs on the man. When Tillman started to speak, Jim said, "I'd advise you to keep quiet, mister. Whatever you have to say, I'll hear it in my office." He shoved the .44 caliber against the small of the man's back. "Get a move on."

He lightly touched the bruise at the corner of Kathryn's mouth. "Mrs. Wallace, I'd appreciate it if you'd walk with Kathryn to the boarding house."

The older woman frowned her concern. She placed an arm around Kathryn's waist. "Come, my dear. We'll ask Lettie and Mrs. Collins to brew us a cup of hot tea, and perhaps lace it with a bit of brandy. To help calm both our nerves, of course."

Chapter Twenty-Eight

Moonlight spilled between the curtains of the window, pale beams lighting Jim's path across the room. He sat down on the edge of the bed, tightening his hold around Kathryn as he held her in his lap. He whispered soothing words in her ear, and rained light kisses along the side of her face until he felt her trembles subside and her ragged breathing slow to normal.

She drew in a deep breath and released it on a shuddering sigh. "I'm sorry, I didn't mean to fall apart. It seems all my life I've run with—and from—men whose only desires were to do me harm." She twisted around to look into his eyes. "All the more reason for me to go to California. I need a place to feel safe."

He brushed a feather-light kiss against her lips, his voice filled with distress. "I'm the one who is sorry. I promised to protect you, and I didn't. When I spotted those men last night at the dance, I should have suspected a connection to you."

Kathryn shook her head, the anguish in his voice tearing at her soul. She cupped one hand against his strong jaw. Her thumb traced the scar marring his cheekbone. "You have protected me, Jim. In more ways than one. Whitey Tillman or any of the gangs I rode with were bound to find me sooner or later. I was having so much fun last night that I let my guard down.

I didn't even see him."

She wrapped her arms tighter around Jim's neck, finding the comfort she so desperately needed from his embrace. Oh, how she loved this man, loved the way he made her feel safe, and…special. "If you don't mind, I'd like to be alone for awhile."

He held her for several minutes before tenderly setting her from his lap onto the bed, then crossing to the door. "Keep the revolver under your pillow, and don't answer the door unless it's me, Lettie, or Millie Collins."

Her voice stopped him. "Jim?"

He turned.

"Will I always be Katie Em?"

In the dimly lit room, she felt his smile. "I believe she's buried in a lonely grave on an abandoned homestead. I seem to recall meeting her a long time ago. The Katie Em I knew could never hold a candle to Kathryn Emerson."

She sighed, too drained to refute his words. "Thank you."

****

Jim crossed the street to his office. He walked to his desk and picked up the Wanted poster on Whitey Tillman. "How's our prisoner?"

Lundy said, "Ah, all he's done since you locked him up is bellyache."

"In the morning, you and Ezra can escort him to Oklahoma City for trial. I'll have the papers ready before you leave."

The deputy's grin spread across his young face. "Hot damn, Marshal, it's about time me and Ezra got to do something besides sitting in the office or making the rounds about town."

Jim turned the poster on Tillman toward the two deputies. "Five-thousand-dollar bounty. Wanted dead or alive. Killed a teller during a bank robbery. Killed a guard and a passenger during a stagecoach holdup." He laid the poster on the desk. "Give Whitey Tillman the opportunity, and he will kill the two of you and laugh about it. You and Ezra never let your guard down. Never take the cuffs off him—even if he has to answer the call of nature. If you don't heed what I say, you won't live to grow gray whiskers on your chin. You hear me, Lundy?"

Lundy nodded his belief as he stroked his chin. "Loud and clear, Marshal Sawyer."

"Good. Now get on out of here. You and Ezra have a couple of long days in the saddle. One of you sleep while the other keeps watch. When you feed Tillman, no forks, no knives. Hell, he could do you in with the end of a spoon."

"You trying to put a scare into me, Marshal?"

"Damn right I am."

Lundy grabbed his hat and slammed it on his head. From the slight tic at the corner of his eye, Jim knew his point had hit home with the young man. The boy's youth made Jim feel old. A lot of years had passed since he'd seen twenty-three.

Alone in the office, and with the only prisoner snoring loudly, Jim poured a cup of coffee. He laced it with a generous splash of whiskey. Still wearing his coat, he walked out to the porch and settled in the chair. The same chair Hank had always used when the town was quiet. Propping a booted foot against the porch rail, he reared the chair back on two legs. Crickets' loud

Loretta C. Rogers

chirps filled the darkness, and hoot owls serenaded the chickens.

Jim frowned as he sipped the mug of whiskey-laced coffee, and stared out at the peacefulness of the night that surrounded him. He thought about his last visit to the graveyard and his conversation with Tessa.

Until today's incident between Kathryn and a man from her past, the idea of giving up his job as a lawman had plagued him.

A heaviness settled in Jim's chest. He sipped the coffee. Kathryn was always there…hovering on the outskirts of his every thought. He thought about how he would feel when she left Oklahoma, or worse, if someone from her past put a bullet in her.

The sudden pain that slammed into his chest choked the breath right out of him, then twisted in his heart when he realized he couldn't risk losing her, too. Kathryn was sweet and beautiful, and he was seriously in love with her. The sudden realization jolted him.

His decision made, he held the cup forward, saluted the night, and finished off the drink. Back inside the office, he locked the door, then filled out forms for his deputies to use when they transferred Whitey Tillman to the district marshal's office. With the paperwork completed, he sat for a moment, contemplating. He pulled several sheets of stationery from the drawer, dipped the pen into the inkwell. The nib scratched across the paper as he wrote. He balled up two sheets and tossed them into the wastebasket. Satisfied with the words he'd penned on the third attempt, he blew the ink dry, folded the letter, and sealed it in an envelope for Ezra to give to the Director of U.S. Marshals.

268

A knock at the door, and a voice called, "Jim, open up. It's me."

He rose to unlock the door. "Kind of late, Hank."

The old marshal harrumphed. "Tell that to Lettie." He set the tray of food on the desk. "Figured you'd need a sandwich and cookies to get you through the night."

Jim removed the checkered napkin and lifted the sandwich from the plate. "I'm glad you stopped by, Hank. Ever since you planted the idea in my mind about giving up marshaling, it's bothered me. I've given it plenty of thought, and after what happened to Kathryn today, I've made up my mind."

Hank cast a wry glance at his friend. He didn't say a word, just waited.

Jim pointed at the envelope. "Ezra and Lundy are transporting Tillman to the district office tomorrow. Both men are good deputies, but young, and inexperienced. Neither are ready to take on the job of marshal. I'm turning in my badge and asking the director to send a replacement as soon as possible."

Hank thrummed gnarled fingers against his knee. "Does this mean what I think it means?"

"Yep. I'm going to California, but before we leave, I plan to ask Kathryn to marry me."

"Danged if I didn't know it all along." Hank fairly cackled with joy. "I'm proud for you, Jim. When you gonna pop the question?"

A sheepish grin spread over Jim's face. "Tell you the truth, I haven't thought that far. Tomorrow, maybe." He polished off the remains of the sandwich and set the cookies aside for later.

****

The moon had risen past the midnight hour. Unable to sleep, Kathryn stood at the window, peering into the darkness.

She didn't blame Jim for what had happened earlier in the day. He couldn't fix her problem. She was who she was and feared her past would plague her until the day she died. It was enough knowing he cared about her and had done so much to help her. She didn't want to burden him any more by making her feelings known to him. He was a Deputy United States Marshal. He had a place of importance in his life, in society. Her reputation would only serve to destroy him. But she also knew she wasn't safe anywhere in Kansas or Oklahoma.

She choked on a sob when a light tap sent chills racing through her. Moving to the bed, she reached for the revolver hidden beneath the pillow. Tiptoeing to the door, she put an ear against it. "Who's there?"

Waves of relief washed over her when Lettie answered, "It's me."

Turning the key, she opened the door to find her friend clad in a blue robe over a nightdress, and holding a tray.

Lettie offered a gracious smile. "I saw the light under your door. Figured after today's ordeal you probably couldn't sleep, so I brought you a mug of warm milk and some cookies."

Kathryn invited Lettie to set the tray on a table next to the bed. She settled on top of the quilt, offering the only chair to her friend. She accepted the cup and sipped. The flavorful liquid brought a smile to her face. "I always figured warm milk might taste like flour mixed with water."

Lettie chuckled. She helped herself to a sugar cookie. "My own special recipe—a touch of cinnamon, a dash of nutmeg, a spoon of honey, and a splash of bourbon."

The women sat quietly until Lettie broke the silence. "It's written all over your face, child. Your emotions are all bottled up inside and busting to come out. If you're of a mind to talk, I'll listen. If not, I'll say good night, and go back to bed."

Kathryn heaved a sorrowful sigh. She brushed crumbs from the front of her nightgown. "I don't remember anyone ever caring enough to bring me milk and cookies. I don't even know what it's like to give love, or how it's supposed to feel.

"Lettie, what am I to do? If what I feel for Jim is love, then it hurts like the dickens to think about leaving him. Yet after what happened today, I can't stay. Hellfire—" Kathryn placed a hand over her mouth to express her regret for allowing the cuss words to slip out. "I don't even know how he feels about me."

"Lawsy me, girl, even a blind man could see Jim Sawyer has deep feelings for you. It pleasures me how his face lights up when he's in the room with you, or hears your name. He loved Tessa with all his heart and soul, there's no denying that. Give him time to completely heal."

"That's just it, Lettie. We're leaving in a few weeks. I don't have time to wait."

Lettie seemed to ponder on her answer. "I don't think Hank really loved me when I pursued him. He cared about me, much the way Jim cares about you. I figured if him and me were friends first, the loving part would come later."

"Did you know when it happened—the loving part?"

Again, Lettie took her time answering. "I saw it in Hank's eyes the day I told him he was going to be a papa, and I saw it again the day we buried our son. The thing is, Kathryn, if we hadn't been friends first, I don't think we'd have lasted through all the long days of him tracking outlaws, or me wondering if he'd come home slung over a saddle. We've seen nigh on forty years together, and the best part is, even though the love is there, we're still friends."

She rose from the chair, and set the empty mug and plate on the tray. "Roosters will start crowing pretty soon. Reckon we'd better catch a few winks." At the door, she turned. "Whatever is meant to happen—will."

Kathryn slid down beneath the quilt. She found comfort in Lettie's words, and decided the best way to be a friend to Jim was to get out of his life.

Chapter Twenty-Nine

Kathryn stepped outside onto the front porch, drawing a deep breath as she looked beyond the town toward distant mountains. So beautiful. So peaceful. She enjoyed the early mornings before the town awakened to a bustle of activities.

In spite of the brisk air, a warm contentment and a freedom she had never thought to feel settled in her soul as she mentally ticked off the remaining days before she would board a California-bound stagecoach. No more running, hiding. No more worries. No more lies. Freedom.

What if something went wrong?

She worried her bottom lip. No, it would be fine. Besides, Jim had promised to watch after her until she left. *Until she left.*

Giving herself a mental shake, she glanced down the street. Jim stood with his back to her, one leg lifted to the stirrup. Her heart pounded faster. She wanted him to know how much she loved him, needed him, wanted him in her life. Chuckling slightly, she admonished herself for desiring the impossible.

He swung into the saddle and turned the appaloosa in her direction. Kathryn swallowed back a rush of emotion as the horse shuffled toward her. She lifted a hand and waved, her pulse racing as Jim stopped in front of the hitching rail.

"You're up early, Kathryn."

She stepped down to rub the appaloosa's velvety nose. "So are you."

"One of the hands from the Bar S rode in with several bullet holes in him. He's at Doc's now, getting patched up."

"What happened?"

"Squatters trying to lay claim to land they don't own, plus slaughtering a couple steers they also don't own."

She gazed up at him. Words locked inside her throat. *I love you. I don't want to be without you.*

Instead, she said, "Be careful."

Jim nodded. "Kathryn, when I return, there's something I'd like to talk over with you."

"Have I done something wrong?"

"On the contrary. With luck, I'll see you before dark."

The mare brushed its head against Kathryn's shoulder and whickered.

"I think Dancer likes you. It's a bit unusual. Normally, she doesn't cotton to anyone."

Kathryn planted a kiss on the horse's nose. "Keep your master safe."

She stepped back and lifted her hand in a wave as Jim backed the horse from the hitching post to trot down the street.

Kathryn spent the day going about her usual chores and then helping prepare supper for the evening boarders and others who preferred dining at the boarding house rather than at the town's only restaurant.

When the day was done, she freshened herself and

donned a woolen cloak. She called out, "Lettie, I'm going for a walk."

Lettie peeked around the kitchen door, and offered a concerned smile. "Got your revolver?"

Kathryn patted the side of her wrap. "In my pocket."

Outside, she watched the evening sun resting above the horizon. Two hours of sunlight left. Without giving heed to the direction, she found herself standing in the graveyard beneath a sprawling oak tree. For a long moment she reveled in the stillness. "Tessa…"

She felt strange, wanting to talking to a grave marker buried in a patch of dirt and winter-dead grass. Keeping her voice to a whisper, she began again. "My name is Kathryn, Tessa. Compared to all the wonderful things I've heard about you, I can never measure up to the woman you were when you lived. The thing is, I love Jim. I think he has feelings for me, but he loved you so deeply, I'm not sure he has room in his heart for me.

"I'm going away in a few weeks, leaving this part of the country forever. It makes my bones ache to know I'll never see him again. He's the only man who's ever treated me decent, never once judging me for who I was, and helping me to become who I am.

"Take care of him, Tessa. But, one day, if Jim finds another woman he can love as much as he did you"— she hesitated, sorrow filling her—"please let him know that he isn't betraying you. I wish it were me, that I was that woman. And if I were, I'd want your blessings, Tessa."

She blinked back the moisture swimming in her eyes. Tension released in her shoulders.

The quiet peace of the graveyard was broken by the blowing snort of a horse. Startled, Kathryn turned.

****

Letting out his breath slowly, Jim attempted to gather his scattered thoughts into some semblance of logical order. His emotions churned unmercifully.

He dropped the appaloosa's reins to stand at the foot of the grave. "Kathryn?" He reached out to brush a tangled web of blonde tresses from her face.

She pressed a trembling hand to her bosom. "Ho-how long have you been standing there?"

He traced a lean finger along her cheek. "Long enough."

Her voice broke on a high note. "Did you hear?"

"I did."

Her cheeks pinked and her mouth formed a perfect O before she said, "You're here. I thought it would take longer to deal with the squatters."

"It was an old man, his woman, and a youngster. They were peaceful enough."

"You arrested them?"

"Nope. Arranged with the rancher to let them work off their debt. At least they'll have a warm place to lay their heads, and food."

Kathryn placed her hand against his chest. She gazed into his eyes. "You are a truly good man, Jim Sawyer."

His heart felt as if it were ready to pound right through his chest at the sight of her. He had made a lot of decisions last night, decisions that would make him the happiest man alive if Kathryn agreed with him.

"I've waited too long to tell you…I love you, Kathryn. I don't want to be without you."

The sparkle in her eyes, the smile that widened her full lips sent pleasure coursing through his veins. He pressed his lips to hers, his heart soaring at her eager response. "I want you in my life, always."

He pulled back and placed his forehead gently against hers. "Kathryn, I can't promise that trouble won't follow you, but I give you my word that I will do everything in my power to make life better for you."

She placed her palms against his cheeks, her eyes gleaming with tears. "I've wanted to hear those words for a long time, Jim, and I thank you for them. But we have no life together as long as I remain in Texhoma."

He reached for her. She backed away from him. He crooked a smile. "I've submitted my resignation. The new marshal should arrive by the end of the week. I plan to start a new life…in California."

A deep frown clouded her face, and she stood without moving.

His throat rippled as he swallowed.

Time seemed to stand still. And then the unexpected happened.

A gust of wind swayed the branches of the oak tree.

Jim looked up, but before he could utter a warning, a blob of snow landed on top of Kathryn's bare head. She huffed a squeal of surprise.

Then, whether by coincidence or design, the appaloosa placed her head in the center of Kathryn's back and shoved, sending her into Jim's arms.

A warm glow spread through his soul. He leaned down, brushing his lips lightly over hers. She responded to his touch and his kiss in a way that a man dreamed of. It was her innocence he loved. He loved her naïve wonder, and her faith in him.

The heavy scent of lilacs wafted around Jim and Kathryn. He lifted his eyes heavenward. *Thank you, Tessa.*

Kathryn stepped back from his embrace. She lifted her head. "Odd, I thought I smelled lilacs, but that can't be. They don't bloom in winter."

He took her hand in his, lacing their fingers together. "It's said that when a spirit finds peace it sends a sign. I believe Tessa Cloud Woman is giving us her blessing."

In the twilight, Kathryn looked up at Jim. She did not smile. She did not scowl. "Will you regret giving up your badge?"

Holding both her hands, he bent down on one knee. "Kathryn Emerson, the only regrets I'll have is if you say no to becoming my wife. Marry me?"

Kathryn pulled him to his feet. Her lips twitched into a smile. "We have Tessa's approval...and Dancer's. Yes. I accept. Let's go tell the others."

Chapter Thirty

The following weeks were a calming period for Jim, and a blissful time for Kathryn. Jim paved the way for the newly appointed marshal, and Kathryn helped Lettie and Millie sew a wedding gown, as well as traveling dresses. She had argued against white.

"I'm not pure." She told the well-meaning friends. "And I don't want silk or taffeta or any of those swishy materials. It doesn't fit who I am."

She and Jim married on the first Sunday of March.

Kathryn was beautiful. More beautiful than he'd ever imagined. In fact, Jim had never imagined her like this. Her butter-hued hair was fashioned atop her head in an elaborate arrangement. He gazed at cheeks he had cupped in his hands, lips he had thoroughly kissed, and eyes that reminded him of a blue summer sky.

She wore a gown of emerald green satiny cotton. A cameo, a gift from Hank and Lettie, rested between the swells of her bosom. In one hand she carried a bouquet of purple coneflowers tied together with purple and green ribbons, her other hand in the crook of Hank's arm as he escorted her down the boarding house stairs to the parlor.

Jim took her hand in his as they stood before the parson. He and Kathryn each pledged to honor, cherish, and protect one another, and then he slipped the gold band on her finger.

The parson spoke. "If anyone has reason why these two should not be joined together in holy wedlock, let them speak now or forever hold their peace."

He pulled his black frock coat back enough to expose the pearl-handled butt of his pistol as if daring anyone to object.

A very tense moment of silence followed.

"You may now kiss the bride."

Jim told Kathryn he loved her, again. And she told him that she loved him, again. He slipped the flannel-lined green cape over her shoulders. The group of friends followed them out to the porch, where she prepared to toss the bridal bouquet to a group of hopeful young women.

A strong wind captured the fullness of Kathryn's skirt, wrapping it around Jim's legs. They smiled at one another, each hearing the laughter, and knew Tessa was with them. To everyone else it was the breeze whistling around the corners of the boarding house.

The stagecoach driver yelled, "You folks 'bout ready? I've got a schedule to keep."

Jim scooped up his new bride and strode down the steps toward the coach. He whispered, "I'm afraid the honeymoon will have to wait until we board the train."

Kathryn laughed with humor. "We've waited this long. A few more days won't hurt."

Lettie and Hank joined Jim and Kathryn inside the coach. The friends waved goodbye to Charlie, Cora Beth, and Millie.

After two days of traveling, the group boarded the train in Dodge City, having settled Dancer and Blaze inside a stock car. Hank said, "Once we find our Pullman, me and Lettie plan to get a bite of supper in the dining car. You two want to join us?"

Jim's eyes gleamed in anticipation. He wrapped his arm around Kathryn's waist, drawing her closer. "If you'll excuse us, I think we'll retire to our own car."

Lettie chuckled softly as she nudged her husband's shoulder. "Come on, ole man. Let's leave these two to do what newlyweds do."

A few minutes later, Jim lifted Kathryn into his arms, and she snuggled against his neck as he crossed the threshold of their private sleeping car. His heartbeat quickened, and he paused to swallow. "Here I am in a room with a bed and a beautiful woman, and I'm as nervous as colt about to be broke to saddle." He brushed his lips against hers. The moment Kathryn returned his gentle kiss, the fire within him flamed, igniting his need for her. He released his hold on her and trailed his fingers up the cotton of her sleeve, feeling the slender limb quiver beneath his touch. "I won't hurt you, Kathryn."

She breathed against him. "I know."

Her cheeks pinked as he followed the narrow line of her shoulder and brushed his hand across her smooth cheek. He circled his hand around the nape of her neck and gently pulled her closer. He ran his tongue around the line of her lips. She opened her mouth at the tender coaxing.

His pulse pounded at the earnest sincerity gleaming in the depths of her blue eyes. She drew a deep breath and released a heavy sigh.

"Are you nervous?"

"A little." She ran her tongue over his lips, driving his blood to a heated level that roared in his head and surged to a throbbing crescendo in his loins. Stepping from his arms, she turned her back as she unbuttoned the gown, letting it puddle to the floor, followed by the chemise and then the bloomers, until she turned to face him. Offering herself.

Jim knew the effort it took for Kathryn to bare her body to him. He stared at the sure confidence that glowed in her eyes, his fired blood coursing with deepened desire. He wanted her more than he wanted his next breath. He lowered her onto the bed, where he kissed her long and deep.

He rode the wave of ecstasy with her, a glorious harmony, a beautiful blending, and when she reached her peak and cried out his name, he didn't hold back any longer, following her over the edge in a searing rhapsody.

"That was wonderful," she whispered, a shy smile lifting the corners of her lips.

"Definitely wonderful." He leaned down and kissed her lips slowly, softly, before he drew back and sat up. He reached for the container of water and wet the cloth that lay next to a porcelain basin.

Tears sprang to her eyes as he tenderly bathed her body. She took the cloth from his hands and returned the gesture, wiping the moisture of their lovemaking from the hard lines of his abdomen and groin.

A low growl drew her attention. He gently pulled her flush against him and dipped his head to claim her mouth. He lowered her back down to the bed, then proceeded to make love to his wife, and consumed the light that had finally begun to shine in his soul again.

A word about the author...

Loretta C. Rogers is an award-winning author who writes historical romance with a twist. When not writing, she enjoys reading and traveling, especially with her husband on their motorcycle.

Loretta enjoys hearing from readers and invites them to visit her website:

www.lorettacrogersbooks.com

~*~

Author's Note

If you enjoyed *Cloud Woman's Spirit*, Loretta would appreciate if readers would post a review at:

www.thewildrosepress.com or amazon.com